Alexandre Dumas Père

Massacres of the South; Celebrated Crimes

in large print

Alexandre Dumas Père

Massacres of the South; Celebrated Crimes

in large print

Reproduction of the original.

1st Edition 2022 | ISBN: 978-3-36832-155-0

Verlag (Publisher): Outlook Verlag GmbH, Zeilweg 44, 60439 Frankfurt, Deutschland
Vertretungsberechtigt (Authorized to represent): E. Roepke, Zeilweg 44, 60439 Frankfurt, Deutschland
Druck (Print): Books on Demand GmbH, In de Tarpen 42, 22848 Norderstedt, Deutschland

MASSACRES OF THE SOUTH

From "Celebrated Crimes" In Eight Volumes

By
Alexandre Dumas, Pere

1910

MASSACRES OF THE SOUTH—1551-1815

CHAPTER I

It is possible that our reader, whose recollections may perhaps go back as far as the Restoration, will be surprised at the size of the frame required for the picture we are about to bring before him, embracing as it does two centuries and a half; but as everything, has its precedent, every river its source, every volcano its central fire, so it is that the spot of earth on which we are going to fix our eyes has been the scene of action and reaction, revenge and retaliation, till the religious annals of the South resemble an account-book kept by double entry, in which fanaticism enters the profits of death, one side being written with the blood of Catholics, the other with that of Protestants.

In the great political and religious convulsions of the South, the earthquake-like throes of which were felt even in the capital, Nimes has always taken the central place; Nimes will therefore be the pivot round which our story will revolve, and though we may sometimes leave it for a moment, we shall always return thither without fail.

Nimes was reunited to France by Louis VIII, the government being taken from its vicomte, Bernard Athon VI, and given to consuls in the year 1207. During the episcopate of Michel Briconnet the relics of St. Bauzile were discovered, and hardly were the rejoicings over this event at an end when the new doctrines began to spread over France. It was in the South that the persecutions began, and in 1551 several persons were publicly burnt as heretics by order of the Seneschal's Court at Nimes, amongst whom was Maurice Secenat, a missionary from the Cevennes, who was taken in the very act of preaching. Thenceforth Nimes rejoiced in two martyrs and two patron saints, one revered by the Catholics, and one by the Protestants; St. Bauzile, after reigning as sole protector for twenty-four years, being forced to share the honours of his guardianship with his new rival.

Maurice Secenat was followed as preacher by Pierre de Lavau; these two names being still remembered among the crowd of obscure and forgotten martyrs. He also was put to death on the Place de la Salamandre, all the difference being that the former was burnt and the latter hanged.

Pierre de Lavau was attended in his last moments by Dominique Deyron, Doctor of Theology; but instead of, as is usual, the dying man being converted by the priest, it was the priest who was converted by de Lavau, and the teaching which it was desired should be suppressed burst forth again. Decrees were issued against Dominique Deyron; he was pursued and tracked down, and only escaped the gibbet by fleeing to the mountains.

The mountains are the refuge of all rising or decaying sects; God has given to the powerful on earth city, plain, and sea, but the mountains are the heritage of the oppressed.

Persecution and proselytism kept pace with each other, but the blood that was shed produced the usual effect: it rendered the soil on which it fell fruitful, and after two or three years of struggle, during which two or three hundred

Huguenots had been burnt or hanged, Nimes awoke one morning with a Protestant majority. In 1556 the consuls received a sharp reprimand on account of the leaning of the city towards the doctrines of the Reformation; but in 1557, one short year after this admonition, Henri II was forced to confer the office of president of the Presidial Court on William de Calviere, a Protestant. At last a decision of the senior judge having declared that it was the duty of the consuls to sanction the execution of heretics by their presence, the magistrates of the city protested against this decision, and the power of the Crown was insufficient to carry it out.

Henri II dying, Catherine de Medicis and the Guises took possession of the throne in the name of Francois II. There is a moment when nations can always draw a long breath, it is while their kings are awaiting burial; and Nimes took advantage of this moment on the death of Henri II, and on September 29th, 1559, Guillaume Moget founded the first Protestant community.

Guillaume Moget came from Geneva. He was the spiritual son of Calvin, and came to Nimes with the firm purpose of converting all the remaining Catholics or of being hanged. As he was eloquent, spirited, and wily, too wise to be violent, ever ready to give and take in the matter of concessions, luck was on his side, and Guillaume Moget escaped hanging.

The moment a rising sect ceases to be downtrodden it becomes a queen, and heresy, already mistress of three-fourths of the city, began to hold up its head with boldness in the streets. A householder called Guillaume Raymond

5

opened his house to the Calvinist missionary, and allowed him to preach in it regularly to all who came, and the wavering were thus confirmed in the new faith. Soon the house became too narrow to contain the crowds which flocked thither to imbibe the poison of the revolutionary doctrine, and impatient glances fell on the churches.

Meanwhile the Vicomte de Joyeuse, who had just been appointed governor of Languedoc in the place of M. de Villars, grew uneasy at the rapid progress made by the Protestants, who so far from trying to conceal it boasted of it; so he summoned the consuls before him, admonished them sharply in the king's name, and threatened to quarter a garrison in the town which would soon put an end to these disorders. The consuls promised to stop the evil without the aid of outside help, and to carry out their promise doubled the patrol and appointed a captain of the town whose sole duty was to keep order in the streets. Now this captain whose office had been created solely for the repression of heresy, happened to be Captain Bouillargues, the most inveterate Huguenot who ever existed.

The result of this discriminating choice was that Guillaume Moget began to preach, and once when a great crowd had gathered in a garden to hear him hold forth, heavy rain came on, and it became necessary for the people either to disperse or to seek shelter under a roof. As the preacher had just reached the most interesting part of his sermon, the congregation did not hesitate an instant to take the latter alternative. The Church of St. Etienne du Capitole was quite near: someone present suggested that this building, if not the most suitable, as at least the most spacious for such a gathering.

The idea was received with acclamation: the rain grew heavier, the crowd invaded the church, drove out the priests, trampled the Holy Sacrament under foot, and broke the sacred images. This being accomplished, Guillaume Moget entered the pulpit, and resumed his sermon with such eloquence that his hearers' excitement redoubled, and not satisfied with what had already been done, rushed off to seize on the Franciscan monastery, where they forthwith installed Moget and the two women, who, according to Menard the historian of Languedoc, never left him day or night; all which proceedings were regarded by Captain Bouillargues with magnificent calm.

The consuls being once more summoned before M. de Villars, who had again become governor, would gladly have denied the existence of disorder; but finding this impossible, they threw themselves on his mercy. He being unable to repose confidence in them any longer, sent a garrison to the citadel of Nimes, which the municipality was obliged to support, appointed a governor of the city with four district captains under him, and formed a body of military police which quite superseded the municipal constabulary. Moget was expelled from Nimes, and Captain Bouillargues deprived of office.

Francis II dying in his turn, the usual effect was produced,—that is, the persecution became less fierce,—and Moget therefore returned to Nimes. This was a victory, and every victory being a step forward, the triumphant preacher organised a Consistory, and the deputies of Nimes demanded from the States-General of Orleans possession of the churches. No notice was taken of this demand; but the Protestants were at no loss how to proceed. On the 21st December 1561 the churches of Ste. Eugenie, St. Augustin, and the Cordeliers were taken by assault, and cleared of their images in a hand's turn; and this time Captain Bouillargues was not satisfied with looking on, but directed the operations.

The cathedral was still safe, and in it were entrenched the remnant of the Catholic clergy; but it was apparent that at the earliest opportunity it too would be turned into a meeting-house; and this opportunity was not long in coming.

One Sunday, when Bishop Bernard d'Elbene had celebrated mass, just as the regular preacher was about to begin his sermon, some children who were playing in the close began to hoot the 'beguinier' [a name of contempt for friars]. Some of the faithful being disturbed in their meditations, came out of the church and chastised the little Huguenots, whose parents considered themselves in consequence to have been insulted in the persons of their children. A great commotion ensued, crowds began to form, and cries of "To the church! to the church!" were heard. Captain Bouillargues happened to be in the neighbourhood, and being very methodical set about organising the insurrection; then putting himself at its head, he charged the cathedral, carrying everything before him, in spite of the barricades which had been hastily erected by the Papists. The assault was over in a few moments; the priests and their flock fled by one door, while the Reformers entered by another. The building was in the twinkling of an eye adapted to the new form of worship: the great crucifix from above the altar was dragged about the streets at the end of a rope and scourged at every cross-roads. In the evening a large fire was lighted in the place before the cathedral, and the archives of the ecclesiastical and religious houses, the sacred images, the relics of the saints, the decorations of the altar, the sacerdotal vestments, even the Host itself, were thrown on it without any remonstrance from the consuls; the very wind which blew upon Nimes breathed heresy.

For the moment Nimes was in full revolt, and the spirit of organisation spread: Moget assumed the titles of pastor and minister of the Christian Church. Captain Bouillargues melted down the sacred vessels of the Catholic churches, and paid in this manner the volunteers of Nimes and the German mercenaries; the stones of the demolished religious houses were used in the construction of fortifications, and before anyone thought of attacking it the city was ready for a siege. It was at this moment that Guillaume Calviere, who was at the head of the Presidial Court, Moget being president of the Consistory, and Captain Bouillargues commander-in-chief of the armed forces, suddenly resolved to create a new authority, which, while sharing the powers hitherto vested solely in the consuls, should be, even more than they, devoted to Calvin: thus the office of les Messieurs came into being. This was neither more nor less than a committee of public safety, and having been formed in the stress of revolution it acted in a revolutionary spirit, absorbing the powers of the consuls, and restricting the authority of the Consistory to things spiritual. In the meantime the Edict of Amboise, was promulgated, and it was announced that the

9

king, Charles IX, accompanied by Catherine de Medicis, was going to visit his loyal provinces in the South.

Determined as was Captain Bouillargues, for once he had to give way, so strong was the party against him; therefore, despite the murmurs of the fanatics, the city of Nimes resolved, not only to open its gates to its sovereign, but to give him such a reception as would efface the bad impression which Charles might have received from the history of recent events. The royal procession was met at the Pont du Gare, where young girls attired as nymphs emerged from a grotto bearing a collation, which they presented to their Majesties, who graciously and heartily partook of it. The repast at an end, the illustrious travellers resumed their progress; but the imagination of the Nimes authorities was not to be restrained within such narrow bounds: at the entrance to the city the king found the Porte de la Couronne transformed into a mountain-side, covered with vines and olive trees, under which a shepherd was tending his flock. As the king approached the mountain parted as if yielding to the magic of his power, the most beautiful maidens and the most noble came out to meet their sovereign, presenting him the keys of the city wreathed with flowers, and singing to the accompaniment of the shepherd's pipe. Passing through the mountain, Charles saw chained to a palm tree in the depths of a grotto a monster crocodile from whose jaws issued flames: this was a representation of the old coat of arms granted to the city by Octavius Caesar Augustus after the battle of Actium, and which Francis I had restored to it in exchange for a model in silver of the amphitheatre presented to him by the city. Lastly, the king found in the Place de la

Salamandre numerous bonfires, so that without waiting to ask if these fires were made from the remains of the faggots used at the martyrdom of Maurice Secenat, he went to bed very much pleased with the reception accorded him by his good city of Nimes, and sure that all the unfavourable reports he had heard were calumnies.

Nevertheless, in order that such rumours, however slight their foundation, should not again be heard, the king appointed Damville governor of Languedoc, installing him himself in the chief city of his government; he then removed every consul from his post without exception, and appointed in their place Guy-Rochette, doctor and lawyer; Jean Beaudan, burgess; Francois Aubert, mason; and Cristol Ligier, farm labourer—all Catholics. He then left for Paris, where a short time after he concluded a treaty with the Calvinists, which the people with its gift of prophecy called "The halting peace of unsure seat," and which in the end led to the massacre of St. Bartholomew.

Gracious as had been the measures taken by the king to secure the peace of his good city of Nimes, they had nevertheless been reactionary; consequently the Catholics, feeling the authorities were now on their side, returned in crowds: the householders reclaimed their houses, the priests their churches; while, rendered ravenous by the bitter bread of exile, both the clergy and the laity pillaged the treasury. Their return was not, however; stained by bloodshed, although the Calvinists were reviled in the open street. A few stabs from a dagger or shots from an arquebus might, however, have been better; such wounds heal while mocking words rankle in the memory.

11

On the morrow of Michaelmas Day—that is, on the 31st September 1567—a number of conspirators might have been seen issuing from a house and spreading themselves through the streets, crying "To arms! Down with the Papists!" Captain Bouillargues was taking his revenge.

As the Catholics were attacked unawares, they did not make even a show of resistance: a number of Protestants—those who possessed the best arms—rushed to the house of Guy-Rochette, the first consul, and seized the keys of the city. Guy Rochette, startled by the cries of the crowds, had looked out of the window, and seeing a furious mob approaching his house, and feeling that their rage was directed against himself, had taken refuge with his brother Gregoire. There, recovering his courage and presence of mind, he recalled the important responsibilities attached to his office, and resolving to fulfil them whatever might happen, hastened to consult with the other magistrates, but as they all gave him very excellent reasons for not meddling, he soon felt there was no dependence to be placed on such cowards and traitors. He next repaired to the episcopal palace, where he found the bishop surrounded by the principal Catholics of the town, all on their knees offering up earnest prayers to Heaven, and awaiting martyrdom. Guy-Rochette joined them, and the prayers were continued.

A few instants later fresh noises were heard in the street, and the gates of the palace court groaned under blows of axe and crowbar. Hearing these alarming sounds, the bishop, forgetting that it was his duty to set a brave example, fled through a breach in the wall of the next house; but Guy-Rochette and his companions valiantly resolved not to run away, but to await their fate with patience. The gates soon yielded, and the courtyard and palace were filled with Protestants: at their head appeared Captain Bouillargues, sword in hand. Guy-Rochette and those with him were seized and secured in a room under the charge of four guards, and the palace was looted. Meantime another band of insurgents had attacked the house of the vicar-general, John Pebereau, whose body pierced by seven stabs of a dagger was thrown out of a window, the same fate as was meted out to Admiral Coligny eight years later at the hands of the Catholics. In the house a sum of 800 crowns was found and taken. The two bands then uniting, rushed to the cathedral, which they sacked for the second time.

Thus the entire day passed in murder and pillage: when night came the large number of prisoners so imprudently taken began to be felt as an encumbrance by the insurgent chiefs, who therefore resolved to take advantage of the darkness to get rid of them without causing too much excitement in the city. They were therefore gathered together from the various houses in which they had been confined, and were brought to a large hall in the Hotel de Ville, capable of containing from four to five hundred persons, and which was soon full. An irregular tribunal arrogating to itself powers of life and death was formed, and a clerk was appointed to register its decrees. A list of all the prisoners was given him, a cross placed before a name indicating that its bearer was condemned to death, and, list in hand, he went from group to group calling out the names distinguished by the fatal sign. Those thus sorted out were then conducted to a spot which had been chosen beforehand as the place of execution.

This was the palace courtyard in the middle of which yawned a well twenty-four feet in circumference and fifty deep. The fanatics thus found a grave ready-digged as it were to their hand, and to save time, made use of it.

The unfortunate Catholics, led thither in groups, were either stabbed with daggers or mutilated with axes, and the bodies thrown down the well. Guy-Rochette was one of the first to be dragged up. For himself he asked neither mercy nor favour, but he begged that the life of his young brother might be spared, whose only crime was the bond of blood which united them; but the assassins, paying no heed to his prayers, struck down both man and boy and flung them into the well. The corpse of the vicar-general, who had been killed the day before, was in its turn dragged thither by a rope and added to the others. All night the massacre went on, the crimsoned water rising in the well as corpse after corpse was thrown in, till, at break of day, it overflowed, one hundred and twenty bodies being then hidden in its depths.

Next day, October 1st, the scenes of tumult were renewed: from early dawn Captain Bouillargues ran from street to street crying, "Courage, comrades! Montpellier, Pezenas, Aramon, Beaucaire, Saint-Andeol, and Villeneuve are taken, and are on our side. Cardinal de Lorraine is dead, and the king is in our power." This aroused the failing energies of the assassins. They joined the captain, and demanded that the houses round the palace should be searched, as it was almost certain that the bishop, who had, as may be remembered, escaped the day before, had taken refuge in one of them. This being agreed to, a house-to-house visitation was begun: when the house of M. de Sauvignargues was reached, he confessed that the bishop was in his cellar, and proposed to treat with Captain Bouillargues for a ransom. This proposition being considered reasonable, was accepted, and after a short discussion the sum of 120 crowns was agreed on. The bishop laid down every penny he had about him, his servants were despoiled, and the sum made up by the Sieur de Sauvignargues, who having the bishop in his house kept him caged. The prelate, however, made no objection, although under other circumstances he would have regarded this restraint as the height of impertinence; but as it was he felt safer in M. de Sauvignargues' cellar than in the palace.

But the secret of the worthy prelate's hiding place was but badly kept by those with whom he had treated; for in a few moments a second crowd appeared, hoping to obtain a second ransom. Unfortunately, the Sieur de Sauvignargues, the bishop, and the bishop's servants had stripped themselves of all their ready money to make up the first, so the master of the house, fearing for his own safety, having barricaded the doors, got out into a lane and escaped, leaving the bishop to his fate. The Huguenots climbed in at the windows, crying, "No quarter! Down with the Papists!" The bishop's servants were cut down, the bishop himself dragged out of the cellar and thrown into the street. There his rings and crozier were snatched from him; he was stripped of his clothes and arrayed in a grotesque and ragged garment which chanced to be at hand; his mitre was replaced by a peasant's cap; and in this condition he was dragged back to the palace and placed on the brink of the well to be thrown in. One of the assassins drew attention to the fact that it was already full. "Pooh!" replied another, "they won't mind a little crowding for a bishop." Meantime the prelate, seeing he need expect no mercy from man, threw himself on his knees and commended his soul to God. Suddenly, however, one of those who had shown himself most ferocious during the massacre, Jean Coussinal by name, was touched as if by miracle with a feeling of compassion at the sight of so much resignation, and threw himself between the bishop and those about to strike, and declaring that whoever touched the prelate must first overcome himself, took him under his protection, his comrades retreating in astonishment. Jean Coussinal raising the bishop, carried him in his arms into a neighbouring house, and drawing his sword, took his stand on the threshold.

The assassins, however, soon recovered from their surprise, and reflecting that when all was said and done they were fifty to one, considered it would be shameful to let themselves be intimidated by a single opponent, so they advanced again on Coussinal, who with a back-handed stroke cut off the head of the first-comer. The cries upon this redoubled, and two or three shots were fired at the obstinate defender of the poor bishop, but they all missed aim. At that moment Captain Bouillargues passed by, and seeing one man attacked by fifty, inquired into the cause. He was told of Coussinal's odd determination to save the bishop. "He is quite right," said the captain; "the bishop has paid ransom, and no one has any right to touch him." Saying this, he walked up to Coussinal, gave him his hand, and the two entered the house, returning in a few moments with the bishop between them. In this order they crossed the town, followed by the murmuring crowd, who were, however, afraid to do more than murmur; at the gate the bishop was provided with an escort and let go, his defenders remaining there till he was out of sight.

The massacres went on during the whole of the second day, though towards evening the search for victims relaxed somewhat; but still many isolated acts of murder took place during the night. On the morrow, being tired of killing, the people began to destroy, and this phase lasted a long time, it being less fatiguing to throw stones about than corpses. All the convents, all the monasteries, all the houses of the priests and canons were attacked in turn; nothing was spared except the cathedral, before which axes and crowbars seemed to lose their power, and the church of Ste. Eugenie, which was turned into a powder-magazine. The day of the great butchery was called "La Michelade," because it took place the day after Michaelmas, and as all this happened in the year 1567 the Massacre of St. Bartholomew must be regarded as a plagiarism.

At last, however, with the help of M. Damville; the Catholics again got the upper hand, and it was the turn of the Protestants to fly. They took refuge in the Cevennes. From the beginning of the troubles the Cevennes had been the asylum of those who suffered for the Protestant faith; and still the plains are Papist, and the mountains Protestant. When the Catholic party is in the ascendant at Nimes, the plain seeks the mountain; when the Protestants come into power, the mountain comes down into the plain.

17

However, vanquished and fugitive though they were, the Calvinists did not lose courage: in exile one day, they felt sure their luck would turn the next; and while the Catholics were burning or hanging them in effigy for contumacy, they were before a notary, dividing the property of their executioners.

But it was not enough for them to buy or sell this property amongst each other, they wanted to enter into possession; they thought of nothing else, and in 1569—that is, in the eighteenth month of their exile—they attained their wish in the following manner:

One day the exiles perceived a carpenter belonging to a little village called Cauvisson approaching their place of refuge. He desired to speak to M. Nicolas de Calviere, seigneur de St. Cosme, and brother of the president, who was known to be a very enterprising man. To him the carpenter, whose name was Maduron, made the following proposition:

In the moat of Nimes, close to the Gate of the Carmelites, there was a grating through which the waters from the fountain found vent. Maduron offered to file through the bars of this grating in such a manner that some fine night it could be lifted out so as to allow a band of armed Protestants to gain access to the city. Nicolas de Calviere approving of this plan, desired that it should be carried out at once; but the carpenter pointed out that it would be necessary to wait for stormy weather, when the waters swollen by the rain would by their noise drown the sound of the file. This precaution was doubly necessary as the box of the sentry was almost exactly above the grating. M. de Calviere tried to make Maduron give way; but the latter, who was risking more than anyone else, was firm. So whether they liked it or not, de Calviere and the rest had to await his good pleasure.

Some days later rainy weather set in, and as usual the fountain became fuller; Maduron seeing that the favourable moment had arrived, glided at night into the moat and applied his file, a friend of his who was hidden on the ramparts above pulling a cord attached to Maduron's arm every time the sentinel, in pacing his narrow round, approached the spot. Before break of day the work was well begun. Maduron then obliterated all traces of his file by daubing the bars with mud and wax, and withdrew. For three consecutive nights he returned to his task, taking the same precautions, and before the fourth was at an end he found that by means of a slight effort the grating could be removed. That was all that was needed, so he gave notice to Messire Nicolas de Calviere that the moment had arrived.

Everything was favourable to the undertaking: as there was no moon, the next night was chosen to carry out the plan, and as soon as it was dark Messire Nicolas de Calviere set out with his men, who, slipping down into the moat without noise, crossed, the water being up to their belts, climbed up the other side, and crept along at the foot of the wall till they reached the grating without being perceived. There Maduron was waiting, and as soon as he caught sight of them he gave a slight blow to the loose bars; which fell, and the whole party entered the drain, led by de Calviere, and soon found themselves at the farther end—that is to say, in the Place de la Fontaine. They immediately formed into companies twenty strong, four of which hastened to the principal gates, while the others patrolled the streets

19

shouting, "The city taken! Down with the Papists! A new world!" Hearing this, the Protestants in the city recognised their co-religionists, and the Catholics their opponents: but whereas the former had been warned and were on the alert, the latter were taken by surprise; consequently they offered no resistance, which, however, did not prevent bloodshed. M. de St. Andre, the governor of the town, who during his short period of office had drawn the bitter hatred of the Protestants on him, was shot dead in his bed, and his body being flung out of the window, was torn in pieces by the populace. The work of murder went on all night, and on the morrow the victors in their turn began an organised persecution, which fell more heavily on the Catholics than that to which they had subjected the Protestants; for, as we have explained above, the former could only find shelter in the plain, while the latter used the Cevennes as a stronghold.

It was about this time that the peace, which was called, as we have said, "the insecurely seated," was concluded. Two years later this name was justified by the Massacre of St. Bartholomew.

When this event took place, the South, strange as it may seem, looked on: in Nimes both Catholics and Protestants, stained with the other's blood, faced each other, hand on hilt, but without drawing weapon. It was as if they were curious to see how the Parisians would get through. The massacre had one result, however, the union of the principal cities of the South and West: Montpellier, Uzes, Montauban, and La Rochelle, with Nimes at their head, formed a civil and military league to last, as is declared in the Act of Federation, until God should raise up a sovereign to be the defender of the Protestant faith. In the year 1775 the Protestants of the South began to turn their eyes towards Henri IV as the coming defender.

At that date Nimes, setting an example to the other cities of the League, deepened her moats, blew up her suburbs, and added to the height of her ramparts. Night and day the work of perfecting the means of defence went on; the guard at every gate was doubled, and knowing how often a city had been taken by surprise, not a hole through which a Papist could creep was left in the fortifications. In dread of what the future might bring, Nimes even committed sacrilege against the past, and partly demolished the Temple of Diana and mutilated the amphitheatre—of which one gigantic stone was sufficient to form a section of the wall. During one truce the crops were sown, during another they were garnered in, and so things went on while the reign of the Mignons lasted. At length the prince raised up by God, whom the Huguenots had waited for so long, appeared; Henri IV ascended the, throne.

But once seated, Henri found himself in the same difficulty as had confronted Octavius fifteen centuries earlier, and which confronted Louis Philippe three centuries later—that is to say, having been raised to sovereign power by a party which was not in the majority, he soon found himself obliged to separate from this party and to abjure his religious beliefs, as others have abjured or will yet abjure their political beliefs; consequently, just as Octavius had his Antony, and Louis Philippe was to have his Lafayette, Henri IV was to have his Biron. When monarchs are in this position they can no longer have a will of their own or personal likes and dislikes; they submit to the force of circumstances, and feel compelled to rely on the masses; no sooner are they freed from the ban under which they laboured than they are obliged to bring others under it.

However, before having recourse to extreme measures, Henri IV with soldierly frankness gathered round him all those who had been his comrades of old in war and in religion; he spread out before them a map of France, and showed them that hardly a tenth of the immense number of its inhabitants were Protestants, and that even that tenth was shut up in the mountains; some in Dauphine, which had been won for them by their three principal leaders, Baron des Adrets, Captain Montbrun, and Lesdiguieres; others in the Cevennes, which had become Protestant through their great preachers, Maurice Secenat and Guillaume Moget; and the rest in the mountains of Navarre, whence he himself had come. He recalled to them further that whenever they ventured out of their mountains they had been beaten in every battle, at Jarnac, at Moncontour, and at Dreux. He concluded by explaining how impossible it was for him, such being the case, to entrust the guidance of the State to their party; but he offered them instead three things, viz., his purse to supply their present needs, the Edict of Nantes to assure their future safety, and fortresses to defend themselves should this edict one day be revoked, for with profound insight the grandfather divined the grandson: Henri IV feared Louis XIV.

The Protestants took what they were offered, but of course like all who accept benefits they went away filled with discontent because they had not been given more.

22

Although the Protestants ever afterwards looked on Henri IV as a renegade, his reign nevertheless was their golden age, and while it lasted Nines was quiet; for, strange to say, the Protestants took no revenge for St. Bartholomew, contenting themselves with debarring the Catholics from the open exercise of their religion, but leaving them free to use all its rites and ceremonies in private. They even permitted the procession of the Host through the streets in case of illness, provided it took place at night. Of course death would not always wait for darkness, and the Host was sometimes carried to the dying during the day, not without danger to the priest, who, however, never let himself be deterred thereby from the performance of his duty; indeed, it is of the essence of religious devotion to be inflexible; and few soldiers, however brave, have equalled the martyrs in courage.

During this time, taking advantage of the truce to hostilities and the impartial protection meted out to all without distinction by the Constable Damville, the Carmelites and Capuchins, the Jesuits and monks of all orders and colours, began by degrees to return to Nines; without any display, it is true, rather in a surreptitious manner, preferring darkness to daylight; but however this may be, in the course of three or four years they had all regained foothold in the town; only now they were in the position in which the Protestants had been formerly, they were without churches, as their enemies were in possession of all the places of worship. It also happened that a Jesuit high in authority, named Pere Coston, preached with such success that the Protestants, not wishing to be beaten, but

23

desirous of giving word for word, summoned to their aid the Rev. Jeremie Ferrier, of Alais, who at the moment was regarded as the most eloquent preacher they had. Needless to say, Alais was situated in the mountains, that inexhaustible source of Huguenot eloquence. At once the controversial spirit was aroused; it did not as yet amount to war, but still less could it be called peace: people were no longer assassinated, but they were anathematised; the body was safe, but the soul was consigned to damnation: the days as they passed were used by both sides to keep their hand in, in readiness for the moment when the massacres should again begin.

CHAPTER II

The death of Henri IV led to new conflicts, in which although at first success was on the side of the Protestants it by degrees went over to the Catholics; for with the accession of Louis XIII Richelieu had taken possession of the throne: beside the king sat the cardinal; under the purple mantle gleamed the red robe. It was at this crisis that Henri de Rohan rose to eminence in the South. He was one of the most illustrious representatives of that great race which, allied as it was to the royal houses of Scotland, France, Savoy, and Lorraine; had taken as their device, "Be king I cannot, prince I will not, Rohan I am."

Henri de Rohan was at this time about forty years of age, in the prime of life. In his youth, in order to perfect his education, he had visited England, Scotland, and Italy. In England Elizabeth had called him her knight; in Scotland James VI had asked him to stand godfather to his son, afterwards Charles I; in Italy he had been so deep in the confidence of the leaders of men, and so thoroughly initiated into the politics of the principal cities, that it was commonly said that, after Machiavel, he was the greatest authority in these matters. He had returned to France in the lifetime of Henry IV, and had married the daughter of Sully, and after Henri's death had commanded the Swiss and the Grison regiments—at the siege of Juliers. This was the man whom the king was so imprudent as to offend by refusing him the reversion of the office of governor of Poitou, which was then held by Sully, his father-in-law. In order to revenge himself for the neglect he met with at court, as he states in his Memoires with military ingenuousness, he espoused the cause of Conde with all his heart, being also drawn in this direction by his liking for Conde's brother and his consequent desire to help those of Conde's religion.

From this day on street disturbances and angry disputes assumed another aspect: they took in a larger area and were not so readily appeased. It was no longer an isolated band of insurgents which roused a city, but rather a conflagration which spread over the whole South, and a general uprising which was almost a civil war.

This state of things lasted for seven or eight years, and during this time Rohan, abandoned by Chatillon and La Force, who received as the reward of their defection the field marshal's baton, pressed by Conde, his old friend, and by Montmorency, his consistent rival, performed prodigies of courage and miracles of strategy. At last, without soldiers, without ammunition, without money, he still appeared to Richelieu to be so redoubtable that all the conditions of surrender he demanded were granted. The maintenance of the Edict of Nantes was guaranteed, all the places of worship were to be restored to the Reformers, and a general amnesty granted to himself and his partisans. Furthermore, he obtained what was an unheard-of thing until then, an indemnity of 300,000 livres for his expenses during the rebellion; of which sum he allotted 240,000 livres to his co-religionists—that is to say, more than three-quarters of the entire amount—and kept, for the purpose of restoring his various chateaux and setting his domestic establishment, which had been destroyed during the war, again on foot, only 60,000 livres. This treaty was signed on July 27th, 1629.

The Duc de Richelieu, to whom no sacrifice was too great in order to attain his ends, had at last reached the goal, but the peace cost him nearly 40,000,000 livres; on the other hand, Saintonge, Poitou, and Languedoc had submitted, and the chiefs of the houses of La Tremouille, Conde, Bouillon, Rohan, and Soubise had came to terms with him; organised armed opposition had disappeared, and the lofty manner of viewing matters natural to the cardinal duke prevented him from noticing private enmity. He therefore left Nimes free to manage her local affairs as she pleased, and very soon the old order, or rather disorder, reigned once more within her walls. At last Richelieu died, and Louis XIII soon followed him, and the long minority of his successor, with its embarrassments, left to Catholics and Protestants in the South more complete liberty than ever to carry on the great duel which down to our own days has never ceased.

But from this period, each flux and reflux bears more and more the peculiar character of the party which for the moment is triumphant; when the Protestants get the upper hand, their vengeance is marked by brutality and rage; when the Catholics are victorious, the retaliation is full of hypocrisy and greed. The Protestants pull down churches and monasteries, expel the monks, burn the crucifixes, take the body of some criminal from the gallows, nail it on a cross, pierce its side, put a crown of thorns round its temples and set it up in the market-place—an effigy of Jesus on Calvary. The Catholics levy contributions, take back what they had been deprived of, exact indemnities, and although ruined by each reverse, are richer than ever after each victory. The Protestants act in the light of day, melting down the church bells to make cannon to the sound of the drum, violate agreements, warm themselves with wood taken from the houses of the cathedral clergy, affix their theses to the cathedral doors, beat the priests who carry the Holy Sacrament to the dying, and, to crown all other insults, turn churches into slaughter-houses and sewers.

The Catholics, on the contrary, march at night, and, slipping in at the gates which have been left ajar for them, make their bishop president of the Council, put Jesuits at the head of the college, buy converts with money from the treasury, and as they always have influence at court, begin by excluding the Calvinists from favour, hoping soon to deprive them of justice.

27

At last, on the 31st of December, 1657, a final struggle took place, in which the Protestants were overcome, and were only saved from destruction because from the other side of the Channel, Cromwell exerted himself in their favour, writing with his own hand at the end of a despatch relative to the affairs of Austria, "I Learn that there have been popular disturbances in a town of Languedoc called Nimes, and I beg that order may be restored with as much mildness as possible, and without shedding of blood." As, fortunately for the Protestants, Mazarin had need of Cromwell at that moment, torture was forbidden, and nothing allowed but annoyances of all kinds. These henceforward were not only innumerable, but went on without a pause: the Catholics, faithful to their system of constant encroachment, kept up an incessant persecution, in which they were soon encouraged by the numerous ordinances issued by Louis XIV. The grandson of Henri IV could not so far forget all ordinary respect as to destroy at once the Edict of Nantes, but he tore off clause after clause.

In 1630—that is, a year after the peace with Rohan had been signed in the preceding reign—Chalons-sur-Saone had resolved that no Protestant should be allowed to take any part in the manufactures of the town.

In 1643, six months after the accession of Louis XIV, the laundresses of Paris made a rule that the wives and daughters of Protestants were unworthy to be admitted to the freedom of their respectable guild.

In 1654, just one year after he had attained his majority, Louis XIV consented to the imposition of a tax on the town of Nimes of 4000 francs towards the support of the Catholic and the Protestant hospitals; and instead of allowing each party to contribute to the support of its own hospital, the money was raised in one sum, so that, of the money paid by the Protestants, who were twice as numerous as the Catholics, two-sixths went to their enemies. On August 9th of the same year a decree of the Council ordered that all the artisan consuls should be Catholics; on the 16th September another decree forbade Protestants to send deputations to the king; lastly, on the 20th of December, a further decree declared that all hospitals should be administered by Catholic consuls alone.

In 1662 Protestants were commanded to bury their dead either at dawn or after dusk, and a special clause of the decree fixed the number of persons who might attend a funeral at ten only.

In 1663 the Council of State issued decrees prohibiting the practice of their religion by the Reformers in one hundred and forty-two communes in the dioceses of Nimes, Uzes, and Mendes; and ordering the demolition of their meetinghouses.

In 1664 this regulation was extended to the meeting-houses of Alencon and Montauban, as Well as their small place of worship in Nimes. On the 17th July of the same year the Parliament of Rouen forbade the master-mercers to engage any more Protestant workmen or apprentices when the number already employed had reached the proportion of one Protestant, to fifteen Catholics; on the 24th of the same month the Council of State declared all certificates of mastership held by a Protestant invalid from whatever source derived; and in October reduced to two the number of Protestants who might be employed at the mint.

In 1665 the regulation imposed on the mercers was extended to the goldsmiths.

In 1666 a royal declaration, revising the decrees of Parliament, was published, and Article 31 provided that the offices of clerk to the consulates, or secretary to a guild of watchmakers, or porter in a municipal building, could only be held by Catholics; while in Article 33 it was ordained that when a procession carrying the Host passed a place of worship belonging to the so-called Reformers, the worshippers should stop their psalm-singing till the procession had gone by; and lastly, in Article 34 it was enacted that the houses and other buildings belonging to those who were of the Reformed religion might, at the pleasure of the town authorities, be draped with cloth or otherwise decorated on any religious Catholic festival.

In 1669 the Chambers appointed by the Edict of Nantes in the Parliaments of Rouen and Paris were suppressed, as well as the articled clerkships connected therewith, and the clerkships in the Record Office; and in August of the same year, when the emigration of Protestants was just beginning, an edict was issued, of which the following is a clause:

"Whereas many of our subjects have gone to foreign countries, where they continue to follow their various trades and occupations, even working as shipwrights, or taking service as sailors, till at length they feel at home and determine never to return to France, marrying abroad and acquiring property of every description: We hereby forbid any member of the so-called Reformed Church to leave this kingdom without our permission, and we command those who have already left France to return forthwith within her boundaries."

In 1670 the king excluded physicians of the Reformed faith from the office of dean of the college of Rouen, and allowed only two Protestant doctors within its precincts. In 1671 a decree was published commanding the arms of France to be removed from all the places of worship belonging to the pretended Reformers. In 1680 a proclamation from the king closed the profession of midwife to women of the Reformed faith. In 1681 those who renounced the Protestant religion were exempted for two years from all contributions towards the support of soldiers sent to their town, and were for the same period relieved from the duty of giving them board and lodging. In the same year the college of Sedan was closed—the only college remaining in the entire kingdom at which Calvinist children could receive instruction. In 1682 the king commanded Protestant notaries; procurators, ushers, and serjeants to lay down their offices, declaring them unfit for such professions; and in September of the same year three months only were allowed them for the sale of the reversion of the said offices. In 1684 the Council of State extended the preceding regulations to those Protestants holding the title of honorary secretary to the king, and in August of the same year Protestants were declared incapable of serving on a jury of experts.

In 1685 the provost of merchants in Paris ordered all Protestant privileged merchants in that city to sell their privileges within a month. And in October of the same year the long series of persecutions, of which we have omitted many, reached its culminating point—the: Revocation of the Edict of Nantes. Henri IV, who foresaw this result, had hoped that it would have occurred in another manner, so that his co-religionists would have been able to retain their fortresses; but what was actually done was that the strong places were first taken away, and then came the Revocation; after which the Calvinists found themselves completely at the mercy of their mortal enemies.

From 1669, when Louis first threatened to aim a fatal blow at the civil rights of the Huguenots, by abolishing the equal partition of the Chambers between the two parties, several deputations had been sent to him praying him to stop the course of his persecutions; and in order not to give him any fresh excuse for attacking their party, these deputations addressed him in the most submissive manner, as the following fragment from an address will prove:

"In the name of God, sire," said the Protestants to the king, "listen to the last breath of our dying liberty, have pity on our sufferings, have pity on the great number of your poor subjects who daily water their bread with their tears: they are all filled with burning zeal and inviolable loyalty to you; their love for your august person is only equalled by their respect; history bears witness that they contributed in no small degree to place your great and magnanimous ancestor on his rightful throne, and since your miraculous birth they have never done anything worthy of blame; they might indeed use much stronger terms, but your Majesty has spared their modesty by addressing to them on many occasions words of praise which they would never have ventured to apply to themselves; these your subjects place their sole trust in your sceptre for refuge and protection on earth, and their interest as well as their duty and conscience impels them to remain attached to the service of your Majesty with unalterable devotion."

But, as we have seen, nothing could restrain the triumvirate which held the power just then, and thanks to the suggestions of Pere Lachaise and Madame de Maintenon, Louis XIV determined to gain heaven by means of wheel and stake.

As we see, for the Protestants, thanks to these numerous decrees, persecution began at the cradle and followed them to the grave.

As a boy, a Huguenot could—enter no public school; as a youth, no career was open to him; he could become neither mercer nor concierge, neither apothecary nor physician, neither lawyer nor consul. As a man, he had no sacred house, of prayer; no registrar would inscribe his marriage or the birth of his children; hourly his liberty and his conscience were ignored. If he ventured to worship God by the singing of psalms, he had to be silent as the Host was carried past outside. When a Catholic festival occurred, he was forced not only to swallow his rage but to let his house be hung with decorations in sign of joy; if he had inherited a fortune from his fathers, having neither social standing nor civil rights, it slipped gradually out of his hands, and went to support the schools and hospitals of his foes. Having reached the end of his life, his deathbed was made miserable; for dying in the faith of his fathers, he could not be laid to rest beside them, and like a pariah he would be carried to his grave at night, no more than ten of those near and dear to him being allowed to follow his coffin.

Lastly, if at any age whatever he should attempt to quit the cruel soil on which he had no right to be born, to live, or to die, he would be declared a rebel, his goads would be confiscated, and the lightest penalty that he had to expect, if he ever fell into the hands of his enemies, was to row for the rest of his life in the galleys of the king, chained between a murderer and a forger.

Such a state of things was intolerable: the cries of one man are lost in space, but the groans of a whole population are like a storm; and this time, as always, the tempest gathered in the mountains, and the rumblings of the thunder began to be heard.

First there were texts written by invisible hands on city walls, on the signposts and cross-roads, on the crosses in the cemeteries: these warnings, like the 'Mene, Mene, Tekel, Upharsin' of Belshazzar, even pursued the persecutors into the midst of their feasts and orgies.

Now it was the threat, "Jesus came not to send peace, but a sword." Then this consolation, "For where two or three are gathered together in My name, there am I in the midst of them." Or perhaps it was this appeal for united action which was soon to become a summons to revolt, "That which we have seen and heard declare we unto you, that ye also may have fellowship with us."

And before these promises, taken from the New Testament, the persecuted paused, and then went home inspired by faith in the prophets, who spake, as St. Paul says

34

in his First Epistle to the Thessalonians, "not the word of men but the word of God."

Very soon these words became incarnate, and what the prophet Joel foretold came to pass: "Your sons and your daughters shall prophesy, your old men shall dream dreams, your young men shall see visions,... and I will show wonders in the heavens and in the earth, blood and fire,... and it shall come to pass that whosoever shall call on the name of the Lord shall be delivered."

In 1696 reports began to circulate that men had had visions; being able to see what was going on in the most distant parts, and that the heavens themselves opened to their eyes. While in this ecstatic state they were insensible to pain when pricked with either pin or blade; and when, on recovering consciousness, they were questioned they could remember nothing.

The first of these was a woman from Vivarais, whose origin was unknown. She went about from town to town, shedding tears of blood. M. de Baville, intendant of Languedoc, had her arrested and brought to Montpellier. There she was condemned to death and burnt at the stake, her tears of blood being dried by fire.

After her came a second fanatic, for so these popular prophets were called. He was born at Mazillon, his name was Laquoite, and he was twenty years of age. The gift of prophecy had come to him in a strange manner. This is the story told about him:—"One day, returning from Languedoc, where he had been engaged in the cultivation of silkworms, on reaching the bottom of the hill of St. Jean he found a man lying on the ground trembling in every limb. Moved by pity, he stopped and asked what ailed him. The man replied, 'Throw yourself on your knees, my son, and trouble not yourself about me, but learn how to attain salvation and save your brethren. This can only be done by the communion of the Holy Ghost, who is in me, and whom by the grace of God I can bestow on you. Approach and receive this gift in a kiss.' At these words the unknown kissed the young man on the mouth, pressed his hand and disappeared, leaving the other trembling in his turn; for the spirit of God was in him, and being inspired he spread the word abroad."

A third fanatic, a prophetess, raved about the parishes of St. Andeol de Clerguemont and St. Frazal de Vantalon, but she addressed herself principally to recent converts, to whom she preached concerning the Eucharist that in swallowing the consecrated wafer they had swallowed a poison as venomous as the head of the basilisk, that they had bent the knee to Baal, and that no penitence on their part could be great enough to save them. These doctrines inspired such profound terror that the Rev. Father Louvreloeil himself tells us that Satan by his efforts succeeded in nearly emptying the churches, and that at the following Easter celebrations there were only half as many communicants as the preceding year.

Such a state of licence, which threatened to spread farther and farther, awoke the religious solicitude of Messire Francois Langlade de Duchayla, Prior of Laval, Inspector of Missions of Gevaudan, and Arch-priest of the Cevennes. He therefore resolved to leave his residence at Mende and to visit the parishes in which heresy had taken the strongest hold, in order to oppose it by every mean's which God and the king had put in his power.

The Abbe Duchayla was a younger son of the noble house of Langlade, and by the circumstances of his birth, in spite of his soldierly instincts, had been obliged to leave epaulet and sword to his elder brother, and himself assume cassock and stole. On leaving the seminary, he espoused the cause of the Church militant with all the ardour of his temperament. Perils to encounter; foes to fight, a religion to force on others, were necessities to this fiery character, and as everything at the moment was quiet in France, he had embarked for India with the fervent resolution of a martyr.

On reaching his destination, the young missionary had found himself surrounded by circumstances which were wonderfully in harmony with his celestial longings: some of his predecessors had been carried so far by religious zeal that the King of Siam had put several to death by torture and had forbidden any more missionaries to enter his dominions; but this, as we can easily imagine, only excited still more the abbe's missionary fervour; evading the watchfulness of the military, and regardless of the terrible penalties imposed by the king, he crossed the frontier, and began to preach the Catholic religion to the heathen, many of whom were converted.

One day he was surprised by a party of soldiers in a little village in which he had been living for three months, and in which nearly all the inhabitants had abjured their false faith, and was brought before the governor of Bankan, where instead of denying his faith, he nobly defended Christianity and magnified the name of God. He was handed over to the executioners to be subjected to torture, and suffered at their hands with resignation everything that a human body can endure while yet retaining life, till at length his patience exhausted their rage; and seeing him become unconscious, they thought he was dead, and with mutilated hands, his breast furrowed with wounds, his limbs half warn through by heavy fetters, he was suspended by the wrists to a branch of a tree and abandoned. A pariah passing by cut him down and succoured him, and reports of his martyrdom having spread, the French ambassador demanded justice with no uncertain voice, so that the King of Siam, rejoicing that the executioners had stopped short in time, hastened to send back to M. de Chaumont, the representative of Louis XIV, a mutilated though still living man, instead of the corpse which had been demanded.

At the time when Louis XIV was meditating the Revocation of the Edict of Nantes he felt that the services of such a man would be invaluable to him, so about 1632, Abbe Duchayla was recalled from India, and a year later was sent to Mende, with the titles of Arch-priest of the Cevennes and Inspector of Missions.

Soon the abbe, who had been so much persecuted, became a persecutor, showing himself as insensible to the sufferings of others as he had been inflexible under his own. His apprenticeship to torture stood him in such good stead that he became an inventor, and not only did he enrich the torture chamber by importing from India several scientifically constructed machines, hitherto unknown in Europe, but he also designed many others. People told with terror of reeds cut in the form of whistles which the abbe pitilessly forced under the nails of malignants; of iron pincers for tearing out their beards, eyelashes, and eyebrows; of wicks steeped in oil and wound round the fingers of a victim's hands, and then set on fire so as to form a pair of five-flamed candelabra; of a case turning on a pivot in which a man who refused to be converted was sometimes shut up, the case being then made to revolve rapidly till the victim lost consciousness; and lastly of fetters used when taking prisoners from one town to another, and brought to such perfection, that when they were on the prisoner could neither stand nor sit.

Even the most fervent panegyrists of Abbe Duchayla spoke of him with bated breath, and, when he himself looked into his own heart and recalled how often he had applied to the body the power to bind and loose which God had only given him over the soul, he was seized with strange tremors, and falling on his knees with folded hands and bowed head he remained for hours wrapt in thought, so motionless that were it not for the drops of sweat which stood on his brow he might have been taken for a marble statue of prayer over a tomb.

Moreover, this priest by virtue of the powers with which he was invested, and feeling that he had the authority of M. de Baville, intendant of Languedoc, and M. de Broglie, commander of the troops, behind him, had done other terrible things.

He had separated children from father and mother, and had shut them up in religious houses, where they had been subjected to such severe chastisement, by way of making them do penance for the heresy of their parents, that many of them died under it.

He had forced his way into the chamber of the dying, not to bring consolation but menaces; and bending over the bed, as if to keep back the Angel of Death, he had repeated the words of the terrible decree which provided that in case of the death of a Huguenot without conversion, his memory should be persecuted, and his body, denied Christian burial, should be drawn on hurdles out of the city, and cast on a dungheap.

Lastly, when with pious love children tried to shield their parents in the death-agony from his threats, or dead from his justice, by carrying them, dead or dying, to some refuge in which they might hope to draw their last breath in peace or to obtain Christian burial, he declared that anyone who should open his door hospitably to such disobedience was a traitor to religion, although among the heathen such pity would have been deemed worthy of an altar.

Such was the man raised up to punish, who went on his way, preceded by terror, accompanied by torture, and followed by death, through a country already exhausted by long and bloody oppression, and where at every step he trod on half repressed religious hate, which like a volcano was ever ready to burst out afresh, but always prepared for martyrdom. Nothing held him back, and years ago he had had his grave hollowed out in the church of St. Germain, choosing that church for his last long sleep because it had been built by Pope Urban IV when he was bishop of Mende.

Abbe Duchayla extended his visitation over six months, during which every day was marked by tortures and executions: several prophets were burnt at the stake; Francoise de Brez, she who had preached that the Host contained a more venomous poison than a basilisk's head, was hanged; and Laquoite, who had been confined in the citadel of Montpellier, was on the point of being broken on the wheel, when on the eve of his execution his cell was found empty. No one could ever discover how he escaped, and consequently his reputation rose higher than ever, it being currently believed that, led by the Holy Spirit as St. Peter by the angel, he had passed through the guards invisible to all, leaving his fetters behind.

This incomprehensible escape redoubled the severity of the Arch-priest, till at last the prophets, feeling that their only chance of safety lay in getting rid of him, began to preach against him as Antichrist, and advocate his death. The abbe was warned of this, but nothing could abate his zeal. In France as in India, martyrdom was his longed-for goal, and with head erect and unfaltering step he "pressed toward the mark."

At last, on the evening of the 24th of July, two hundred conspirators met in a wood on the top of a hill which overlooked the bridge of Montvert, near which was the Arch-priest's residence. Their leader was a man named Laporte, a native of Alais, who had become a master-blacksmith in the pass of Deze. He was accompanied by an inspired man, a former wool-carder, born at Magistavols, Esprit Seguier by name. This man was, after Laquoite, the most highly regarded of the twenty or thirty prophets who were at that moment going up and down the Cevennes in every direction.

41

The whole party was armed with scythes, halberts, and swords; a few had even pistols and guns.

On the stroke of ten, the hour fixed for their departure, they all knelt down and with uncovered heads began praying as fervently as if they were about to perform some act most pleasing to God, and their prayers ended, they marched down the hill to the town, singing psalms, and shouting between the verses to the townspeople to keep within their homes, and not to look out of door or window on pain of death.

The abbe was in his oratory when he heard the mingled singing and shouting, and at the same moment a servant entered in great alarm, despite the strict regulation of the Arch-priest that he was never to be interrupted at his prayers. This man announced that a body of fanatics was coming down the hill, but the abbe felt convinced that it was only an unorganised crowd which was going to try and carry off six prisoners, at that moment in the 'ceps.' [A terrible kind of stocks—a beam split in two, no notches being made for the legs: the victim's legs were placed between the two pieces of wood, which were then, by means of a vice at each end, brought gradually together. Translators Note.]

These prisoners were three young men and three girls in men's clothes, who had been seized just as they were about to emigrate. As the abbe was always protected by a guard of soldiers, he sent for the officer in command and ordered him to march against, the fanatics and disperse them. But the officer was spared the trouble of obeying, for the fanatics were already at hand. On reaching the gate of the courtyard he heard them outside, and perceived that

42

they were making ready to burst it in. Judging of their numbers by the sound of their voices, he considered that far from attacking them, he would have enough to do in preparing for defence, consequently he bolted and barred the gate on the inside, and hastily erected a barricade under an arch leading to the apartments of the abbe. Just as these preparations were complete, Esprit Seguier caught sight of a heavy beam of wood lying in a ditch; this was raised by a dozen men and used as a battering-ram to force in the gate, which soon showed a breach. Thus encouraged, the workers, cheered by the chants of their comrades, soon got the gate off the hinges, and thus the outside court was taken. The crowd then loudly demanded the release of the prisoners, using dire threats.

The commanding officer sent to ask the abbe what he was to do; the abbe replied that he was to fire on the conspirators. This imprudent order was carried out; one of the fanatics was killed on the spot, and two wounded men mingled their groans with the songs and threats of their comrades.

The barricade was next attacked, some using axes, others darting their swords and halberts through the crevices and killing those behind; as for those who had firearms, they climbed on the shoulders of the others, and having fired at those below, saved themselves by tumbling down again. At the head of the besiegers were Laporte and Esprit Seguier, one of whom had a father to avenge and the other a son, both of whom had been done to death by the abbe. They were not the only ones of the party who were

43

fired by the desire of vengeance; twelve or fifteen others were in the same position.

The abbe in his room listened to the noise of the struggle, and finding matters growing serious, he gathered his household round him, and making them kneel down, he told them to make their confession, that he might, by giving them absolution, prepare them for appearing before God. The sacred words had just been pronounced when the rioters drew near, having carried the barricade, and driven the soldiers to take refuge in a hall on the ground floor just under the Arch-priest's room.

But suddenly, the assault was stayed, some of the men going to surround the house, others setting out on a search for the prisoners. These were easily found, for judging by what they could hear that their brethren had come to their rescue, they shouted as loudly as they could.

The unfortunate creatures had already passed a whole week with their legs caught and pressed by the cleft beams which formed these inexpressibly painful stocks. When the unfortunate victims were released, the fanatics screamed with rage at the sight of their swollen bodies and half-broken bones. None of the unhappy people were able to stand. The attack on the soldiers was renewed, and these being driven out of the lower hall, filled the staircase leading to the abbe's apartments, and offered such determined resistance that their assailants were twice forced to fall back. Laporte, seeing two of his men killed and five or six wounded, called out loudly, "Children of God, lay down your arms: this way of going to work is too slow; let us burn the abbey and all in it. To work! to work!" The advice was good, and they all hastened to follow it: benches, chairs, and furniture of all sorts were heaped up in the hall, a palliasse thrown on the top, and the pile fired. In a moment the whole building was ablaze, and the Arch-priest, yielding to the entreaties of his servants, fastened his sheets to the window-bars, and by their help dropped into the garden. The drop was so great that he broke one of his thigh bones, but dragging himself along on his hands and one knee, he, with one of his servants, reached a recess in the wall, while another servant was endeavouring to escape through the flames, thus falling into the hands of the fanatics, who carried him before their captain. Then cries of "The prophet! the prophet!" were heard on all sides. Esprit Seguier, feeling that something fresh had taken place, came forward, still holding in his hand the blazing torch with which he had set fire to the pile.

"Brother," asked Laporte, pointing to the prisoner, "is this man to die?"

Esprit Seguier fell on his knees and covered his face with his mantle, like Samuel, and sought the Lord in prayer, asking to know His will.

In a short time he rose and said, "This man is not to die; for inasmuch as he has showed mercy to our brethren we must show mercy to him."

Whether this fact had been miraculously revealed to Seguier, or whether he had gained his information from other sources, the newly released prisoners confirmed its truth, calling out that the man had indeed treated them with humanity. Just then a roar as of a wild beast was heard: one of the fanatics, whose brother had been put to death by the abbe, had just caught sight of him, the whole neighbourhood

45

being lit up by the fire; he was kneeling in an angle of the wall, to which he had dragged himself.

"Down with the son of Belial!" shouted the crowd, rushing towards the priest, who remained kneeling and motionless like a marble statue. His valet took advantage of the confusion to escape, and got off easily; for the sight of him on whom the general hate was concentrated made the Huguenots forget everything else:

Esprit Seguier was the first to reach the priest, and spreading his hands over him, he commanded the others to hold back. "God desireth not the death of a sinner,'" said he, "'but rather that he turn from his wickedness and live.'"

"No, no!" shouted a score of voices, refusing obedience for the first time, perhaps, to an order from the prophet; "let him die without mercy, as he struck without pity. Death to the son of Belial, death!"

"Silence!" exclaimed the prophet in a terrible voice, "and listen to the word of God from my mouth. If this man will join us and take upon him the duties of a pastor, let us grant him his life, that he may henceforward devote it to the spread of the true faith."

"Rather a thousand deaths than apostasy!" answered the priest.

"Die, then!" cried Laporte, stabbing him; "take that for having burnt my father in Nimes."

And he passed on the dagger to Esprit Seguier.

Duchayla made neither sound nor gesture: it would have seemed as if the dagger had been turned by the priest's gown as by a coat of mail were it not that a thin stream of blood appeared. Raising his eyes to heaven, he repeated the

46

words of the penitential psalm: "Out of the depths have I cried unto Thee, O Lord! Lord, hear my voice!"

Then Esprit Seguier raised his arm and struck in his turn, saying, "Take that for my son, whom you broke on the wheel at Montpellier."

And he passed on the dagger.

But this blow also was not mortal, only another stream of blood appeared, and the abbe said in a failing voice, "Deliver me, O my Saviour, out of my well-merited sufferings, and I will acknowledge their justice; far I have been a man of blood."

The next who seized the dagger came near and gave his blow, saying, "Take that for my brother, whom you let die in the 'ceps.'"

This time the dagger pierced the heart, and the abbe had only time to ejaculate, "Have mercy on me, O God, according to Thy great mercy!" before he fell back dead.

But his death did not satisfy the vengeance of those who had not been able to strike him living; one by one they drew near and stabbed, each invoking the shade of some dear murdered one and pronouncing the same words of malediction.

In all, the body of the abbe received fifty-two dagger thrusts, of which twenty-four would have been mortal.

Thus perished, at the age of fifty-five, Messire Francois de Langlade Duchayla, prior of Laval, inspector of missions in Gevaudan, and Arch-priest of the Cevennes and Mende.

Their vengeance thus accomplished, the murderers felt that there was no more safety for them in either city or plain, and fled to the mountains; but in passing near the residence

47

of M. de Laveze, a Catholic nobleman of the parish of Molezon, one of the fugitives recollected that he had heard that a great number of firearms was kept in the house. This seemed a lucky chance, for firearms were what the Huguenots needed most of all. They therefore sent two envoys to M. de Laveze to ask him to give them at, least a share of his weapons; but he, as a good Catholic, replied that it was quite true that he had indeed a store of arms, but that they were destined to the triumph and not to the desecration of religion, and that he would only give them up with his life. With these words, he dismissed the envoys, barring his doors behind them.

But while this parley was going on the conspirators had approached the chateau, and thus received the valiant answer to their demands sooner than M. de Laveze had counted on. Resolving not to leave him time to take defensive measures, they dashed at the house, and by standing on each other's shoulders reached the room in which M. de Laveze and his entire family had taken refuge. In an instant the door was forced, and the fanatics, still reeking with the life-blood of Abbe Duchayla, began again their work of death. No one was spared; neither the master of the house, nor his brother, nor his uncle, nor his sister, who knelt to the assassins in vain; even his old mother, who was eighty years of age, having from her bed first witnessed the murder of all her family, was at last stabbed to the heart, though the butchers might have reflected that it was hardly worth while thus to anticipate the arrival of Death, who according to the laws of nature must have been already at hand.

The massacre finished, the fanatics spread over the castle, supplying themselves with arms and under-linen, being badly in need of the latter; for when they left their homes they had expected soon to return, and had taken nothing with them. They also carried off the copper kitchen utensils, intending to turn them into bullets. Finally, they seized on a sum of 5000 francs, the marriage-portion of M. de Laveze's sister, who was just about to be married, and thus laid the foundation of a war fund.

The news of these two bloody events soon reached not only Nimes but all the countryside, and roused the authorities to action. M. le Comte de Broglie crossed the Upper Cevennes, and marched down to the bridge of Montvert, followed by several companies of fusiliers. From another direction M. le Comte de Peyre brought thirty-two cavalry and three hundred and fifty infantry, having enlisted them at Marvejols, La Canourgue, Chiac, and Serverette. M. de St. Paul, Abbe Duchayla's brother, and the Marquis Duchayla, his nephew, brought eighty horsemen from the family estates. The Count of Morangiez rode in from St. Auban and Malzieu with two companies of cavalry, and the town of Mende by order of its bishop despatched its nobles at the head of three companies of fifty men each.

But the mountains had swallowed up the fanatics, and nothing was ever known of their fate, except that from time to time a peasant would relate that in crossing the Cevennes he had heard at dawn or dusk, on mountain peak or from valley depths, the sound going up to heaven of songs of praise. It was the fanatic assassins worshipping God.

Or occasionally at night, on the tops of the lofty mountains, fires shone forth which appeared to signal one to another, but on looking the next night in the same direction all was dark.

So M. de Broglie, concluding that nothing could be done against enemies who were invisible, disbanded the troops which had come to his aid, and went back to Montpellier, leaving a company of fusiliers at Collet, another at Ayres, one at the bridge of Montvert, one at Barre, and one at Pompidon, and appointing Captain Poul as their chief.

This choice of such a man as chief showed that M. de Broglie was a good judge of human nature, and was also perfectly acquainted with the situation, for Captain Poul was the very man to take a leading part in the coming struggle. "He was," says Pere Louvreloeil, priest of the Christian doctrine and cure of Saint-Germain de Calberte, "an officer of merit and reputation, born in Ville-Dubert, near Carcassonne, who had when young served in Hungary and Germany, and distinguished himself in Piedmont in several excursions against the Barbets, [A name applied first to the Alpine smugglers who lived in the valleys, later to the insurgent peasants in the Cevennes.—Translator's Note.] notably in one of the later ones, when, entering the tent of their chief, Barbanaga, he cut off his head. His tall and agile figure, his warlike air, his love of hard work, his hoarse voice, his fiery and austere character, his carelessness in regard to dress, his mature age, his tried courage, his taciturn habit, the length and weight of his sword, all combined to render him formidable. Therefore no one could have been chosen more suitable for putting down the rebels, for forcing their entrenchments, and for putting them to flight."

Hardly had he taken up a position in the market town of Labarre, which was to be his headquarters, than he was informed that a gathering of fanatics had been seen on the little plain of Fondmorte, which formed a pass between two valleys. He ordered out his Spanish steed, which he was accustomed to ride in the Turkish manner—that is, with very short stirrups, so that he could throw himself forward to the horse's ears, or backward to the tail, according as he wished to give or avoid a mortal blow. Taking with him eighteen men of his own company and twenty-five from the town, he at once set off for the place indicated, not considering any larger number necessary to put to rout a band of peasants, however numerous.

The information turned out to be correct: a hundred Reformers led by Esprit Seguier had encamped in the plain of Fondmorte, and about eleven o'clock in the morning one of their sentinels in the defile gave the alarm by firing off his gun and running back to the camp, shouting, "To arms!" But Captain Poul, with his usual impetuosity, did not give the insurgents time to form, but threw himself upon them to the beat of the drum, not in the least deterred by their first volley. As he had expected, the band consisted of undisciplined peasants, who once scattered were unable to rally. They were therefore completely routed. Poul killed several with his own hand, among whom were two whose heads he cut off as cleverly as the most experienced executioner could have done, thanks to the marvellous temper of his Damascus blade. At this sight all who had till

51

then stood their ground took to flight, Poul at their heels, slashing with his sword unceasingly, till they disappeared among the mountains. He then returned to the field of battle, picked up the two heads, and fastening them to his saddlebow, rejoined his soldiers with his bloody trophies,— that is to say, he joined the largest group of soldiers he could find; for the fight had turned into a number of single combats, every soldier fighting for himself. Here he found three prisoners who were about to be shot; but Poul ordered that they should not be touched: not that he thought for an instant of sparing their lives, but that he wished to reserve them for a public execution. These three men were Nouvel, a parishioner of Vialon, Moise Bonnet of Pierre-Male, and Esprit Seguier the prophet.

Captain Poul returned to Barre carrying with him his two heads and his three prisoners, and immediately reported to M. Just de Baville, intendant of Languedoc, the important capture he had made. The prisoners were quickly tried. Pierre Nouvel was condemned to be burnt alive at the bridge of Montvert, Molise Bonnet to be broken on the wheel at Deveze, and Esprit Seguier to be hanged at Andre-de-Lancise. Thus those who were amateurs in executions had a sufficient choice.

However, Moise Bonnet saved himself by becoming Catholic, but Pierre Nouvel and Esprit Seguier died as martyrs, making profession of the new faith and praising God.

Two days after the sentence on Esprit Seguier had been carried out, the body disappeared from the gallows. A nephew of Laporte named Roland had audaciously carried it off, leaving behind a writing nailed to the gibbet. This was a challenge from Laporte to Poul, and was dated from the "Camp of the Eternal God, in the desert of Cevennes," Laporte signing himself "Colonel of the children of God who seek liberty of conscience." Poul was about to accept the challenge when he learned that the insurrection was spreading on every side. A young man of Vieljeu, twenty-six years of age, named Solomon Couderc, had succeeded Esprit Seguier in the office of prophet, and two young lieutenants had joined Laporte. One of these was his nephew Roland, a man of about thirty, pock-marked, fair, thin, cold, and reserved; he was not tall, but very strong, and of inflexible courage. The other, Henri Castanet of Massevaques, was a keeper from the mountain of Laygoal, whose skill as a marksman was so well known that it was said he never missed a shot. Each of these lieutenants had fifty men under him.

Prophets and prophetesses too increased apace, so that hardly a day passed without reports being heard of fresh ones who were rousing whole villages by their ravings.

In the meantime a great meeting of the Protestants of Languedoc had been held in the fields of Vauvert, at which it had been resolved to join forces with the rebels of the Cevennes, and to send a messenger thither to make this resolution known.

Laporte had just returned from La Vaunage, where he had been making recruits, when this good news arrived; he at once sent his nephew Roland to the new allies with power to pledge his word in return for theirs, and to describe to them, in order to attract them, the country which he had

53

chosen as the theatre of the coming war, and which, thanks to its hamlets, its woods, its defiles, its valleys, its precipices, and its caves, was capable of affording cover to as many bands of insurgents as might be employed, would be a good rallying-ground after repulse, and contained suitable positions for ambuscades. Roland was so successful in his mission that these new "soldiers of the Lord," as they called themselves, on learning that he had once been a dragoon, offered him the post of leader, which he accepted, and returned to his uncle at the head of an army.

Being thus reinforced, the Reformers divided themselves into three bands, in order to spread abroad their beliefs through the entire district. One went towards Soustele and the neighbourhood of Alais, another towards St. Privat and the bridge of Montvert, while the third followed the mountain slope down to St. Roman le Pompidou, and Barre.

The first was commanded by Castanet, the second by Roland, and the third by Laporte.

Each party ravaged the country as it passed, returning deathblow for deathblow and conflagration for conflagration, so that hearing one after another of these outrages Captain Poul demanded reinforcements from M. de Broglie and M. de Baville, which were promptly despatched.

As soon as Captain Poul found himself at the head of a sufficient number of troops, he determined to attack the rebels. He had received intelligence that the band led by Laporte was just about to pass through the valley of Croix, below Barre, near Temelague. In consequence of this information, he lay in ambush at a favourable spot on the route. As soon as the Reformers who were without suspicion, were well within the narrow pass in which Poul awaited them, he issued forth at the head of his soldiers, and charged the rebels with such courage and impetuosity that they, taken by surprise, made no attempt at resistance, but, thoroughly demoralised, spread over the mountain-side, putting a greater and greater distance at, every instant between themselves and the enemy, despite the efforts of Laporte to make them stand their ground. At last, seeing himself deserted, Laporte began to think of his own safety. But it was already too late, for he was surrounded by dragoons, and the only way of retreat open to him lay over a large rock. This he successfully scaled, but before trying to get down the other side he raised his hands in supplication to Heaven; at that instant a volley was fired, two bullets struck him, and he fell head foremost down the precipice.

When the dragoons reached the foot of the rock, they found him dead. As they knew he was the chief of the rebels, his body was searched: sixty Louis was found in his pockets, and a sacred chalice which he was in the habit of using as an ordinary drinking-cup. Poul cut off his head and the heads of twelve other Reformers found dead on the field of battle, and enclosing them in a wicker basket, sent them to M. Just de Baville.

The Reformers soon recovered from this defeat and death, joined all their forces into one body, and placed Roland at their head in the place of Laporte. Roland chose a young man called Couderc de Mazel-Rozade, who had assumed the name of Lafleur, as his lieutenant, and the rebel forces were not only quickly reorganised, but made complete by the addition of a hundred men raised by the new lieutenant, and soon gave a sign that they were again on the war-path by burning down the churches of Bousquet, Cassagnas, and Prunet.

Then first it was that the consuls of Mende began to realise that it was no longer an insurrection they had on hand but a war, and Mende being the capital of Gevaudan and liable to be attacked at any moment, they set themselves to bring into repair their counterscarps, ravelins, bastions, gates, portcullises, moats, walls, turrets, ramparts, parapets, watchtowers, and the gear of their cannon, and having laid in a stock of firearms, powder and ball, they formed eight companies each fifty strong, composed of townsmen, and a further band of one hundred and fifty peasants drawn from the neighbouring country. Lastly, the States of the province sent an envoy to the king, praying him graciously to take measures to check the plague of heresy which was spreading from day to day. The king at once sent M. Julien in answer to the petition. Thus it was no longer simple governors of towns nor even chiefs of provinces who were engaged in the struggle; royalty itself had come to the rescue.

M de Julien, born a Protestant, was a, member of the nobility of Orange, and in his youth had served against France and borne arms in England and Ireland when William of Orange succeeded James II as King of England, Julien was one of his pages, and received as a reward for his fidelity in the famous campaign of 1688 the command of a regiment which was sent to the aid of the Duke of Savoy, who had begged both England and Holland to help him. He bore himself so gallantly that it was in great part due to him that the French were forced to raise the siege of Cony.

Whether it was that he expected too much from this success, or that the Duke of Savoy did not recognise his services at their worth, he withdrew to Geneva, where Louis XIV hearing of his discontent, caused overtures to be made to him with a view to drawing him into the French service. He was offered the same rank in the French army as he had held in the English, with a pension of 3000 livres.

M de Julien accepted, and feeling that his religious belief would be in the way of his advancement, when he changed his master he changed his Church. He was given the command of the valley of Barcelonnette, whence he made many excursions against the Barbets; then he was transferred to the command of the Avennes, of the principality of Orange, in order to guard the passes, so that the French Protestants could not pass over the frontier for the purpose of worshipping with their Dutch Protestant brethren; and after having tried this for a year, he went to Versailles to report himself to the king. While he was there, it chanced that the envoy from Gevaudan arrived, and the king being satisfied with de Julien's conduct since he had entered his service, made him major-general, chevalier of the military order of St. Louis; and commander-in-chief in the Vivarais and the Cevennes.

M de Julien from the first felt that the situation was very grave, and saw that his predecessors had felt such great contempt for the heretics that they had not realised the danger of the revolt. He immediately proceeded to inspect in person the different points where M. de Broglie had placed detachments of the Tournon and Marsily regiments. It is true that he arrived by the light of thirty burning village churches.

M de Broglie, M. de Baville, M. de Julien, and Captain Poul met together to consult as to the best means of putting an end to these disorders. It was agreed that the royal troops should be divided into two bodies, one under the command of M. de Julien to advance on Alais, where it was reported large meetings of the rebels were taking place, and the other under M. de Brogue, to march about in the neighbourhood of Nimes.

Consequently, the two chiefs separated. M. le Comte de Broglie at the head of sixty-two dragoons and some companies of foot, and having under him Captain Poul and M. de Dourville, set out from Cavayrac on the 12th of January at 2 a. m., and having searched without finding anything the vineyards of Nimes and La Garrigue de Milhau, took the road to the bridge of Lunel. There he was informed that those he was in search of had been seen at the chateau of Caudiac the day before; he therefore at once set out for the forest which lies around it, not doubting to find the fanatics entrenched there; but, contrary to his expectations, it was vacant. He then pushed on to Vauvert, from Vauvert to Beauvoisin, from Beauvoisin to Generac, where he learned that a troop of rebels had passed the night there, and in the morning had left for Aubore. Resolved to give them no rest, M. de Broglie set out at once for this village.

When half-way there, a member of his staff thought he could distinguish a crowd of men near a house about half a league distant; M. de Broglie instantly ordered Sieur de Gibertin, Captain Paul's lieutenant, who was riding close by, at the head of his company, to take eight dragoons and make a reconnaissance, in order to ascertain who these men were, while the rest of the troops would make a halt.

This little band, led by its officer, crossed a clearing in the wood, and advanced towards the farmhouse, which was called the Mas de Gafarel, and which now seemed deserted. But when they were within half a gun-shot of the wall the charge was sounded behind it, and a band of rebels rushed towards them, while from a neighbouring house a second troop emerged, and looking round, he perceived a third lying on their faces in a small wood. These latter suddenly stood up and approached him, singing psalms. As it was impossible for M. de Gibertin to hold his ground against so large a force, he ordered two shots to be fired as a warning to de Brogue to advance to meet him, and fell back on his comrades. Indeed, the rebels had only pursued him till they had reached a favourable position, on which they took their stand.

M de Brogue having surveyed the whole position with the aid of a telescope, held a council of war, and it was decided that an attack should be made forthwith. They therefore advanced on the rebels in line: Captain Poul on the right, M. de Dourville on the left, and Count Broglie in the centre.

As they got near they could see that the rebels had chosen their ground with an amount of strategical sagacity they had never till then displayed. This skill in making their dispositions was evidently due to their having found a new leader whom no one knew, not even Captain Poul, although they could see him at the head of his men, carbine in hand.

However, these scientific preparations did not stop M. de Brogue: he gave the order to charge, and adding example to precept, urged his horse to a gallop. The rebels in the first rank knelt on one knee, so that the rank behind could take aim, and the distance between the two bodies of troops disappeared rapidly, thanks to the impetuosity of the dragoons; but suddenly, when within thirty paces of the enemy, the royals found themselves on the edge of a deep ravine which separated them from the enemy like a moat. Some were able to check their horses in time, but others, despite desperate efforts, pressed upon by those behind, were pushed into the ravine, and rolled helplessly to the bottom. At the same moment the order to fire was given in a sonorous voice, there was a rattle of musketry, and several dragoons near M. de Broglie fell.

"Forward!" cried Captain Poul, "forward!" and putting his horse at a part of the ravine where the sides were less steep, he was soon struggling up the opposite side, followed by a few dragoons.

"Death to the son of Belial!" cried the same voice which had given the order to fire. At that moment a single shot rang out, Captain Poul threw up his hands, letting his sabre go, and fell from his horse, which instead of running away, touched his master with its smoking nostrils, then lifting its head, neighed long and low. The dragoons retreated.

"So perish all the persecutors of Israel!" cried the leader, brandishing his carbine. He then dashed down into the ravine, picked up Captain Poul's sabre and jumped upon his horse. The animal, faithful to its old master, showed some signs of resistance, but soon felt by the pressure of its rider's

60

knees that it had to do with one whom it could not readily unseat. Nevertheless, it reared and bounded, but the horseman kept his seat, and as if recognising that it had met its match, the noble animal tossed its head, neighed once more, and gave in. While this was going on, a party of Camisards [Name given to the insurgent Calvinists after the Revocation of the Edict of Nantes.—Translator's Note.] and one of the dragoons had got down into the ravine, which had in consequence been turned into a battlefield; while those who remained above on either side took advantage of their position to fire down at their enemies. M. de Dourville, in command of the dragoons, fought among the others like a simple soldier, and received a serious wound in the head; his men beginning to lose ground, M. de Brogue tried to rally them, but without avail, and while he was thus occupied his own troop ran away; so seeing there was no prospect of winning the battle, he and a few valiant men who had remained near him dashed forward to extricate M. Dourville, who, taking advantage of the opening thus made, retreated, his wound bleeding profusely. On the other hand, the Camisards perceiving at some distance bodies of infantry coming up to reinforce the royals, instead of pursuing their foes, contented themselves with keeping up a thick and well-directed musketry-fire from the position in which they had won such a quick and easy victory.

As soon as the royal forces were out of reach of their weapons, the rebel chief knelt down and chanted the song the Israelites sang when, having crossed the Red Sea in safety, they saw the army of Pharaoh swallowed up in the waters, so that although no longer within reach of bullets the defeated troops were still pursued by songs of victory. Their thanksgivings ended, the Calvinists withdrew into the forest, led by their new chief, who had at his first assay shown the great extent of his knowledge, coolness, and courage.

This new chief, whose superiors were soon to become his lieutenants, was the famous Jean Cavalier.

Jean Cavalier was then a young man of twenty-three, of less than medium height, but of great strength. His face was oval, with regular features, his eyes sparkling and beautiful; he had long chestnut hair falling on his shoulders, and an expression of remarkable sweetness. He was born in 1680 at Ribaute, a village in the diocese of Alais, where his father had rented a small farm, which he gave up when his son was about fifteen, coming to live at the farm of St. Andeol, near Mende.

Young Cavalier, who was only a peasant and the son of a peasant, began life as a shepherd at the Sieur de Lacombe's, a citizen of Vezenobre, but as the lonely life dissatisfied a young man who was eager for pleasure, Jean gave it up, and apprenticed himself to a baker of Anduze.

There he developed a great love for everything connected with the military; he spent all his free time watching the soldiers at their drill, and soon became intimate with some of them, amongst others with a fencing-master who gave him lessons, and a dragoon who taught him to ride.

On a certain Sunday, as he was taking a walk with his sweetheart on his arm, the young girl was insulted by a dragoon of the Marquis de Florae's regiment. Jean boxed the dragoon's ears, who drew his sword. Cavalier seized a sword from one of the bystanders, but the combatants were prevented from fighting by Jean's friends. Hearing of the quarrel, an officer hurried up: it was the Marquis de Florae himself, captain of the regiment which bore his name; but when he arrived on the scene he found, not the arrogant peasant who had dared to attack a soldier of the king, but only the young girl, who had fainted, the townspeople having persuaded her lover to decamp.

The young girl was so beautiful that she was commonly called la belle Isabeau, and the Marquis de Florac, instead of pursuing Jean Cavalier, occupied himself in reviving Isabeau.

As it was, however, a serious affair, and as the entire regiment had sworn Cavalier's death, his friends advised him to leave the country for a time. La belle Isabeau, trembling for the safety of her lover, joined her entreaties to those of his friends, and Jean Cavalier yielded. The young girl promised him inviolable fidelity, and he, relying on this promise, went to Geneva.

There he made the acquaintance of a Protestant gentleman called Du Serre, who having glass-works at the Mas Arritas, quite near the farm of St. Andeol, had undertaken several times, at the request of Jean's father, Jerome, to convey money to Jean; for Du Serre went very often to Geneva, professedly on business affairs, but really in the interests of the Reformed faith. Between the outlaw and the apostle union was natural. Du Serre found in Cavalier a young man of robust nature, active imagination, and irreproachable courage; he confided to him his hopes of converting all Languedoc and Vivarais. Cavalier felt himself drawn back there by many ties, especially by patriotism and love. He crossed the frontier once more, disguised as a servant, in the suite of a Protestant gentleman; he arrived one night at Anduze, and immediately directed his steps to the house of Isabeau.

He was just about to knock, although it was one o'clock in the morning, when the door was opened from within, and a handsome young man came out, who took tender leave of a woman on the threshold. The handsome young man was the Marquis de Florac; the woman was Isabeau. The promised wife of the peasant had become the mistress of the noble.

Our hero was not the man to suffer such an outrage quietly. He walked straight up to the marquis and stood right in his way. The marquis tried to push him aside with his elbow, but Jean Cavalier, letting fall the cloak in which he was wrapped, drew his sword. The marquis was brave, and did not stop to inquire if he who attacked him was his equal or not. Sword answered sword, the blades crossed, and at the end of a few instants the marquis fell, Jean's sword piercing his chest.

Cavalier felt sure that he was dead, for he lay at his feet motionless. He knew he had no time to lose, for he had no mercy to hope for. He replaced his bloody sword in the scabbard, and made for the open country; from the open country he hurried into the mountains, and at break of day he was in safety.

The fugitive remained the whole day in an isolated farmhouse whose inmates offered him hospitality. As he very soon felt that he was in the house of a co-religionist, he confided to his host the circumstances in which he found himself, and asked where he could meet with an organised band in which he could enrol himself in order to fight for the propagation of the Reformed religion. The farmer mentioned Generac as being a place in which he would probably find a hundred or so of the brethren gathered together. Cavalier set out the same evening for this village, and arrived in the middle of the Camisards at the very moment when they had just caught sight of M. de Broglie and his troops in the distance. The Calvinists happening to have no leader, Cavalier with governing faculty which some men possess by nature, placed himself at their head and took those measures for the reception of the royal forces of which we have seen the result, so that after the victory to which his head and arm had contributed so much he was confirmed in the title which he had arrogated to himself, by acclamation.

Such was the famous Jean Cavalier when the Royalists first learned of his existence, through the repulse of their bravest troops and the death of their most intrepid captain.

The news of this victory soon spread through the Cevennes, and fresh conflagrations lit up the mountains in sign of joy. The beacons were formed of the chateau de la Bastide, the residence of the Marquis de Chambonnas, the church of Samson, and the village of Grouppieres, where of eighty houses only seven were left standing.

Thereupon M. de Julien wrote to the king, explaining the serious turn things had taken, and telling him that it was no longer a few fanatics wandering through the mountains and flying at the sight of a dragoon whom they had to put down, but organised companies well led and officered, which if united would form an army twelve to fifteen hundred strong. The king replied by sending M. le Comte de Montrevel to

Nimes. He was the son of the Marechal de Montrevel, chevalier of the Order of the Holy Spirit, major-general, lieutenant of the king in Bresse and Charolais, and captain of a hundred men-at-arms.

In their struggle against shepherds, keepers, and peasants, M. de Brogue, M. de Julien, and M. de Baville were thus joined together with the head of the house of Beaune, which had already at this epoch produced two cardinals, three archbishops, two bishops, a viceroy of Naples, several marshals of France, and many governors of Savoy, Dauphine, and Bresse.

He was followed by twenty pieces of ordnance, five thousand bullets, four thousand muskets, and fifty thousand pounds of powder, all of which was carried down the river Rhone, while six hundred of the skilful mountain marksmen called 'miquelets' from Roussillon came down into Languedoc.

M de Montrevel was the bearer of terrible orders. Louis XIV was determined, no matter what it cost, to root out heresy, and set about this work as if his eternal salvation depended on it. As soon as M. de Baville had read these orders, he published the following proclamation:

"The king having been informed that certain people without religion bearing arms have been guilty of violence, burning down churches and killing priests, His Majesty hereby commands all his subjects to hunt these people down, and that those who are taken with arms in their hands or found amongst their bands, be punished with death without any trial whatever, that their houses be razed to the ground and their goods confiscated, and that all buildings in

66

which assemblies of these people have been held, be demolished. The king further forbids fathers, mothers, brothers, sisters, and other relations of the fanatics, or of other rebels, to give them refuge, food, stores, ammunition, or other assistance of any kind, under any pretext whatever, either directly or indirectly, on pain of being reputed accessory to the rebellion, and he commands the Sieur de Baville and whatever officers he may choose to prosecute such and pronounce sentence of death on them. Furthermore, His Majesty commands that all the inhabitants of Languedoc who may be absent at the date of the issue of this proclamation, return home within a week, unless their absence be caused by legitimate business, in which case they shall declare the same to the commandant, the Sieur de Montrevel, or to the intendant, the Sieur de Baville, and also to the mayors and consuls of the places where they may be, receiving from the latter certificates that there is a sufficient reason for their delay, which certificates they shall forward to the above-mentioned commandant or intendant. And His Majesty furthermore commands the said commandant and intendant to admit no foreigner or inhabitant of any other province into Languedoc for commercial purposes or for any other reason whatsoever, unless provided with certificates from the commandants or intendants of the provinces whence they come, or from the judges of the royal courts in the places whence they come, or from the nearest place containing such courts. Foreigners must be provided with passports from the ambassadors or ministers of the king accredited to the countries to which they belong, or from the commandants or intendants of the provinces, or from the judges of the royal courts of the places in which they may be at the date of this proclamation. Furthermore, it is His Majesty's will that those who are found in the, aforesaid province of Languedoc without such certificates be regarded as fanatics and rebels, and that they be prosecuted as such, and punished with death, and that they be brought for this purpose before the aforesaid Sieur de Baville or the officers whom he may choose.

"(Signed) "(Countersigned) "LOUIS PHILIPPEAU

"Given at Versailles the 25th day, of the month of February 1703."

M de Montrevel obeyed this proclamation to the letter. For instance, one day—the 1st of April 1703—as he was seated at dinner it was reported to him that about one hundred and fifty Reformers were assembled in a mill at Carmes, outside Nimes, singing psalms. Although he was told at the same time that the gathering was composed entirely of old people and children, he was none the less furious, and rising from the table, gave orders that the call to horse should be sounded. Putting himself at the head of his dragoons, he advanced on the mill, and before the Huguenots knew that they were about to be attacked they were surrounded on every side. It was no combat which ensued, for the Huguenots were incapable of resistance, it was simply a massacre; a certain number of the dragoons entered the mill sword in hand, stabbing all whom they could reach, whilst the rest of the force stationed outside before the windows received those who jumped out on the points of their swords. But soon this butchery tired the butchers, and to get over the business more quickly, the marshal, who was anxious to return to his dinner, gave orders that the mill should be set on fire. This being done, the dragoons, the marshal still at their head, no longer exerted themselves so violently, but were satisfied with pushing back into the flames the few unfortunates who, scorched and burnt, rushed out, begging only for a less cruel death.

Only one victim escaped. A beautiful young girl of sixteen was saved by the marshal's valet: both were taken and condemned to death; the young girl was hanged, and the valet was on the point of being executed when some Sisters of Mercy from the town threw themselves at the marshal's feet end begged for his life: after long supplication, he granted their prayer, but he banished the valet not only from his service, but from Nimes.

The very same evening at supper word was brought to the marshal that another gathering had been discovered in a garden near the still smoking mill. The indefatigable marshal again rose from table, and taking with him his faithful dragoons, surrounded the garden, and caught and shot on the spot all those who were assembled in it. The next day it turned out that he had made a mistake: those whom he had shot were Catholics who had gathered together to rejoice over the execution of the Calvinists. It is true that they had assured the marshal that they were Catholics, but he had refused to listen to them. Let us, however, hasten to assure the reader that this mistake caused no further annoyance to the marshal, except that he received a paternal remonstrance from the Bishop of Nimes, begging him in future not to confound the sheep with the wolves.

In requital of these bloody deeds, Cavalier took the chateau of Serras, occupied the town of Sauve, formed a company of horse, and advancing to Nimes, took forcible possession of sufficient ammunition for his purposes. Lastly, he did something which in the eyes of the courtiers seemed the most incredible thing of all, he actually wrote a long letter to Louis XIV himself. This letter was dated from the "Desert, Cevennes," and signed "Cavalier, commander of the troops sent by God"; its purpose was to prove by numerous passages from Holy Writ that Cavalier and his comrades had been led to revolt solely from a sense of duty, feeling that liberty of conscience was their right; and it dilated on the subject of the persecutions under which Protestants had suffered, and asserted that it was the infamous measures put in force against them which had driven them to take up arms, which they were ready to lay down if His Majesty would grant them that liberty in matters of religion which they sought and if he would liberate all who were in prison for their faith. If this were accorded, he assured the king His Majesty would have no more faithful subjects than themselves, and would henceforth be ready to shed their last drop of blood in his service, and wound up by saying that if their just demands were refused they would obey God rather than the king, and would defend their religion to their last breath.

Roland, who, whether in mockery or pride, began now to call himself "Comte Roland," did not lag behind his young brother either as warrior or correspondent. He had entered the town of Ganges, where a wonderful reception awaited him; but not feeling sure that he would be equally well received at St. Germain and St. Andre, he had written the following letters:—

"Gentlemen and officers of the king's forces, and citizens of St. Germain, make ready to receive seven hundred troops who have vowed to set Babylon on fire; the seminary and the houses of MM. de Fabregue, de Sarrasin, de Moles, de La Rouviere, de Musse, and de Solier, will be burnt to the ground. God, by His Holy Spirit, has inspired my brother Cavalier and me with the purpose of entering your town in a few days; however strongly you fortify yourselves, the children of God will bear away the victory. If ye doubt this, come in your numbers, ye soldiers of St. Etienne, Barre, and Florac, to the field of Domergue; we shall be there to meet you. Come, ye hypocrites, if your hearts fail not. "COMTE ROLAND."

The second letter was no less violent. It was as follows:—

"We, Comte Roland, general of the Protestant troops of France assembled in the Cevennes in Languedoc, enjoin on the inhabitants of the town of St. Andre of Valborgne to give proper notice to all priests and missionaries within it, that we forbid them to say mass or to preach in the afore-mentioned town, and that if they will avoid being burnt alive with their adherents in their churches and houses, they are to withdraw to some other place within three days. "COMTE ROLAND."

Unfortunately for the cause of the king, though the rebels met with some resistance in the villages of the plain, such as St. Germain and St. Andre, it was otherwise with those situated in the mountains; in those, when beaten, the

Protestants found cover, when victorious rest; so that M. de Montrevel becoming aware that while these villages existed heresy would never be extirpated, issued the following ordinance:—

"We, governor for His most Christian Majesty in the provinces of Languedoc and Vivarais, do hereby make known that it has pleased the king to command us to reduce all the places and parishes hereinafter named to such a condition that they can afford no assistance to the rebel troops; no inhabitants will therefore be allowed to remain in them. His Majesty, however, desiring to provide for the subsistence of the afore-mentioned inhabitants, orders them to conform to the following regulations. He enjoins on the afore-mentioned inhabitants of the hereinafter-mentioned parishes to repair instantly to the places hereinafter appointed, with their furniture, cattle, and in general all their movable effects, declaring that in case of disobedience their effects will be confiscated and taken away by the troops employed to demolish their houses. And it is hereby forbidden to any other commune to receive such rebels, under pain of having their houses also razed to the ground and their goods confiscated, and furthermore being regarded and treated as rebels to the commands of His Majesty."

To this proclamation were appended the following instructions:—

"I. The officers who may be appointed to perform the above task shall first of all make themselves acquainted with the position of the parishes and villages which are to be destroyed and depopulated, in order to an effective

72

disposition of the troops, who are to guard the militia engaged in the work of destruction.

"II. The attention of the officers is called to the following:—When two or more villages or hamlets are so near together that they may be protected at the same time by the same troops, then in order to save time the work is to be carried on simultaneously in such villages or hamlets.

"III. When inhabitants are found still remaining in any of the proscribed places, they are to be brought together, and a list made of them, as well as an inventory taken of their stock and corn.

"IV. Those inhabitants who are of the most consequence among them shall be selected to guide the others to the places assigned.

"V. With regard to the live stock, the persons who may be found in charge of it shall drive it to the appointed place, save and except mules and asses, which shall be employed in the transport of corn to whatever places it may be needed in. Nevertheless, asses may be given to the very old, and to women with child who may be unable to walk.

"VI. A regular distribution of the militia is to be made, so that each house to be destroyed may have a sufficient number, for the task; the foundations of such houses may be undermined or any other method employed which may be most convenient; and if the house can be destroyed by no other means, it is to be set on fire.

"VII. No damage is to be done to the houses of former Catholics until further notice, and to ensure the carrying out of this order a guard is to be placed in them, and an inventory of their contents taken and sent to Marechal de Montrevel.

"VIII. The order forbidding the inhabitants to return to their houses is to be read to the inhabitants of each village; but if any do return they shall not be harmed, but simply driven away with threats; for the king does not desire that blood be shed; and the said order shall be affixed to a wall or tree in each village.

"IX. Where no inhabitants are found, the said order shall simply be affixed as above-mentioned in each place.

"(Signed) "MARECHAL DE MONTREVEL"

Under these instructions the list of the villages to be destroyed was given. It was as follows:

18 in the parish of Frugeres,

5 " " Fressinet-de-Lozere,

4 " " Grizac,

15 " " Castagnols,

11 " " Vialas,

6 " " Saint-Julien,

8 " " Saint-Maurice de Vantalon,

14 " " Frezal de Vantalon,

7 " " Saint-Hilaire de Laret,

6 " " Saint-Andeol de Clergues,

28 " " Saint-Privat de Vallongues,

10 " " Saint-Andre de Lancise,

19 " " Saint-Germain de Calberte,

26 " " Saint-Etienne de Valfrancesque,

9 " " parishes of Prunet and Montvaillant,

16 " " parish of Florac.
—-
202

A second list was promised, and was shortly afterwards published: it included the parishes of Frugeres, Pompidon, Saint-Martin, Lansuscle, Saint-Laurent, Treves, Vebron, Ronnes, Barre, Montluzon, Bousquet, La Barthes, Balme, Saint-Julien d'Aspaon Cassagnas, Sainte-Croix de Valfrancesque, Cabriac, Moissac, Saint-Roman, Saint Martin de Robaux, La Melouse, le Collet de Deze, Saint-Michel de Deze, and the villages of Salieges, Rampon, Ruas, Chavrieres, Tourgueselle, Ginestous, Fressinet, Fourques, Malbos, Jousanel, Campis, Campredon, Lous-Aubrez, La Croix de Fer, Le Cap de Coste, Marquayres, Le Cazairal, and Le Poujal.

In all, 466 market towns, hamlets, and villages, with 19,500 inhabitants, were included.

All these preparations made Marechal de Montrevel set out for Aix, September 26th, 1703, in order that the work might be carried out under his personal supervision. He was accompanied by MM. de Vergetot and de Marsilly, colonels of infantry, two battalions of the Royal-Comtois, two of the Soissonnais infantry, the Languedoc regiment of dragoons, and two hundred dragoons from the Fimarcon regiment. M. de Julien, on his side, set out for the Pont-de-Montvert at the same time with two battalions from Hainault, accompanied by the Marquis of Canillac, colonel of infantry, who brought two battalions of his own regiment, which was stationed in Rouergue, with him, and Comte de Payre, who brought fifty-five companies of militia from Gevaudan, and followed by a number of mules loaded with crowbars, axes, and other iron instruments necessary for pulling down houses.

The approach of all these troops following close on the terrible proclamations we have given above, produced exactly the contrary effect to that intended. The inhabitants of the proscribed districts were convinced that the order to gather together in certain places was given that they might be conveniently massacred together, so that all those capable of bearing arms went deeper into the mountains, and joined the forces of Cavalier and Roland, thus reinforcing them to the number of fifteen hundred men. Also hardly had M. de Julien set his hand to the work than he received information from M. de Montrevel, who had heard the news through a letter from Flechier, that while the royal troops were busy in the mountains the Camisards had come down into the plain, swarmed over La Camargue, and had been seen in the neighbourhood of Saint-Gilles. At the same time word was sent him that two ships had been seen in the offing, from Cette, and that it was more than probable that they contained troops, that England and Holland were sending to help the Camisards.

M de Montrevel; leaving the further conduct of the expedition to MM. de Julien and de Canillac, hastened to Cette with eight hundred men and ten guns. The ships were still in sight, and were really, as had been surmised, two vessels which had been detached from the combined fleets of England and Holland by Admiral Schowel, and were the bearers of money, arms, and ammunition to the Huguenots. They continued to cruise about and signal, but as the rebels were forced by the presence of M. de Montrevel to keep away from the coast, and could therefore make no answer, they put off at length into the open, and rejoined the fleet. As M. de Montrevel feared that their retreat might be a feint, he ordered all the fishermen's huts from Aigues-Morte to Saint-Gilles to be destroyed, lest they should afford shelter to the Camisards. At the same time he carried off the inhabitants of the district of Guillan and shut them up in the chateau of Sommerez, after having demolished their villages. Lastly, he ordered all those who lived in homesteads, farms, or hamlets, to quit them and go to some large town, taking with them all the provisions they were possessed of; and he forbade any workman who went outside the town to work to take more than one day's provisions with him.

These measures had the desired effect, but they were terrible in their results; they deprived the Camisards of shelter indeed, but they ruined the province. M. de Baville, despite his well-known severity tried remonstrances, but they were taken in bad part by M. de Montrevel, who told the intendant to mind his own business, which was confined to civil matters, and to leave military matters in his, M. de Montrevel's, hands; whereupon the commandant joined M. de Julien, who was carrying on the work of destruction with indefatigable vigour.

In spite of all the enthusiasm with which M. de Julien went to work to accomplish his mission, and being a new convert, it was, of course, very great. Material hindrances hampered him at every step. Almost all the doomed houses were built on vaulted foundations, and were therefore difficult to lay low; the distance of one house from another, too, their almost inaccessible position, either on the peak of a high mountain or in the bottom of a rocky valley, or buried in the depths of the forest which hid then like a veil, made the difficulty still greater; whole days were often lost by the workmen and militia in searching for the dwellings they came to destroy.

The immense size of the parishes also caused delay: that of Saint-Germain de Calberte, for instance, was nine leagues in circumference, and contained a hundred and eleven hamlets, inhabited by two hundred and seventy-five families, of which only nine were Catholic; that of Saint-Etienne de Valfrancesque was of still greater extent, and its population was a third larger, so that obstacles to the work multiplied in a remarkable manner. For the first few days the soldiers and workmen found food in and around the villages, but this was soon at an end, and as they could hardly expect the peasants to keep up the supply, and the provisions they had brought with them being also exhausted, they were soon reduced to

78

biscuit and water; and they were not even able to make it into a warm mess by heating the water, as they had no vessels; moreover, when their hard day's work was at an end, they had but a handful of straw on which to lie. These privations, added to their hard and laborious life, brought on an endemic fever, which incapacitated for work many soldiers and labourers, numbers of whom had to be dismissed. Very soon the unfortunate men, who were almost as much to be pitied as those whom they were persecuting, waited no longer to be sent away, but deserted in numbers.

M de Julien soon saw that all his efforts would end in failure if he could not gain the king's consent to a slight change in the original plan. He therefore wrote to Versailles, and represented to the king how long the work would take if the means employed were only iron tools and the human hand, instead of fire, the only true instrument employed by Heaven in its vengeance. He quoted in support of his petition the case of Sodom and Gomorrah—those cities accursed of the Lord. Louis XIV, impressed by the truth of this comparison, sent him back a messenger post-haste authorising him to employ the suggested means.

"At once," says Pere Louvreloeil, "the storm burst, and soon of all the happy homesteads nothing was left: the hamlets, with their barns and outhouses, the isolated farmhouses, the single huts and cottages, every species of building in short, disappeared before the swift advancing flames as wild flowers, weeds, and roots fall before the ploughshare."

This destruction was accompanied by horrible cruelty. For instance, twenty-five inhabitants of a certain village took refuge in a chateau; the number consisted of children and very old people, and they were all that was left of the entire population. Palmerolle, in command of the miquelets, hearing of this, hastened thither, seized the first eight he could lay hold of, and shot them on the spot, "to teach them," as he says in his report, "not to choose a shelter which was not on the list of those permitted to them."

The Catholics also of St. Florent, Senechas, Rousson, and other parishes, becoming excited at seeing the flames which enveloped the houses of their old enemies, joined together, and arming themselves with everything that could be made to serve as an instrument of death, set out to hunt the conscripts down; they carried off the flocks of Perolat, Fontareche, and Pajolas, burned down a dozen houses at the Collet-de-Deze, and from there went to the village of Brenoux, drunk with the lust of destruction. There they massacred fifty-two persons, among them mothers with unborn children; and with these babes, which they tore from them, impaled on their pikes and halberts, they continued their march towards the villages of St. Denis and Castagnols.

Very soon these volunteers organised themselves into companies, and became known under the name of Cadets de la Croix, from a small white cross which they wore on their coats; so the poor Huguenots had a new species of enemy to contend with, much more bloodthirsty than the dragoons and the miquelets; for while these latter simply obeyed orders from Versailles, Nimes, or Montpellier, the former gratified a personal hate—a hate which had come down to them from their fathers, and which they would pass on to their children.

On the other hand, the young Huguenot leader, who every day gained more influence over his soldiers, tried to make the dragoons and Cadets de la Croix suffer in return everything they inflicted on the Huguenots, except the murders. In the night from the 2nd to the 3rd October, about ten o'clock, he came down into the plain and attacked Sommieres from two different points, setting fire to the houses. The inhabitants seizing their arms, made a sortie, but Cavalier charged them at the head of the Cavalry and forced them to retreat. Thereupon the governor, whose garrison was too small to leave the shelter of the walls, turned his guns on them and fired, less in the hope of inflicting injury on them than in that of being heard by the neighbouring garrisons.

The Camisards recognising this danger, retired, but not before they had burnt down the hotels of the Cheval-Blanc, the Croix-d'Or, the Grand-Louis, and the Luxembourg, as well as a great number of other houses, and the church and the presbytery of Saint-Amand.

Thence the Camisards proceeded to Cayla and Vauvert, into which they entered, destroying the fortifications. There they provided themselves abundantly with provisions for man and beast. In Vauvert, which was almost entirely inhabited by his co-religionists, Cavalier assembled the inhabitants in the market-place, and made them join with him in prayer to God, that He would prevent the king from following evil counsel; he also exhorted his brethren to be ready to sacrifice their goods and their lives for the re-establishment of their religion, affirming that the Holy Spirit had revealed to him that the arm of the Lord, which had always come to their aid, was still stretched out over them.

Cavalier undertook these movements in the hope of interrupting the work of destruction going on in Upper Cevennes; and partly obtained the desired result; for M. de Julien received orders to come down into the open country and disperse the Camisards.

The troops tried to fulfil this task, but, thanks to the knowledge that the rebels had of the country, it was impossible to come up with them, so that Fleshier, who was in the thick of the executions, conflagrations, and massacres, but who still found time to write Latin verse and gallant letters, said, in speaking of them, "They were never caught, and did all the damage they wished to do without let or hindrance. We laid their mountains waste, and they laid waste our plain. There are no more churches left in our dioceses, and not being able either to plough or sow our lands, we have no revenues. We dread serious revolt, and desire to avoid a religious civil war; so all our efforts are relaxing, we let our arms fall without knowing why, and we are told, 'You must have patience; it is not possible to fight against phantoms.'" Nevertheless, from time to time, these phantoms became visible. Towards the end of October, Cavalier came down to Uzes, carried off two sentinels who were guarding the gates, and hearing the call to arms within, shouted that he would await the governor of the city, M. de Vergetot, near Lussan.

And indeed Cavalier, accompanied by his two lieutenants, Ravanel and Catinat, took his way towards this little town, between Uzes and Bargeac, which stands upon an eminence surrounded upon all sides by cliffs, which serve it as ramparts and render it very difficult of access. Having arrived within three gun-shots of Lussan, Cavalier sent Ravanel to demand provisions from the inhabitants; but they, proud of their natural ramparts, and believing their town impregnable, not only refused to comply with the requisition, but fired several shots on the envoy, one of which wounded in the arm a Camisard of the name of La Grandeur, who had accompanied Ravanel. Ravanel withdrew, supporting his wounded comrade, followed by shots and the hootings of the inhabitants. When they rejoined Cavalier and made their report, the young commander issued orders to his soldiers to make ready to take the town the next morning; for, as night was already falling, he did not venture to start in the dark. In the meantime the besieged sent post-haste to M. de Vergetot to warn him of their situation; and resolving to defend themselves as long as they could, while waiting for a response to their message they set about barricading their gates, turned their scythes into weapons, fastened large hooks on long poles, and collected all the instruments they could find that could be used in attack or defence. As to the Camisards, they encamped for the night near an old chateau called Fan, about a gun-shot from Lussan.

At break of day loud shouts from the town told the Camisards that the expected relief was in sight, and looking out they saw in the distance a troop of soldiers advancing towards them; it was M. de Vergetat at the head of his regiment, accompanied by forty Irish officers.

The Protestants prepared themselves, as usual, by reciting psalms and prayers, notice without taking of the shouts and threats of any of the townspeople, and having finished their invocations, they marched out to meet the approaching column. The cavalry, commanded by Catinat, made a detour, taking a sheltered way to an unguarded bridge over a small river not far off, so as to outflank the royal forces, which they were to attack in the rear as soon as Cavalier and Ravanel should have engaged them in front.

M de Vergetot, on his side, continued to advance, so that the Calvinists and the Catholics were soon face to face. The battle began on both sides by a volley; but Cavalier having seen his cavalry emerging from a neighbouring wood, and counting upon their assistance, charged the enemy at the double quick. Catinat judging by the noise of the firing that his presence was necessary, charged also at a gallop, falling on the flank of the Catholics.

In this charge, one of M. de Vergetot's captains was killed by a bullet, and the other by a sabre-cut, and the grenadiers falling into disorder, first lost ground and then fled, pursued by Catinat and his horsemen, who, seizing them by the hair, despatched them with their swords. Having tried in vain to rally his men, M. de Vergetot, surrounded by a few Irish, was forced in his turn to fly; he was hotly pursued, and on the point of being taken, when by good luck he reached the height of Gamene, with its walls of rock. Jumping off his horse, he entered the narrow pathway which led to the top, and entrenched himself with about a hundred men in this natural fort. Cavalier perceiving that further pursuit would be dangerous, resolved to rest satisfied with his victory; as he knew by his own experience that neither men nor horses had eaten for eighteen hours, he gave the signal far retreat, and retired on Seyne, where he hoped to find provisions.

This defeat mortified the royal forces very deeply, and they resolved to take their revenge. Having learnt by their spies that on a certain night in November Cavalier and his band intended to sleep on a mountain called Nages, they surrounded the mountain during the night, so that at dawn Cavalier found himself shut in on every side. As he wished to see with his own eyes if the investment was complete, he ordered his troops to fall into rank on the top of the mountain, giving the command to Ravanel and Catinat, and with a pair of pistols in his belt and his carbine on his shoulder, he glided from bush to bush and rock to rock, determined, if any weak spot existed, to discover it; but the information he had received was perfectly correct, every issue was guarded.

Cavalier now set off to rejoin his troops, passing through a ravine, but he had hardly taken thirty steps when he found himself confronted by a cornet and two dragoons who were lying in ambush. There was no time to run away, and indeed such a thought never entered the young commander's head; he walked straight up to them. On their side, the dragoons advanced towards him, and the cornet covering him with his pistol, called out, "Halt! you are Cavalier; I know you. It is not possible for you to escape; surrender at discretion." Cavalier's answer was to blow out the cornet's brains with a shot from his carbine, then throwing it behind him as of no further use, he drew his two pistols from his belt, walked up to the two dragoons, shot them both dead, and rejoined his comrades unwounded. These, who had believed him lost, welcomed him with cheers.

But Cavalier had something else to do than to celebrate his return; mounting his horse, he put himself at the head of his men, and fell upon the royal troops with such impetuosity that they gave way at the first onset. Then a strange incident occurred. About thirty women who had come to the camp with provisions, carried away by their enthusiasm at the sight of this success, threw themselves upon the enemy, fighting like men. One young girl of about seventeen, Lucrese Guigon by name, distinguished herself amongst the others by her great valour. Not content with encouraging her brethren by the cry of "The sword of the Lord and of Gideon!" she tore sabres from the hands of the dead dragoons to despatch the dying. Catinat, followed by ten of his men, pursued the flying troops as far as the plain of Calvisson. There they were able to rally, thanks to the advance of the garrison to meet them.

Eighty dragoons lay dead on the field of battle, while Cavalier had only lost five men.

As we shall see, Cavalier was not only a brave soldier and a skilful captain, but also a just judge. A few days after the deed of arms which we have just related, he learned that a horrible murder had been committed by four Camisards, who had then retired into the forest of Bouquet. He sent a detachment of twenty men with orders to arrest the murderers and bring them before him. The following are the details of the crime:

The daughter of Baron Meyrargues, who was not long married to a gentleman named M. de Miraman, had set out on the 29th November for Ambroix to join her husband, who was waiting for her there. She was encouraged to do this by her coachman, who had often met with Camisards in the neighbourhood, and although a Catholic, had never received any harm from them. She occupied her own carriage, and was accompanied by a maid, a nurse, a footman, and the coachman who had persuaded her to undertake the journey. Two-thirds of the way already lay safely behind them, when between Lussan and Vaudras she was stopped by four, men, who made her get out of her carriage and accompany them into the neighbouring forest. The account of what then happened is taken from the deposition of the maid. We copy it word for word:

"These wretches having forced us," says she, "to walk into the forest till we were at some distance from the high road, my poor mistress grew so tired that she begged the man who walked beside her to allow her to lean on his shoulder. He looking round and seeing that they had reached a lonely spot, replied, 'We need hardly go any farther,' and made us sit dawn on a plot of grass which was to be the scene of our martyrdom. My poor mistress began to plead with the barbarians in the most touching manner, and so sweetly that she would have softened the heart of a demon. She offered them her purse, her gold waistband, and a fine diamond which she drew from her finger; but nothing could move these tigers, and one of them said, 'I am going to kill all the Catholics at once, and shall be gin with you.' 'What will you gain by my death?' asked my mistress. 'Spare my life.'—

'No; shut up!' replied he. 'You shall die by my hand. Say your prayers.' My good mistress threw herself at once on her knees and prayed aloud that God would show mercy to her and to her murderers, and while she was thus praying she received a pistol-shot in her left breast, and fell; a second assassin cut her across the face with his sword, and a third dropped a large stone on her head, while the fourth killed the nurse with a shot from his pistol. Whether it was that they had no more loaded firearms, or that they wished to save their ammunition, they were satisfied with only giving me several bayonet wounds. I pretended to be dead: they thought it was really the case, and went away. Some time after, seeing that everything had become quiet, and hearing no sound, I dragged myself, dying as I was, to where my dear mistress lay, and called her. As it happened, she was not quite dead, and she said in a faint voice, 'Stay with me, Suzon, till I die.' She added, after a short pause, for she was hardly able to speak, 'I die for my religion, and I hope that God will have pity on me. Tell my husband that I confide our little one to his care.' Having said this, she turned her thoughts from the world, praying to God in broken and tender words, and drew her last breath as the night fell."

In obedience to Cavalier's orders, the four criminals were taken and brought before him. He was then with his troops near Saint-Maurice de Casevielle; he called a council of war, and having had the prisoners tried for their atrocious deed, he summed up the evidence in as clear a manner as any lawyer could have done, and called upon the judges to pronounce sentence. All the judges agreed that the prisoners should be put to death, but just as the sentence was made known one of the assassins pushed aside the two men who guarded him, and jumping down a rock, disappeared in the forest before any attempt could be made to stop him. The three others were shot.

The Catholics also condemned many to be executed, but the trials conducted by then were far from being as remarkable for honour and justice as was that which we have just described. We may instance the trial of a poor boy of fourteen, the son of a miller of Saint-Christol who had been broken the wheel just a month before. For a moment the judges hesitated to condemn so young a boy to death, but a witness presented himself who testified that the little fellow was employed by the fanatics to strangle Catholic children. Although no one believed the evidence, yet it was seized-on as a pretext: the unfortunate boy was condemned to death, and hanged without mercy an hour later.

A great many people from the parishes devastated by M. de Julien had taken refuge in Aussilargues, in the parish of St. Andre. Driven by hunger and misery, they went beyond the prescribed limits in search of means of subsistence. Planque hearing of this, in his burning zeal for the Catholic faith resolved not to leave such a crime unpunished. He despatched a detachment of soldiers to arrest the culprits: the task was easy, for they were all once more inside the barrier and in their beds. They were seized, brought to St. Andre's Church and shut in; then, without trial of any kind,— they were taken, five at a time, and massacred: some were shot and some cut down with sword or axe; all were killed without exception—old and young women and children. One of the latter, who had received three shots was still able to raise his head and cry, "Where is father? Why doesn't he come and take me away."

Four men and a young girl who had taken refuge in the town of Lasalle, one of the places granted to the houseless villagers as an asylum, asked and received formal permission from the captain of the Soissonais regiment, by name Laplace, to go home on important private business, on condition that they returned the same night. They promised, and in the intention of keeping this promise they all met on their way back at a small farmhouse. Just as they reached it a terrible storm came on. The men were for continuing their way in spite of the weather, but the young girl besought them to wait till daylight, as she did not dare to venture out in the dark during such a storm, and would die of fright if left alone at the farm. The men, ashamed to desert their companion, who was related to one of them, yielded to her entreaties and remained, hoping that the storm would be a sufficient excuse for the delay. As soon as it was light, the five resumed their journey. But the news of their crime had reached the ears of Laplace before they got back. They were arrested, and all their excuses were of no avail. Laplace ordered the men to be taken outside the town and shot. The young girl was condemned to be hanged; and the sentence was to be carried out that very day, but some nuns who had been sent for to prepare her for death, having vainly begged Laplace to show mercy, entreated the girl to declare that she would soon become a mother. She indignantly refused to save her life at the cost of her good name, so the nuns took the lie on themselves and made the necessary declaration before the captain, begging him if he had no pity for the mother to spare the child at least, by granting a reprieve till it should be born. The captain was not for a moment deceived, but he sent for a midwife and ordered her to examine the young girl. At the end of half an hour she declared that the assertion of the nuns was true.

"Very well," said the captain: "let them both be kept in prison for three months; if by the end of that time the truth of this assertion is not self-evident, both shall be hanged." When this decision was made known to the poor woman, she was overcome by fear, and asked to see the, captain again, to whom she confessed that, led away by the entreaties of the nuns, she had told a lie.

Upon this, the woman was sentenced to be publicly whipped, and the young girl hanged on a gibbet round which were placed the corpses of the four men of whose death she was the cause.

As may easily be supposed, the "Cadets of the Cross" vied with both Catholics and Protestants in the work of destruction. One of their bands devoted itself to destroying everything belonging to the new converts from Beaucaire to Nimes. They killed a woman and two children at Campuget, an old man of eighty at a farm near Bouillargues, several persons at Cicure, a young girl at Caissargues, a gardener at Nimes, and many other persons, besides carrying off all the flocks, furniture, and other property they could lay hands on, and burning down the farmhouses of Clairan, Loubes, Marine, Carlot, Campoget Miraman, La Bergerie, and Larnac—all near St. Gilies and Manduel. "They stopped travellers on the highways," says Louvreloeil, "and by way of finding out whether they were Catholic or not, made them say in Latin the Lord's Prayer, the Ave Maria, the Symbol of the Faith, and the General Confession, and those who were unable to do this were put to the sword. In Dions nine corpses were found supposed to have been killed by their hands, and when the body of a shepherd who had been in the service of the Sieur de Roussiere, a former minister, was found hanging to a tree, no one doubted who were the murderers. At last they went so far that one of their bands meeting the Abbe de Saint Gilles on the road, ordered him to deliver up to them one of his servants, a new convert, in order to put him to death. It was in vain that the abbe remonstrated with them, telling them it was a shame to put such an affront on a man of his birth and rank; they persisted none the less in their determination, till at last the abbe threw his arms round his servant and presented his own body to the blows directed at the other."

The author of The Troubles in the Cevennes relates something surpassing all this which took place at Montelus on the 22nd February "There were a few Protestants in the place," he says, "but they were far outnumbered by the Catholics; these being roused by a Capuchin from Bergerac, formed themselves into a body of 'Cadets of the Cross,' and hastened to serve their apprenticeship to the work of assassination at the cost of their countrymen. They therefore entered the house of one Jean Bernoin, cut off his ears and further mutilated him, and then bled him to death like a pig. On coming out of this house they met Jacques Clas, and shot him in the abdomen, so that his intestines obtruded; pushing them back, he reached his house in a terrible condition, to the great alarm of his wife, who was near her confinement, and her children, who hastened to the help of husband and father. But the murderers appeared on the threshold, and, unmoved by the cries and tears of the unfortunate wife and the poor little children, they finished the wounded man, and as the wife made an effort to prevent them, they murdered her also, treating her dead body, when they discovered her condition, in a manner too revolting for description; while a neighbour, called Marie Silliot, who tried to rescue the children, was shot dead; but in her case they did not pursue their vengeance any further. They then went into the open country and meeting Pierre and Jean Bernard, uncle and nephew, one aged forty-five and the other ten, seized on them both, and putting a pistol into the hands of the child, forced him to shoot his uncle. In the meantime the boy's father had come up, and him they tried to constrain to shoot his son; but finding that no threats had any effect, they ended by killing both, one by the sword, the other by the bayonet.

"The reason why they put an end to father and son so quickly was that they had noticed three young girls of Bagnols going towards a grove of mulberry trees, where they were raising silk-worms. The men followed them, and as it was broad daylight and the girls were therefore not afraid, they soon came up with them. Having first violated them, they hung them by the feet to a tree, and put them to death in a horrible manner."

All this took place in the reign of Louis the Great, and for the greater glory of the Catholic religion.

History has preserved the names of the five wretches who perpetrated these crimes: they were Pierre Vigneau, Antoine Rey, Jean d'Hugon, Guillaume, and Gontanille.

CHAPTER III

Such crimes, of which we have only described a few, inspired horror in the breasts of those who were neither maddened by fanaticism nor devoured by the desire of vengeance. One of these, a Protestant, Baron d'Aygaliers, without stopping to consider what means he had at his command or what measures were the best to take to accomplish his object, resolved to devote his life to the pacification of the Cevennes. The first thing to be considered was, that if the Camisards were ever entirely destroyed by means of Catholic troops directed by de Baville, de Julien, and de Montrevel, the Protestants, and especially the Protestant nobles who had never borne arms, would be regarded as cowards, who had been prevented by fear of death or persecution from openly taking the part of the Huguenots: He was therefore convinced that the only course to pursue was to get, his co-religionists to put an end to the struggle themselves, as the one way of pleasing His Majesty and of showing him how groundless were the suspicions aroused in the minds of men by the Catholic clergy.

This plan presented, especially to Baron d'Aygaliers, two apparently insurmountable difficulties, for it could only be carried out by inducing the king to relax his rigorous measures and by inducing the Camisards to submit. Now the baron had no connection with the court, and was not personally acquainted with a single Huguenot chief.

The first thing necessary to enable the baron to begin his efforts was a passport for Paris, and he felt sure that as he was a Protestant neither M. de Baville nor M. de Montrevel would give him one. A lucky accident, however, relieved his embarrassment and strengthened his resolution, for he thought he saw in this accident the hand of Providence.

Baron d'Aygaliers found one day at the house of a friend a M. de Paratte, a colonel in the king's army, and who afterwards became major-general, but who at the time we are speaking of was commandant at Uzes. He was of a very impulsive disposition, and so zealous in matters relating to the Catholic religion and in the service of the king, that he never could find himself in the presence of a Protestant without expressing his indignation at those who had taken up arms against their prince, and also those who without taking up arms encouraged the rebels in their designs. M. d'Aygaliers understood that an allusion was meant to himself, and he resolved to take advantage of it.

So the next day he paid a visit to M. de Paratte, and instead of demanding satisfaction, as the latter quite expected, for the rudeness of his remarks on the previous day, he professed himself very much obliged for what he had said, which had made such a deep impression on him that he had made up his mind to give proof of his zeal and loyalty by going to Paris and petitioning the king for a position at court.

De Paratte, charmed with what he had heard, and enchanted with his convert, embraced d'Aygaliers, and gave him, says the chronicler, his blessing; and with the blessing a passport, and wished him all the success that a father could wish for his son. D'Aygaliers had now attained his object, and furnished with the lucky safe-conduct, he set out for Paris, without having communicated his intentions to anyone, not even to his mother.

On reaching Paris he put up at a friend's house, and drew up a statement of his plan: it was very short and very clear.

"The undersigned has the honour to point out humbly to His Majesty:

"That the severities and the persecutions which have been employed by some of the village priests have caused many people in the country districts to take up arms, and that the suspicions which new converts excited have driven a great many of them to join the insurgents. In taking this step they were also impelled by the desire to avoid imprisonment or removal from their homes, which were the remedies chosen to keep them in the old faith. This being the case, he thinks that the best means of putting an end to this state of things would be to take measures exactly the contrary of those which produced it, such as putting an end to the persecutions and permitting a certain number of those of the Reformed religion to bear arms, that they might go to the rebels and tell them that far from approving of their actions the Protestants as a whole wished to bring them back to the right way by setting them a good example, or to fight against them in order to show the king and France, at the risk of their lives, that they disapproved of the conduct of their co-religionists, and that the priests had been in the wrong in writing to the court that all those of the Reformed religion were in favour of revolt."

D'Aygaliers hoped that the court would adopt this plan; for if they did, one of two things must happen: either the Camisards, by refusing to accept the terms offered to them, would make themselves odious to their brethren (for d'Aygaliers intended to take with him on his mission of persuasion only men of high reputation among the Reformers, who would be repelled by the Camisards if they refused to submit), or else; by laying down their arms and submitting, they would restore peace to the South of France, obtain liberty of worship, set free their brethren from the prisons and galleys, and come to the help of the king in his war against the allied powers, by supplying him in a moment with a large body of disciplined troops ready to take the field against his enemies; for not only would the Camisards, if they were supplied with officers, be available for this purpose, but also those troops which were at the moment employed in hunting down the Camisards would be set free for this important duty.

This proposition was so clear and promised to produce such useful results, that although the prejudice against the Reformers was very strong, Baron d'Aygaliers found supporters who were at once intelligent and genuine in the Duke de Chevreuse and the Duke de Montfort, his son. These two gentlemen brought about a meeting between the baron and Chamillard, and the latter presented him to the Marechal de Villars, to whom he showed his petition, begging him to bring it to the notice of the king; but M. de Villars, who was well acquainted with the obstinacy of Louis, who, as Baron de Peken says, "only saw the Reformers through the spectacles of Madame de Maintenon," told d'Aygaliers that the last thing he should do would be to give the king any hint of his plans, unless he wished to see them come to nothing; on the contrary, he advised him to go at once to Lyons and wait there for him, M. de Villars; for he would probably be passing through that town in a few days, being almost certain to be appointed governor of Languedoc in place of M. de Montrevel, who had fallen under the king's displeasure and was about to be recalled. In the course of the three interviews which d'Aygaliers had had with M. de Villars, he had become convinced that de Villars was a man capable of understanding his object; he therefore followed his advice, as he believed his knowledge of the king to be correct, and left Paris for Lyons.

The recall of M. de Montrevel had been brought about in the following manner:—M. de Montrevel having just come to Uzes, learned that Cavalier and his troops were in the neighbourhood of Sainte-Chatte; he immediately sent M. de La Jonquiere, with six hundred picked marines and some companies of dragoons from the regiment of Saint-Sernin, but half an hour later, it having occurred to him that these forces were not sufficient, he ordered M. de Foix, lieutenant of the dragoons of Fimarqon, to join M. de La Jonquiere at Sainte-Chatte with a hundred soldiers of his regiment, and to remain with him if he were wanted; if not, to return the same night.

M de Foix gave the necessary orders, chose a hundred of his bravest men, put himself at their head, and joined M. de La Jonquiere, showing him his orders; but the latter, confiding in the courage of his soldiers and unwilling to share with anyone the glory of a victory of which he felt assured, not only sent away M. de Foix, but begged him to go back to Uzes, declaring to him that he had enough troops to fight and conquer all the Camisards whom he might encounter; consequently the hundred dragoons whom the lieutenant had brought with him were quite useless at Sainte-Chatte, while on the contrary they might be very necessary somewhere else. M. de Foix did not consider that it was his duty to insist on remaining under these circumstances, and returned to Uzes, while M. de La Jonquiere continued his route in order to pass the night at Moussac. Cavalier left the town by one gate just as M. de La Jonquiere entered at the other. The wishes of the young Catholic commander were thus in a fair way to be fulfilled, for in all probability he would come up with his enemy the next day.

As the village was inhabited for the most part by new converts, the night instead of being spent in repose was devoted to pillage.

The next day the Catholic troops reached Moussac, which they found deserted, so they went on to Lascours-de-Gravier, a little village belonging to the barony of Boucairan, which M. de La Jonquiere gave up to pillage, and where he had four Protestants shot—a man, a woman, and two young girls. He then resumed his route. As it had rained, he soon came on the trail of the Camisards, the terrible game which

99

he was hunting down. For three hours he occupied himself in this pursuit, marching at the head of his troops, lest someone else less careful than he should make some mistake, when, suddenly raising his eyes, he perceived the Camisards on a small eminence called Les Devois de Maraignargues. This was the spot they had chosen to await attack in, being eager for the approaching combat.

As soon as Cavalier saw the royals advancing, he ordered his men, according to custom, to offer up prayers to God, and when these were finished he disposed his troops for battle. His plan was to take up position with the greater part of his men on the other side of a ravine, which would thus form a kind of moat between him and the king's soldiers; he also ordered about thirty horsemen to make a great round, thus reaching unseen a little wood about two hundred yards to his left, where they could conceal themselves; and lastly, he sent to a point on the right sixty foot-soldiers chosen from his best marksmen, whom he ordered not to fire until the royal forces were engaged in the struggle with him.

M de La Jonquiere having approached to within a certain distance, halted, and sent one of his lieutenants named de Sainte-Chatte to make a reconnaissance, which he did, advancing beyond the men in ambush, who gave no sign of their existence, while the officer quietly examined the ground. But Sainte-Chatte was an old soldier of fortune and not easily taken in, so on his return, while explaining the plan of the ground chosen by Cavalier for the disposition of his troops to M. de La Jonquiere, he added that he should be very much astonished if the young Camisard had not employed the little wood on his left and the lie of the ground on his right as cover for soldiers in ambush; but M. de La Jonquiere returned that the only thing of importance was to know the position of the principal body of troops in order to attack it at once. Sainte-Chatte told him that the principal body was that which was before his eyes, and that on this subject there could be no mistake; for he had approached near enough to recognise Cavalier himself in the front rank.

This was enough for M. de La Jonquiere: he put himself at the head of his men and rode straight to the ravine, beyond which Cavalier and his comrades awaited him in order of battle. Having got within a pistol-shot, M. de La Jonquiere gave the order to fire, but he was so near that Cavalier heard the words and saw the motion made by the men as they made ready; he therefore gave a rapid sign to his men, who threw themselves on their faces, as did their leader, and the bullets passed over them without doing any harm M.M. de La Jonquiere, who believed them all dead, was astonished when Cavalier and his Camisards rose up and rushed upon the royal troops, advancing to the sound of a psalm. At a distance of ten paces they fired, and then charged the enemy at the point of the bayonet. At this moment the sixty men in ambush to the right opened fire, while the thirty horsemen to the left, uttering loud shouts, charged at a gallop. Hearing this noise, and seeing death approach them in three different directions, the royals believed themselves surrounded, and did not attempt to make a stand; the men, throwing away their weapons, took to their heels, the officers alone and a few dragoons whom they had succeeded in rallying making a desperate resistance.

101

Cavalier was riding over the field of battle, sabring all the fugitives whom he met, when he caught sight of a group, composed of ten naval officers; standing close together and back to back, spontoon in hand, facing the Camisards, who surrounded them. He spurred up to them, passing through the ranks of his soldiers, and not pausing till he was within fifteen paces of them, although they raised their weapons to fire. Then making a sign with his hand that he wished to speak to them, he said, "Gentlemen, surrender. I shall give quarter, and in return for the ten lives I now spare you, will ask that my father, who is in prison at Nimes, be released."

For sole answer, one of the officers fired and wounded the young chief's horse in the head. Cavalier drew a pistol from his belt, took aim at the officer and killed him, then turning again to the others, he asked, "Gentlemen, are you as obstinate as your comrade, or do you accept my offer?" A second shot was the reply, and a bullet grazed his shoulder. Seeing that no other answer was to be hoped for, Cavalier turned to his soldiers. "Do your duty," said he, and withdrew, to avoid seeing the massacre. The nine officers were shot.

M de La Jonquiere, who had received a slight wound in the cheek, abandoned his horse in order to climb over a wall. On the other side he made a dragoon dismount and give him his horse, on which he crossed the river Gardon, leaving behind him on the battlefield twenty-five officers and six hundred soldiers killed. This defeat was doubly disastrous to the royal cause, depriving it of the flower of its officers, almost all of those who fell belonging to the noblest families of France, and also because the Camisards gained what they so badly needed, muskets, swords, and bayonets in great quantities, as well as eighty horses, these latter enabling Cavalier to complete the organisation of a magnificent troop of cavalry.

The recall of the Marechal de Montrevel was the consequence of this defeat, and M. de Villars, as he had anticipated, was appointed in his place. But before giving up his governorship Montrevel resolved to efface the memory of the check which his lieutenant's foolhardiness had caused, but for which, according to the rules of war, the general had to pay the penalty. His plan was by spreading false rumours and making feigned marches to draw the Camisards into a trap in which they, in their turn, would be caught. This was the less difficult to accomplish as their latest great victory had made Cavalier over confident both in himself and his men.

In fact, since the incident connected with the naval officers the troops of Cavalier had increased enormously in numbers, everyone desiring to serve under so brave a chief, so that he had now under him over one thousand infantry and two hundred cavalry; they were furnished, besides, just like regular troops, with a bugler for the cavalry, and eight drums and a fife for the infantry.

The marechal felt sure that his departure would be the signal for some expedition into the level country under Cavalier, so it was given out that he had left for Montpellier, and had sent forward some of his baggage-waggons to that place. On April 15th he was informed that Cavalier, deceived by the false news, had set out on the 16th April, intending to pass the night at Caveyrac, a small town about a league from Nimes, that he might be ready next day to make a descent on

La Vannage. This news was brought to M. de Montrevel by a village priest called Verrien, who had in his pay vigilant and faithful spies in whom he had every confidence.

Montrevel accordingly ordered the commandant of Lunel, M. de Grandval, to set out the next day, very early in the morning, with the Charolais regiment and five companies of the Fimarcon and Saint-Sernin dragoons, and to repair to the heights of Boissieres, where instructions would await him. Sandricourt, governor of Nimes, was at the same time directed to withdraw as many men as possible from the garrison, both Swiss and dragoons, and send them by night towards Saint-Come and Clarensac; lastly, he himself set out, as he had said, but instead of going on to Montpellier, he stopped at Sommieres, whence he could observe the movements of Cavalier.

Cavalier, as M. de Montrevel already knew, was to sleep on the 15th at Caveyrac. On this day Cavalier reached the turning-point in his magnificent career. As he entered the town with his soldiers, drums beating and flags flying, he was at the zenith of his power. He rode the splendid horse M. de La Jonquiere had abandoned in his flight; behind him, serving as page, rode his young brother, aged ten, followed by four grooms; he was preceded by twelve guards dressed in red; and as his colleague Roland had taken the title of Comte, he allowed himself to be called Duke of the Cevennes.

At his approach half of the garrison, which was commanded by M. de Maillan, took possession of the church and half of the citadel; but as Cavalier was more bent on obtaining food and rest for his soldiers than of disturbing the town, he billeted his men on the townspeople, and placed sentinels at the church and fortress, who exchanged shots all the night through with the royal troops. The next morning, having destroyed the fortifications, he marched out of the town again, drums beating and flags flying as before. When almost in sight of Nimes he made his troops, which had never before been so numerous or so brilliant, perform a great many evolutions, and then continued his way towards Nages.

M de Montrevel received a report at nine o'clock in the morning of the direction Cavalier and his troops had taken, and immediately left Sommieres, followed by six companies of Fimarqon dragoons, one hundred Irish free-lances, three hundred rank and file of the Hainault regiment, and one company each of the Soissonnais, Charolais, and Menon regiments, forming in all a corps over nine hundred strong. They took the direction of Vaunages, above Clarensac; but suddenly hearing the rattle of musketry behind them, they wheeled and made for Langlade.

They found that Grandval had already encountered the Camisards. These being fatigued had withdrawn into a hollow between Boissieres and the windmill at Langlade, in order to rest. The infantry lay down, their arms beside them; the cavalry placed themselves at the feet of their horses, the bridle on arm. Cavalier himself, Cavalier the indefatigable, broken by the fatigues of the preceding days, had fallen asleep, with his young brother watching beside him. Suddenly he felt himself shaken by the arm, and rousing up, he heard on all sides cries of "Kill! Kill!" and "To arms! To arms!" Grandval and his men, who had been sent to find out where the Camisards were, had suddenly come upon them.

The infantry formed, the cavalry sprang to their saddles, Cavalier leaped on his horse, and drawing his sword, led his soldiers as usual against the dragoons, and these, as was also usual, ran away, leaving twelve of their number dead on the field. The Camisard cavalry soon gave up the pursuit, as they found themselves widely separated from the infantry and from their leader; for Cavalier had been unable to keep up with them, his horse having received a bullet through its neck.

Still they followed the flying dragoons for a good hour, from time to time a wounded dragoon falling from his horse, till at last the Camisard cavalry found itself confronted by the Charolais regiment, drawn up in battle array, and behind them the royal dragoons, who had taken refuge there, and were re-forming.

Carried on by the rapidity of their course, the Camisards could not pull up till they were within a hundred yards of the enemy; they fired once, killing several, then turned round and retreated.

When a third of the way, back had been covered, they met their chief, who had found a fresh horse by the wayside standing beside its dead master. He arrived at full gallop, as he was anxious to unite his cavalry and infantry at once, as he had seen the forces of the marechal advancing, who, as we have already said, had turned in the direction of the firing. Hardly had Cavalier effected the desired junction of his forces than he perceived that his retreat was cut off. He had the royal troops both before and behind him.

The young chief saw that a desperate dash to right or left was all that remained to him, and not knowing this country as well as the Cevennes, he asked a peasant the way from Soudorgues to Nages, that being the only one by which he could escape. There was no time to inquire whether the peasant was Catholic or Protestant; he could only trust to chance, and follow the road indicated. But a few yards from the spot where the road from Doudorgues to Nages joins the road to Nimes he found himself in face of Marechal Montrevel's troops under the command of Menon. However, as they hardly outnumbered the Camisards, these did not stop to look for another route, but bending forward in their saddles, they dashed through the lines at full gallop, taking the direction of Nages, hoping to reach the plain round Calvisson. But the village, the approaches, the issues were all occupied by royal troops, and at the same time Grandval and the marechal joined forces, while Menon collected his men together and pushed forward. Cavalier was completely surrounded: he gave the situation a comprehensive glance—his foes, were five to one.

Rising in his stirrups, so that he could see over every head, Cavalier shouted so loud that not only his own men heard but also those of the enemy: "My children, if our hearts fail us now, we shall be taken and broken on the wheel. There is only one means of safety: we must cut our way at full gallop through these people. Follow me, and keep close order!"

So speaking, he dashed on the nearest group, followed by all his men, who formed a compact mass; round which the three corps of royal troops closed. Then there was everywhere a hand-to-hand battle there was no time to load and fire; swords flashed and fell, bayonets stabbed, the

107

royals and the Camisards took each other by the throat and hair. For an hour this demoniac fight lasted, during which Cavalier lost five hundred men and slew a thousand of the enemy. At last he won through, followed by about two hundred of his troops, and drew a long breath; but finding himself in the centre of a large circle of soldiers, he made for a bridge, where alone it seemed possible to break through, it being only guarded by a hundred dragoons.

He divided his men into two divisions, one to force the bridge, the other to cover the retreat. Then he faced his foes like a wild boar driven to bay.

Suddenly loud shouts behind him announced that the bridge was forced; but the Camisards, instead of keeping the passage open for their leader, scattered over the plain and sought safety in flight. But a child threw himself before them, pistol in hand. It was Cavalier's young brother, mounted on one of the small wild horses of Camargues of that Arab breed which was introduced into Languedoc by the Moors from Spain. Carrying a sword and carbine proportioned to his size, the boy addressed the flying men. "Where are you going?" he cried, "Instead of running away like cowards, line the river banks and oppose the enemy to facilitate my brother's escape." Ashamed of having deserved such reproaches, the Camisards stopped, rallied, lined the banks of the river, and by keeping up a steady fire, covered Cavalier's retreat, who crossed without having received a single wound, though his horse was riddled with bullets and he had been forced to change his sword three times.

Still the combat raged; but gradually Cavalier managed to retreat: a plain cut by trenches, the falling darkness, a wood which afforded cover, all combined to help him at last. Still his rearguard, harassed by the enemy, dotted the ground it passed over with its dead, until at last both victors and vanquished were swallowed up by night. The fight had lasted ten hours, Cavalier had lost more than five hundred men, and the royals about a thousand.

"Cavalier," says M. de Villars, in his Memoirs, "acted on this day in a way which astonished everyone. For who could help being astonished to see a nobody, inexperienced in the art of warfare, bear himself in such difficult and trying circumstances like some great general? At one period of the day he was followed everywhere by a dragoon; Cavalier shot at him and killed his horse. The dragoon returned the shot, but missed. Cavalier had two horses killed under him; the first time he caught a dragoon's horse, the second time he made one of his own men dismount and go on foot."

M de Montrevel also showed himself to be a gallant soldier; wherever there was danger there was he, encouraging officers and soldiers by his example: one Irish captain was killed at his side, another fatally wounded, and a third slightly hurt. Grandval, on his part, had performed miracles: his horse was shot under him, and M. de Montrevel replaced it by one of great value, on which he joined in the pursuit of the Camisards. After this affair M. de Montrevel gave up his place to M. de Villars, leaving word for Cavalier that it was thus he took leave of his friends.

Although Cavalier came out of this battle with honour, compelling even his enemies to regard him as a man worthy of their steel, it had nevertheless destroyed the best part of his hopes. He made a halt near Pierredon to gather together the remnant of his troops, and truly it was but a remnant which remained. Of those who came back the greater number were without weapons, for they had thrown them away in their flight. Many were incapacitated for service by their wounds; and lastly, the cavalry could hardly be said to exist any longer, as the few men who survived had been obliged to abandon their horses, in order to get across the high ditches which were their only cover from the dragoons during the flight.

Meantime the royalists were very active, and Cavalier felt that it would be imprudent to remain long at Pierredon, so setting out during the night, and crossing the Gardon, he buried himself in the forest of Hieuzet, whither he hoped his enemies would not venture to follow him. And in fact the first two days were quiet, and his troops benefited greatly by the rest, especially as they were able to draw stores of all kinds—wheat, hay, arms, and ammunition—from an immense cave which the Camisards had used for a long time as a magazine and arsenal. Cavalier now also employed it as a hospital, and had the wounded carried there, that their wounds might receive attention.

Unfortunately, Cavalier was soon obliged to quit the forest, in spite of his hopes of being left in peace; for one day on his way back from a visit to the wounded in the cave, whose existence was a secret, he came across a hundred miquelets who had penetrated thus far, and who would have taken him prisoner if he had not, with his, accustomed presence of mind and courage, sprung from a rock twenty feet high. The miquelets fired at him, but no bullet reached him. Cavalier rejoined his troops, but fearing to attract the rest of the royalists to the place,—retreated to some distance from the cave, as it was of the utmost importance that it should not be discovered, since it contained all his resources.

Cavalier had now reached one of those moments when Fortune, tired of conferring favours, turns her back on the favourite. The royalists had often noticed an old woman from the village of Hieuzet going towards the forest, sometimes carrying a basket in her hand, sometimes with a hamper on her head, and it occurred to them that she was supplying the hidden Camisards with provisions. She was arrested and brought before General Lalande, who began his examination by threatening that he would have her hanged if she did not at once declare the object of her frequent journeys to the forest without reserve. At first she made use of all kinds of pretexts, which only strengthened the suspicions of Lalande, who, ceasing his questions, ordered her to be taken to the gallows and hanged. The old woman walked to the place of execution with such a firm step that the general began to think he would get no information from her, but at the foot of the ladder her courage failed. She asked to be taken back before the general, and having been promised her life, she revealed everything.

M de Lalande put himself at once at the head of a strong detachment of miquelets, and forced the woman to walk before them till they reached the cavern, which they never would have discovered without a guide, so cleverly was the entrance hidden by rocks and brushwood. On entering, the first thing that met their eye was the wounded, about thirty in number. The miquelets threw themselves upon them and slaughtered them. This deed accomplished, they went

111

farther into the cave, which to their great surprise contained a thousand things they never expected to find there—heaps of grain, sacks of flour, barrels of wine, casks of brandy, quantities of chestnuts and potatoes; and besides all this, chests containing ointments, drugs and lint, and lastly a complete arsenal of muskets, swords, and bayonets, a quantity of powder ready-made, and sulphur, saltpetre, and charcoal-in short, everything necessary for the manufacture of more, down to small mills to be turned by hand. Lalande kept his word: the life of an old woman was not too much to give in return for such a treasure.

Meantime M. de Villars, as he had promised, took up Baron d'Aygaliers in passing through Lyons, so that during the rest of the journey the peacemaker had plenty of time to expatiate on his plans. As M. de Villars was a man of tact and a lover of justice, and desired above all things to bring a right spirit to bear on the performance of the duties of his new office, in which his two predecessors had failed, he promised the baron "to keep," as he expressed himself, his "two ears open" and listen to both sides, and as a first proof of impartiality—he refused to give any opinion until he had heard M. de Julien, who was coming to meet him at Tournon.

When they arrived at Tournon, M. de Julien was there to receive them, and had a very different story to tell from that which M. de Villars had heard from d'Aygaliers. According to him, the only pacific ration possible was the complete extermination of the Camisards. He felt himself very hardly treated in that he had been allowed to destroy only four hundred villages and hamlets in the Upper Cevennes,— assuring de Villars with the confidence of a man who had

112

studied the matter profoundly, that they should all have been demolished without exception, and all the peasants killed to the last man.

So it came to pass that M. de Villars arrived at Beaucaire placed like Don Juan between the spirits of good and evil, the one advising clemency and the other murder. M. de Villars not being able to make up his mind, on reaching Nimes, d'Aygaliers assembled the principal Protestants of the town, told them of his plan, showing them its practicability, so that also joined in the good work, and drew up a document in which they asked the marechal to allow them to take up arms and march against the rebels, as they were determined either to bring them back into the good way by force of example or to fight them as a proof of their loyalty.

This petition, which was signed by several nobles and by almost all the lawyers and merchants of the city of Nimes, was presented to M. de Villars on Tuesday, 22nd April, 1704, by M. de Albenas, at the head of seven or eight hundred persons of the Reformed religion. M. de Villars received the request kindly, thanked its bearer and those who accompanied him, assuring them that he had no doubt of the sincerity of their professions, and that if he were in want of help he would have recourse to them with as much confidence as if they were old Catholics. He hoped, however, to win the rebels back by mildness, and he begged them to second his efforts in this direction by spreading abroad the fact that an amnesty was offered to all those who would lay down arms and return to their houses within a week. The very next day but one, M. de Villars set out from Nimes to visit all the principal towns, in order to make himself acquainted with men, things, and places.

Although the answer to the petition had been a delicate refusal, d'Aygaliers was not discouraged, but followed M. de Villars everywhere. When the latter arrived at Alais, the new governor sent for MM. de Lalande and de Baville, in order to consult them as to the best means of inducing the Camisards to lay down their arms. Baron d'Aygaliers was summoned to this consultation, and described his plan to the two gentlemen. As he expected, both were opposed to it; however, he tried to bring them over to his side by presenting to them what seemed to him to be cogent reasons for its adoption. But de Lalande and de Baville made light of all his reasons, and rejected his proposals with such vehemence, that the marechal, however much inclined to the side of d'Aygaliers, did not venture to act quite alone, and said he would not decide on any course until he reached Uzes.

D'Aygaliers saw clearly that until he had obtained the approbation of either the general or the intendant, he would get nothing from the marechal. He therefore considered which of the two he should try to persuade, and although de Baville was his personal enemy, having several times shown his hatred for him and his family, he decided to address himself to him.

In consequence, the next day, to the great astonishment of M. de Baville, d'Aygaliers paid him a visit. The intendant received him coldly but politely, asked him to sit down, and when he was seated begged to know the motive which had brought him. "Sir," replied the baron, "you have given my family and me such cause of offence that I had come to the firm resolution never to ask a favour of you, and as perhaps you may have remarked during the journey we have taken with M. le marechal, I would rather have died of thirst than accept a glass of water from you. But I have come here to-day not upon any private matter, to obtain my own ends, but upon a matter which concerns the welfare of the State. I therefore beg you to put out of your mind the dislike which you have to me and mine, and I do this the more earnestly that your dislike can only have been caused by the fact that our religion is different from yours—a thing which could neither have been foreseen nor prevented. My entreaty is that you do not try to set M. le marechal against the course which I have proposed to him, which I am convinced would bring the disorders in our province to an end, stop the occurrence of the many unfortunate events which I am sure you look on with regret, and spare you much trouble and embarrassment."

The intendant was much touched by this calm speech, and above all by the confidence which M. d'Aygaliers had shown him, and replied that he had only offered opposition to the plan of pacification because he believed it to be impracticable. M. d'Aygaliers then warmly pressed him to try it before rejecting it for ever, and in the end M. de Baville withdrew his opposition.

M d'Aygaliers hastened to the marechal, who finding himself no longer alone in his favourable opinion, made no further delay, but told the baron to call together that very day all the people whom he thought suitable for the required service, and desired that they should be presented to him the next morning before he set out for Nimes.

The next day, instead of the fifty men whom the marachal had thought could be gathered together, d'Aygaliers came to him followed by eighty, who were almost all of good and many of noble family. The meeting took place, by the wish of the baron, in the courtyard of the episcopal palace. "This palace," says the baron in his Memoirs, "which was of great magnificence, surrounded by terraced gardens and superbly furnished, was occupied by Monseigneur Michel Poncet de La Riviere. He was a man passionately devoted to pleasures of all kinds, especially to music, women, and good cheer. There were always to be found in his house good musicians, pretty women, and excellent wines. These latter suited him so well that he never left the table without being in a pleasant humour, and at such a moment if it came into his head that anyone in his diocese was not as good a Christian as himself, he would sit down and write to M. de Baville, urging that the delinquent ought to be sent into exile. He often did this honour to my late father." M. d'Aygaliers goes on to say that "on seeing such a great number of Huguenots in the court who were all declaring that they were better servants of the king than the Catholics, he almost fell from his balcony with vexation and surprise. This vexation increased when he saw M. de Villars and M. de Baville, who had apartments in the palace, come down into the court and talk to these people. One hope still remained to him: it was that the marechal and the intendant had come down to send them away; but this last hope was cruelly disappointed when he heard M. de Villars say that he

116

accepted their service and expected them to obey d'Aygaliers in all matters concerning the service of the king."

But this was not all that had to be accomplished arms were necessary for the Protestants, and though their number was not great, there was a difficulty in finding them weapons. The unfortunate Calvinists had been disarmed so often that even their table-knives had been carried off, so it was useless to search their houses for guns and sabres. D'Aygaliers proposed that they should take the arms of the townspeople, but M. de Villars considered that it would offend the Catholics to have their arms taken from them and given to the Protestants. In the end, however, this was the course that had to be adopted: M. de Paratte was ordered to give fifty muskets and the same number of bayonets to M. d'Aygaliers, who also received, as the reward of his long patience, from M. de Villars, before the latter left for Nimes, the following commission:

"We, Marechal de Villars, general in the armies of the king, etc., etc., have given permission to M. d'Aygaliers, nobleman and Protestant of the town of Uzes, and to fifty men chosen by him, to make war on the Camisards.

"(Signed) "VILLARS

"Given at Uzes, the 4th of May 1704"

Hardly had M. de Villars set out for Nimes than d'Aygaliers met with fresh difficulties. The bishop, who could not forget that his episcopal palace had been turned into barracks for Huguenots, went from house to house threatening those who had promised to countenance d'Aygaliers' plans, and strictly forbidding the captains of the town troops to deliver any weapons to the Protestants.

Fortunately, d'Aygaliers had not accomplished so much without having learned not to draw back when the road grew rough, so he also on his side went about confirming the strong and encouraging the feeble, and called on M. de Paratte to beg him to carry out the orders of M. de Villars. De Paratte was happily an old soldier, whose one idea was that discipline should be maintained, so that he gave the guns and bayonets to d'Aygaliers on the spot, without a word of objection, and thus enabled the latter to start at five o'clock next morning with his little band.

Meantime de Baville and de Lalande had been reflecting what great influence d'Aygaliers would gain in the province should he succeed in his aims, and their jealousy had made them resolve to forestall him in his work, by themselves inducing Cavalier to abandon his present course. They did not conceal from themselves that this would be difficult, but as they could command means of corruption which were not within the power of d'Aygaliers, they did not despair of success.

They therefore sent for a countryman called Lacombe, in order to enlist him on their side; for Cavalier, when a boy, had been his shepherd for two years, and both had remained friends ever since: this man undertook to try and bring about a meeting between the two gentlemen and Cavalier— an enterprise which would have been dangerous for anyone else. He promised first of all to explain to Cavalier the offers of MM. de Baville and de Lalande.

Lacombe kept his word: he set off the same day, and two days later appeared before Cavalier. The first feeling of the young chief was astonishment, the second pleasure.

118

Lacombe could not have chosen a better moment to speak of peace to his former shepherd.

"Indeed," says Cavalier in his Memoirs, "the loss which I had just sustained at Nages was doubly painful to me because it was irreparable. I had lost at one blow not only a great number of weapons, all my ammunition, and all my money, but also a body of men, inured to danger and fatigue, and capable of any undertaking;—besides all this, I had been robbed of my stores—a loss which made itself felt more than all the others put together, because as long as the secret of the cavern was kept, in all our misfortunes we were never without resources; but from the moment it got into the possession of our enemies we were quite destitute. The country was ravaged, my friends had grown cold, their purses were empty, a hundred towns had been sacked and burned, the prisons were full of Protestants, the fields were uncultivated. Added to all this, the long promised help from England had never arrived, and the new marechal had appeared in the province accompanied by fresh troops."

Nevertheless, in spite of his desperate position, Cavalier listened to the propositions laid before him by Lacombe with cold and haughty front, and his reply was that he would never lay down arms till the Protestants had obtained the right to the free exercise of their religion.

Firm as was this answer, Lalande did not despair of inducing Cavalier to come to terms: he therefore wrote him a letter with his own hand, asking him for an interview, and pledging his word that if they came to no agreement Cavalier should be free to retire without any harm being done him; but he added that, if he refused this request, he should regard him as an enemy to peace, and responsible for all the blood which might be shed in future.

This overture, made with a soldier's frankness, had a great effect on Cavalier, and in order that neither his friends nor his enemies should have the least excuse for blaming him, he resolved to show everyone that he was eager to seize the first chance of making peace on advantageous terms.

He therefore replied to Lalande, that he would come to the bridge of Avene on that very day, the 12th May, at noon, and sent his letter by Catinat, ordering him to deliver it into the hands of the Catholic general himself.

Catinat was worthy of his mission. He was a peasant from Cayla, whose real name was Abdias Maurel. He had served under Marshal Catinat in Italy, the same who had maintained so gallant a struggle against Prince Eugene. When Maurel returned home he could talk of nothing but his marshal and his campaigns, so that he soon went among his neighbours by the name of "Catinat." He was, as we have seen, Cavalier's right hand, who had placed him in command of his cavalry, and who now entrusted him with a still more dangerous post, that of envoy to a man who had often said that he would give 2000 livres to him who would bring him the head of Cavalier, and 1000 livres each for the heads of his two lieutenants. Catinat was quite well aware of this offer of Lalande's, yet he appeared before the general perfectly cool and calm; only, either from a feeling of propriety or of pride, he was dressed in full uniform.

The bold and haughty expression of the man who presented Cavalier's letter astonished the general, who asked him his name.

"I am Catinat," he answered.

"Catinat!" exclaimed Lalande in surprise.

"Yes, Catinat, commander of the cavalry of Cavalier."

"What!" said Lalande, "are you the Catinat who massacred so many people in Beaucaire?"

"Yes, I am. I did it, but it was my duty."

"Well," exclaimed M. de Lalande, "you show great hardihood in daring to appear before me."

"I came," said Catinat proudly, "trusting to your honour and to the promise that Brother Cavalier gave me that nothing should happen to me."

"He was quite right," returned Lalande, taking the letter. Having read it, he said, "Go back to Cavalier and assure him that I shall be at the bridge of Avene at noon, accompanied only by a few officers and thirty dragoons. I expect to find him there with a similar number of men."

"But," answered Catinat, "it is possible that Brother Cavalier may not wish-to come with so poor a following."

"If so," returned Lalande, "then tell him that he may bring his whole army if he likes, but that I shall not take a single man with me more than I have said; as Cavalier has confidence in me, I have confidence in him."

Catinat reported Lalande's answer to his chief it was of a kind that he understood and liked, so leaving the rest of his troops at Massanes, he chose sixty men from his infantry, and eight horsemen as escort. On coming in sight of the bridge, he saw Lalande approaching from the other side. He at once ordered his sixty men to halt, went a few steps farther with his eight horsemen, and then ordered them in their turn to stop, and advanced alone towards the bridge.

121

Lalande had acted in the same manner with regard to his dragoons and officers, and now dismounting, came towards Cavalier.

The two met in the middle of the bridge, and saluted with the courtesy of men who had learned to esteem each other on the field of battle. Then after a short silence, during which they examined each other, Lalande spoke.

"Sir," said he, "the king in his clemency desires to put an end to the war which is going on between his subjects, and which can only result in the ruin of his kingdom. As he knows that this war has been instigated and supported by the enemies of France, he hopes to meet no opposition to his wishes among those of his subjects who were momentarily led astray, but to whom he now offers pardon."

"Sir," answered Cavalier, "the war not having been begun by the Protestants, they are always ready for peace— but a real peace, without restriction or reserve. They have no right, I know, to lay down conditions, but I hope they will be permitted to discuss those which may be laid down for them. Speak openly, sir, and let me know what the offers are that you have been authorised to make to us, that I may judge if we can accept them."

"But how would it be," said Lalande, "if you were mistaken, and if the king desired to know what conditions you would consider reasonable?"

"If that is so," answered Cavalier, "I will tell you our conditions at once, in order not to prolong the negotiations; for every minute's delay, as you know, costs someone his life or fortune."

"Then tell me what your conditions are," returned Lalande.

"Well," said Cavalier, "our demands are three first, liberty of conscience; secondly, the release of all prisoners who have been condemned to imprisonment or the galleys because of their religion; and thirdly, that if we are not granted liberty of conscience we may be at least permitted to leave the kingdom."

"As far as I can judge," replied Lalande, "I do not believe that the king will accept the first proposition, but it is possible that he may accede to the third. In that case, how many Protestants would you take with you?"

"Ten thousand of all ages and both sexes."

"The number is excessive, sir. I believe that His Majesty is not disposed to go beyond three thousand."

"Then," replied Cavalier, "there is nothing more to be said, for I could not accept passports for any smaller number, and I could accept for the ten thousand only on condition that the king would grant us three months in which to dispose of our possessions and withdraw from the country without being molested. Should His Majesty, however, not be pleased to allow us to leave the kingdom, then we beg that our edicts be re-enacted and our privileges restored, whereupon we shall become once more, what we were formerly, His Majesty's loyal and obedient servants."

"Sir," said Lalande, "I shall lay your conditions before M. le Marechal, and if no satisfactory conclusion can be arrived at, it will be to me a matter of profound regret. And now, sir, will you permit me to inspect more closely the gallant men with whose help you have done such astounding deeds?"

Cavalier smiled; for these "gallant men" when caught had been broken on the wheel, burnt at the stake, or hanged like brigands. His sole answer was an inclination of the head as he turned and led the way to his little escort. M. de Lalande followed him with perfect confidence, and, passing by the eight horsemen who were grouped on the road, he walked up to the infantry, and taking out of his pocket a handful of gold, he scattered it before them, saying:

"There, my men! that is to drink the king's health with."

Not a man stooped to pick the money up, and one of them said, shaking his head,

"It is not money we want, but liberty of conscience."

"My men," answered Lalande, "it is unfortunately not in my power to grant your demand, but I advise you to submit to the king's will and trust in his clemency."

"Sir," answered Cavalier, "we are all ready to obey him, provided that he graciously grant us our just demands; if not, we shall die weapon in hand, rather than expose ourselves once more to such outrages as have already been inflicted on us."

"Your demands shall be transmitted word for word to M. de Villars, who will lay them before the king," said Lalande, "and you may be sure, sir, that my most sincere wish is that His Majesty may not find them exorbitant."

With these words, M. de Lalande saluted Cavalier, and turned to rejoin his escort; but Cavalier, wishing to return confidence with confidence, crossed the bridge with him, and accompanied the general to where his soldiers had halted. There, with another salute, the two chiefs parted, M.

de Lalande taking the road to Uzes, while Cavalier rejoined his comrades.

Meantime d'Aygaliers, who, as we have seen, had not left Uzes until the 5th May, in order to join Cavalier, did not come up with him until the 13th, that is to say, the day after his conference with Lalande. D'Aygaliers gives us an account of their interview, and we cannot do better than quote it.

"Although it was the first time that we had met face to face, we embraced each other as if we were old acquaintances. My little band mixed with his and sang psalms together, while Cavalier and I talked. I was very much pleased with what, he said, and convinced him without difficulty that he should submit for the sake of the brethren, who could then choose whichever course best suited them, and either leave the kingdom or serve the king. I said that I believed the last course to be the best, provided we were allowed to worship God according to our consciences; because I hoped that, seeing their faithful service, His Majesty would recognise that he had been imposed upon by those who had described us as disloyal subjects, and that we should thus obtain for the whole nation that liberty of conscience which had been granted to us; that in no other way, as far as I could see, could our deplorable condition be ameliorated, for although Cavalier and his men might be able to exist for some time longer in the forests and mountains, they would never be strong enough to save the inhabitants of towns and other enclosed places from perishing.

"Upon this he replied, that although the Catholics seldom kept a promise made to those of our religion, he was willing to risk his life for the welfare of his brethren and the province but that he trusted if he confided in the clemency of the king for whom he had never ceased to pray, no harm would happen him."

Thereupon d'Aygaliers, delighted to find him so well inclined, begged him to give him a letter for M. de Villars, and as Cavalier knew the marechal to be loyal and zealous, and had great confidence in him, he wrote without any hesitation the following letter:

"MONSEIGNEUR,—Permit me to address your Excellency in order to beg humbly for the favour of your protection for myself and for my soldiers. We are filled with the most ardent desire to repair the fault which we have committed by bearing arms, not against the king, as our enemies have so falsely asserted, but to defend our lives against those who persecuted us, attacking us so fiercely that we believed it was done by order of His Majesty. We know that it was written by St. Paul that subjects ought to submit themselves to their king, and if in spite of these sincere protestations our sovereign should still demand our blood, we shall soon be ready to throw ourselves on his justice or his mercy; but we should, Monseigneur, regard ourselves as happy, if His Majesty, moved by our repentance, would grant us his pardon and receive us into his service, according to the example of the God of mercy whose representative His Majesty is on earth. We trust, Monseigneur, by our faithfulness and zeal to acquire the honour of your protection, and we glory in the thought of being permitted, under the command of such an illustrious and noble-minded general as yourself, to shed our blood for the king; this being so, I hope that your Excellency will be pleased to allow me to

126

inscribe myself with profound respect and humility, Monseigneur, your most humble and obedient servant, "CAVALIER."

D'Aygaliers, as soon as he got possession of this letter, set out for Nimes in the best of spirits; for he felt sure that he was bringing M. de Villars more than he had expected. And, indeed, as soon as the marechal saw how far things had gone, in spite of everything that Lalande could say, who in his jealousy asserted that d'Aygaliers would spoil everything, he sent him back to Cavalier with an invitation to come to Nimes. D'Aygaliers set out at once, promising to bring the young chief back with him, at which Lalande laughed loudly, pretending to be very much amused at the baron's confident way of speaking, and protesting that Cavalier would not come.

In the meantime events were happening in the mountains which might easily have changed the state of mind of the young chief. The Comte de Tournan, who was in command at Florae, had encountered Roland's army in the plain of Fondmortes, and had lost two hundred men, a considerable sum of money, and eighty mules loaded with provisions. The anxiety which this news caused to M. de Villars was soon relieved; for six days after the defeat he received a letter from Cavalier by the hands of Lacombe, the same who had brought about the interview on the bridge of Avenes. In this letter Cavalier expressed the greatest regret for what had just happened.

D'Aygaliers therefore found Cavalier in the best of humours when he joined him at Tarnac. The first feeling that the young chief felt on receiving the invitation was one of stupefaction; for an interview with the marechal was an honour so unexpected and so great, that his impression was that some treason lay behind it; but he was soon reassured when he recalled the character for loyalty which the marechal bore, and how impossible it was that d'Aygaliers should lend himself to treachery. So Cavalier sent back word that he would obey the marechal's orders; and that he put himself entirely into his hands in what concerned the arrangements for the interview. M. de Villars let him know that he would expect him on the 16th in the garden of the convent of the Recollets of Nimes, which lay just outside the city, between the gates of Beaucaire and the Madeleine, and that Lalande would meet him beyond Carayrac to receive him and to bring him hostages.

CHAPTER IV

On the 15th May Cavalier set out from Tarnac at the head of one hundred and sixty foot-soldiers and fifty horse; he was accompanied by his young brother and by d'Aygaliers and Lacombe. They all passed the night at Langlade.

The next day they set out for Nimes, and, as had been agreed upon, were met by Lalande between Saint-Cesaire and Carayrac. Lalande advanced to greet Cavalier and present the hostages to him. These hostages were M. de La Duretiere, captain of the Fimarcon regiment, a captain of infantry, several other officers, and ten dragoons. Cavalier passed them over to his lieutenant, Ravanel, who was in command of the infantry, and left them in his charge at Saint-Cesaire. The cavalry accompanied him to within a musket-shot of Nimes, and encamped upon the heights. Besides this, Cavalier posted sentinels and mounted orderlies at all the approaches to the camp, and even as far off as the fountain of Diana and the tennis-court. These precautions taken, he entered the city, accompanied by his brother, d'Aygaliers, Lacombe, and a body-guard of eighteen cavalry, commanded by Catinat. Lalande rode on before to announce their arrival to the marechal, whom he found waiting with MM. de Baville and Sandricourt, in the garden of the Recollets, dreading every moment to receive word that Cavalier had refused to come; for he expected great results from this interview. Lalande, however, reassured him by telling him the young Huguenot was behind.

In a few minutes a great tumult was heard: it was the people hastening to welcome their hero. Not a Protestant, except paralytic old people and infants in the cradle, remained indoors; for the Huguenots, who had long looked on Cavalier as their champion, now considered him their saviour, so that men and women threw themselves under the feet of his horse in their efforts to kiss the skirts of his coat. It was more like a victor making his entry into a conquered town than a rebel chief coming to beg for an amnesty for himself and his adherents. M. de Villars heard the outcry from the garden of Recollets, and when he learned its cause his esteem for Cavalier rose higher, for every day since his arrival as governor had showed him more and more clearly how great was the young chief's

129

influence. The tumult increased as Cavalier came nearer, and it flashed through the marechal's mind that instead of giving hostages he should have claimed them. At this moment Cavalier appeared at the gate, and seeing the marechal's guard drawn up in line, he caused his own to form a line opposite them. The memoirs of the time tell us that he was dressed in a coffee-coloured coat, with a very full white muslin cravat; he wore a cross-belt from which depended his sword, and on his head a gold-laced hat of black felt. He was mounted on a magnificent bay horse, the same which he had taken from M. de La Jonquiere on the bloody day of Vergenne.

The lieutenant of the guard met him at the gate. Cavalier quickly dismounted, and throwing the bridle of his horse to one of his men, he entered the garden, and advanced towards the expectant group, which was composed, as we have said, of Villars, Baville, and Sandricourt. As he drew near, M. de Villars regarded him with growing astonishment; for he could not believe that in the young man, or rather boy, before him he saw the terrible Cevenol chief, whose name alone made the bravest soldiers tremble. Cavalier at this period had just completed his twenty-fourth year, but, thanks to his fair hair which fell in long locks over his shoulders, and to the gentle expression of his eyes he did not appear more than eighteen. Cavalier was acquainted with none of the men in whose presence he stood, but he noticed M. de Villars' rich dress and air of command. He therefore saluted him first; afterwards, turning towards the others, he bowed to each, but less profoundly, then somewhat embarrassed and with downcast eyes he stood motionless and silent. The marechal still continued to look at him in silent astonishment, turning from time to time to Baville and Sandricourt, as if to assure himself that there was no mistake and that it was really the man whom they expected who stood before them. At last, doubting still, in spite of the signs they made to reassure him, he asked—

"Are you really Jean Cavalier?"

"Yes, monseigneur," was the reply, given in an unsteady voice.

"But I mean Jean Cavalier, the Camisard general, he who has assumed the title of Duke of the Cevennes."

"I have not assumed that title, monseigneur, only some people call me so in joke: the king alone has the right to confer titles, and I rejoice exceedingly, monseigneur, that he has given you that of governor of Languedoc."

"When you are speaking of the king, why do you not say 'His Majesty'?" said M. de Baville. "Upon my soul, the king is too good to treat thus with a rebel."

The blood rushed to Cavalier's head, his face flamed, and after a moment's pause, fixing his eye boldly upon M. de Baville, and speaking in a voice which was now as firm as it had been tremulous a moment before, he said, "If you have only brought me here, sir, to speak to me in such a manner, you might better have left me in my mountains, and come there yourself to take a lesson in hospitality. If I am a rebel, it is not I who am answerable, for it was the tyranny and cruelty of M. de Baville which forced us to have recourse to arms; and if history takes exception to anything connected with the great monarch for whose pardon I sue to-day, it will be, I hope, not that he had foes like me, but friends like him."

131

M de Baville grew pale with anger; for whether Cavalier knew to whom he was speaking or not, his words had the effect of a violent blow full in his face; but before he could reply M. de Villars interposed.

"Your business is only with me, sir," he said; "attend to me alone, I beg: I speak in the name of the king; and the king, of his clemency, wishes to spare his subjects by treating them with tenderness."

Cavalier opened his mouth to reply, but the intendant cut him short.

"I should hope that that suffices," he said contemptuously: "as pardon is more than you could have hoped for, I suppose you are not going to insist on the other conditions you laid down?"

"But it is precisely those other conditions," said Cavalier, addressing himself to M. de Villars, and not seeming to see that anyone else was present, "for which we have fought. If I were alone, sir, I should give myself up, bound hand and foot, with entire confidence in your good faith, demanding no assurances and exacting no conditions; but I stand here to defend the interests of my brethren and friends who trust me; and what is more, things have gone so far that we must either die weapon in hand, or obtain our rights."

The intendant was about to speak, but the marechal stopped him with such an imperative gesture that he stepped back as if to show that he washed his hands of the whole matter.

"What are those rights? Are they those which M. Lalande has transmitted to me by word of mouth?"

"Yes, sir."

"It would be well to commit them to writing."

"I have done so, monseigneur, and sent a copy to M. d'Aygaliers."

"I have not seen it, sir; make me another copy and place it in my hands, I beg."

"I shall go and set about it directly, monseigneur," stepping back as if about to withdraw.

"One moment!" said the marechal, detaining him by a smile. "Is it true that you are willing to enter the king's army?"

"I am more than willing, I desire it with all my heart," exclaimed Cavalier, with the frank enthusiasm natural to his age, "but I cannot do so till our just demands are granted."

"But if they were granted—?"

"Then, sir," replied Cavalier, "the king has never had more loyal subjects than we shall be."

"Well, have a little patience and everything will be arranged, I hope."

"May God grant it!" said Cavalier. "He is my witness that we desire peace beyond everything." And he took another step backwards.

"You will not go too far away, I hope," said the marechal.

"We shall remain wherever your excellency may appoint," said Cavalier.

"Very well," continued M. de Villars; "halt at Calvisson, and try all you can to induce the other leaders to follow your example."

"I shall do my best, monseigneur; but while we await His Majesty's reply shall we be allowed to fulfil our religious duties unimpeded?"

"Yes, I shall give orders that you are to have full liberty in that respect."

"Thanks, monseigneur."

Cavalier bowed once more, and was about to go; but M. de Villars accompanied him and Lalande, who had now joined them, and who stood with his hand on Cavalier's shoulder, a few steps farther. Catinat seeing that the conference was at an end, entered the garden with his men. Thereupon M. de Villars took leave, saying distinctly, "Adieu, Seigneur Cavalier," and withdrew, leaving the young chief surrounded by a dozen persons all wanting to speak to him at once. For half an hour he was detained by questions, to all of which he replied pleasantly. On one finger was an emerald taken from a naval officer named Didier, whom he had killed with his own hand in the action at Devois de Martignargues; he kept time by a superb watch which had belonged to M. d'Acqueville, the second in command of the marines; and he offered his questioners from time to time perfumed snuff from a magnificent snuffbox, which he had found in the holsters when he took possession of M. de La Jonquiere's horse. He told everyone who wished to listen that he had never intended to revolt against the king; and that he was now ready to shed the last drop of his blood in his service; that he had several times offered to surrender on condition that liberty of conscience was granted to those of the new faith, but that M. de Montrevel had always rejected his offers, so that he had been obliged to remain under arms, in order to deliver those who were in prison, and to gain permission for those who were free to worship God in their own way.

He said these things in an unembarrassed and graceful manner, hat in hand; then passing through the crowd which had gathered outside the garden of the Recollets, he repaired to the Hotel de la Poste for lunch, and afterwards walked along the Esplanade to the house of one Guy Billard, a gardener, who was his head prophet's father. As he thus moved about he was preceded by two Camisards with drawn swords, who made way for him; and several ladies were presented to him who were happy to touch his doublet. The visit over, he once again passed along the Esplanade, still preceded by his two Camisards, and just as he passed the Little Convent he and those with him struck up a psalm tune, and continued singing till they reached Saint-Cesaire, where the hostages were. These he at once sent back.

Five hundred persons from Nimes were awaiting him; refreshments were offered to him, which he accepted gratefully, thanking all those who had gathered together to meet him. At last he went off to St. Denoise, where he was to sup and sleep; but before going to bed he offered up supplications in a loud voice for the king, for M. de Villars, for M. de Lalande, and even for M. de Baville.

The next morning, Cavalier, according to promise, sent a copy of his demands to M. de Villars, who caused it to be laid before the king, along with a full report of all that had passed at the interview at Nimes. As soon as the young chief had sent off his missive, he rejoined his troops at Tarnac, and related all that had passed to Roland, urging him to follow his example. That night he slept at Sauves, having passed through Durfort at the head of his men; a captain of dragoons named Montgros, with twenty-five soldiers, accompanying him everywhere, by M. de Villars' orders, and seeing that the villages through which they passed furnished him with all that was needed. They left Sauves on May 16th very early in the morning, in order to get to Calvisson, which, as our readers may remember, was the place appointed for the residence of Cavalier during the truce. In passing through Quissac, where they stopped for refreshments, they were joined by Castanet who delivered a long sermon, at which all the Protestants of the neighbourhood were present.

The two battalions of the Charolais regiment which were quartered at Calvisson had received orders on the evening of the 17th to march out next morning, so as to make room for the Camisards.

On the 18th the head of the commissary department, Vincel, ordered suitable accommodation to be provided for Cavalier and his troops; the muster roll being in the hands of M. d'Aygaliers, it would be sent by him or brought in the course of the day. In the meantime, vans were arriving filled with all sorts of provisions, followed by droves of cattle, while a commissary and several clerks, charged with the distribution of rations, brought up the rear.

On the 19th, Catinat, accompanied by twelve Camisards, rode into the town, and was met at the barrier by the commandant and eighty townspeople. As soon as the little band came in sight the commandant reiterated his orders that nothing should be said or done in the town, on pain of corporal punishment, that could offend the Camisards.

At one o'clock P. M. Baron d'Aygaliers arrived, followed in his turn by the chief of the commissariat, Vincel, by Captain Cappon, two other officers named Viala and Despuech, and six dragoons. These were the hostages Cavalier had given.

At six o'clock there was heard a great noise; and shouts of "Cavalier! Cavalier!" resounded on all sides. The young Cevenol was in sight, and the whole population hastened to meet him. He rode at the head of his cavalry, the infantry following, and the whole number—about six hundred men—sang psalms in a loud voice.

When they reached the church, Cavalier drew up before it with all his men in review order, and for some time the singing went on. When it stopped, a long prayer was offered up, which was most edifying to all the bystanders; and this being over, Cavalier went to the quarters assigned him, which were in the best house in Calvisson. Arrived there, he sent out for a dozen loaves that he might judge how his men were going to be fed; not finding them white enough, he complained to M. Vincel, whom he sent for, and who promised that in future the bread should be of a better quality. Having received this assurance, Cavalier gave orders that the loaves in hand should be distributed for that day, but probably fearing poison, he first made M. de Vincel and his clerks taste them in his presence. These duties accomplished, he visited in person all the gates of the town, placed guards and posted sentinels at all the entrances and along all the avenues, the most advanced being three-quarters of a league from the town. Besides this, he placed guards in the streets, and a sentinel at each door of the house he occupied; in addition, thirty guards always slept outside the door of his bedroom, and these accompanied him as an escort when he went out; not that he was afraid, for he was not of a mistrustful character, but that he thought it politic to give people an exalted idea of his importance. As to his soldiers, they were billeted on the inhabitants, and received each as daily rations a pound of meat, a quart of wine, and two and a half pounds of bread.

The same day a convocation was held on the site of the old meeting-house which had been destroyed by the Catholics. It was a very numerous assembly, to which crowds of people came from all parts; but on the following days it was still more numerous; for, as the news spread, people ran with great eagerness to hear the preaching of the word of which they had been so long deprived. D'Aygaliers tells us in his Memoirs that—"No one could help being touched to see a whole people just escaped from fire and sword, coming together in multitudes to mingle their tears and sighs. So famished were they for the manna divine, that they were like people coming out of a besieged city, after a long and cruel famine, to whom peace has brought food in abundance, and who, first devouring it with their eyes, then throw themselves on it, devouring it bodily—meat, bread, and fruit—as it comes to hand. So it was with the unfortunate inhabitants of La Vannage, and even of places more distant still. They saw their brethren assembling in the meadows and at the gates of Calvisson, gathering in crowds and pressing round anyone who started singing a psalm, until at last four or five thousand persons, singing, weeping, and praying, were gathered together, and remained there all day, supplicating God with a devotion that went to every heart and made a deep impression. All night the same things went on; nothing was to be heard but preaching, singing, praying, and prophesying."

But if it was a time of joy for the Protestants, it was a time of humiliation for the Catholics. "Certainly," says a contemporary historian, "it was a very surprising thing, and quite a novelty, to see in a province like Languedoc, where so many troops were quartered, such a large number of villains—all murderers, incendiaries, and guilty of sacrilege—gathered together in one place by permission of those in command of the troops; tolerated in their eccentricities, fed at the public expense, flattered by everyone, and courteously, received by people sent specially to meet them."

One of those who was most indignant at this state of things was M. de Baville. He was so eager to put an end to it that he went to see the governor, and told him the scandal was becoming too great in his opinion: the assemblies ought to be put an end to by allowing the troops to fall upon them and disperse them; but the governor thought quite otherwise, and told Baville that to act according to his advice would be to set fire to the province again and to scatter for ever people whom they had got together with such difficulty. In any case, he reminded Baville that what he objected to would be over in a few days. His opinion was that de Baville might stifle the expression of his dissatisfaction for a little, to bring about a great good. "More than that," added the marechal, "the impatience of the priests is most ridiculous. Besides your remonstrances, of which I hope I have now heard the last, I have received numberless letters full of such complaints that it would seem as if the prayers of the Camisards not only grated on the ears of the clergy but flayed them alive. I should like above everything to find out the writers of these letters, in order to have them flogged; but they have taken good care to put no signatures. I regard it as a very great impertinence for those who caused these disturbances to grumble and express their disapproval at my efforts to bring them to an end." After this speech, M. de Baville saw there was nothing for him to do but to let things take their course.

The course that they took turned Cavalier's head more and more; for thanks to the injunctions of M. de Villars, all the orders that Cavalier gave were obeyed as if they had been issued by the governor himself. He had a court like a prince, lieutenants like a general, and secretaries like a statesman. It was the duty of one secretary to give leave of absence to those Camisards who had business to attend to or who desired to visit their relations. The following is a copy of the form used for these passports:

"We, the undersigned, secretary to Brother Cavalier, generalissimo of the Huguenots, permit by this order given by him to absent himself on business for three days.

"(Signed) DUPONT.

"Calvisson, this——"

And these safe-conducts were as much respected as if they had been signed "Marechal de Villars."

On the 22nd M. de Saint-Pierre arrived from the court, bringing the reply of the king to the proposals which Cavalier had submitted to M. de Lalande. What this reply was did not transpire; probably it was not in harmony with the pacific intentions of the marechal. At last, on the 25th, the answer to the demands which Cavalier had made to M. de Villars himself arrived. The original paper written by the Camisard chief himself had been sent to Louis XIV, and he returned it with notes in his own writing; thus these two hands, to one of which belonged the shepherd's crook and to the other the sceptre, had rested on the same sheet of paper. The following is the text of the agreement as given by Cavalier in his Memoirs:

"THE HUMBLE PETITION OF THE REFORMERS OF LANGUEDOC TO THE KING

"1. That it may please the king to grant us liberty of conscience throughout the province, and to permit us to hold religious meetings in every suitable place, except fortified places and walled cities.

'Granted, on condition that no churches be built.

"2. That all those in prison or at the galleys who have been sent there since the revocation of the Edict of Nantes, because of their religion, be set at liberty within six weeks from the date of this petition.

'Granted.

"3. That all those who have left the kingdom because of their religion be allowed to return in freedom and safety, and that their goods and privileges be restored to them.

'Granted on condition that they take the oath of fidelity to the king.

"4. That the Parliament of Languedoc be reestablished on its ancient footing, and with all its former privileges.

'The king reserves decision on this point.

"5. That the province of Languedoc be exempted from the poll tax for ten years, this to apply, to Catholics and Protestants alike, both sides having equally suffered.

'Refused.

"6. That the cities of Perpignan, Montpellier, Cette, and Aiguemortes be assigned us as cities of refuge.

'Refused.

"7. That the inhabitants of the Cevennes whose houses were burnt or otherwise destroyed during the war be exempt from taxes for seven years.

'Granted.

"8. That it may please His Majesty to permit Cavalier to choose 2000 men, both from among his own troops and from among those who may be delivered from the prisons and galleys, to form a regiment of dragoons for the service of His Majesty, and that this regiment when formed may at once be ordered to serve His Majesty in Portugal.

'Granted: and on condition that all the Huguenots everywhere lay down their arms, the king will permit them to live quietly in the free exercise of their religion.'"

"I had been a week at Calvisson," says Cavalier in his Memoirs, "when I received a letter from M. le Marechal de Villars ordering me to repair to Nimes, as he wished to see me, the answer to my demands having arrived. I obeyed at once, and was very much displeased to find that several of my demands, and in particular the one relating to the cities of refuge, had been refused; but M. le marechal assured me that the king's word was better than twenty cities of refuge, and that after all the trouble we had given him we should regard it as showing great clemency on his part that he had granted us the greater part of what we had asked. This reasoning was not entirely convincing, but as there was no more time for deliberation, and as I was as anxious for peace as the king himself, I decided to accept gracefully what was offered."

All the further advantage that Cavalier could obtain from M. de Villars was that the treaty should bear the date of the day on which it had been drawn up; in this manner the prisoners who were to be set at liberty in six weeks gained one week.

M de Villars wrote at the bottom of the treaty, which was signed the same day by him and M. de Baville on the part of the king, and by Cavalier and Daniel Billard on the part of the Protestants, the following ratification:

"In virtue of the plenary powers which we have received from the king, we have granted to the Reformers of Languedoc the articles above made known.

"MARECHAL DE VILLARS J. CAVALIER "LAMOIGNON DE BAVILLE DANIEL BILLARD

"Given at Nimes, the 17th of May 1704"

These two signatures, all unworthy as they were to stand beside their own, gave such great delight to MM. de Villars and de Baville, that they at once sent off fresh orders to Calvisson that the wants of the Camisards should be abundantly supplied until the articles of the treaty were executed—that is to say, until the prisoners and the galley slaves were set at liberty, which, according to article 2 of the treaty, would be within the next six weeks. As to Cavalier, the marechal gave him on the spot a commission as colonel, with a pension of 1200 livres attached, and the power of nominating the subordinate officers in his regiment, and at the same time he handed him a captain's commission for his young brother.

Cavalier drew up the muster-roll of the regiment the same day, and gave it to the marechal. It was to consist of seven hundred and twelve men, forming fifteen companies, with sixteen captains, sixteen lieutenants, a sergeant-major, and a surgeon-major.

While all this was happening, Roland, taking advantage of the suspension of hostilities, was riding up and down the province as if he were viceroy of the Cevennes, and wherever he appeared he had a magnificent reception. Like Cavalier, he gave leave of absence and furnished escorts, and held himself haughtily, sure that he too would soon be negotiating treaties on terms of equality with marshals of France and governors of provinces. But Roland was much mistaken: M. de Villars had made great concessions to the popularity of Cavalier, but they were the last he intended to make. So, instead of being in his turn summoned to Nimes, or Uzes, to confer with M. de Villars, Roland merely received an intimation from Cavalier that he desired to speak with him on important business.

They met near Anduze, and Cavalier, faithful to the promise given to M. de Villars, neglected no argument that he could think of to induce Roland to follow his example; but Roland would listen to nothing. Then, when Cavalier saw that arguments and promises were of no avail, he raised his voice in anger; but Roland, laying his hand on his shoulder, told him that his head was turned, that he should remember that he, Roland, was his senior in command, and therefore bound by nothing that had been promised in his name by his junior, and that he had registered a vow in Heaven that nothing would persuade him to make peace unless complete liberty of conscience were granted to all. The young Cevenol, who was unaccustomed to such language, laid his hand on the hilt of his sword, Roland, stepping back, drew his, and the consultation would have ended in a duel if the prophets had not thrown themselves between them, and succeeded in getting Roland to consent to one of their number, a man much esteemed among the Huguenots, named Salomon, going back to Nimes with Cavalier to learn from M. de Villars' own mouth what the exact terms were which Cavalier had accepted and now offered to Roland.

In a couple of hours Cavalier and Salomon set out together, and arrived at Nimes on the 27th May, escorted by twenty-five men; they halted at the tower of Magne, and the Protestants of the city came out to meet them, bringing refreshments; then, after prayers and a hasty meal, they advanced to the barracks and crossed the courtyards. The concourse of people and the enthusiasm was no whit less than on Cavalier's first entry, more than three hundred persons kissing his hands and knees. Cavalier was dressed on this occasion in a doublet of grey cloth, and a beaver hat, laced with gold, and adorned with a white feather.

Cavalier and his travelling-companion went direct to the garden of the Recollets, and hardly had they got there than MM. de Villars and de Baville, accompanied by Lalande and Sandricourt, came out to meet them: the conference lasted three hours, but all that could be learned of the result was that Salomon had declared that his brethren would

145

never lay down their arms till full liberty of conscience had been secured to them. In consequence of this declaration, it was decided that Cavalier and his regiment should be despatched to Spain without delay, in order to weaken the Calvinist forces to that extent; meantime Salomon was sent back to Roland with a positive promise that if he would surrender, as Cavalier had done, he would be granted the same conditions—that is to say, receive a commission as colonel, have the right to name the officers of his regiment, and receive a pension of 1200 livres. On quitting the garden of the Recollets, Cavalier found as great a crowd as ever waiting for him, and so closely did they press on him that two of his men were obliged to ride before him with drawn sabres to clear a way for him till the Montpellier road was reached. He lay that night at Langlade, in order to rejoin his troops early next morning.

But during his absence things had happened among these men, who had hitherto obeyed him blindly, which he little expected. He had left, as usual, Ravanel in command; but hardly had he ridden away when Ravanel began to take all kinds of precautions, ordering the men not to lay aside their arms. The negotiations with M. de Villars had made him most anxious; he looked upon all the promises given as snares, and he regarded the compromise favoured by his chief as a defection on Cavalier's part. He therefore called all the officers and men together, told them of his fears, and ended by imbuing them with his suspicions. This was all the more easily done, as it was very well known that Cavalier had joined the Huguenots less from devotion to the cause than to avenge a private wrong, and on many occasions had

146

given rise to the remark that he had more genius than religion.

So, on getting back to Calvisson, the young chief found his principal officers, Ravanel at their head, drawn up in the market-place, waiting for him. As soon as he drew near they told him that they were determined to know at once what were the conditions of the treaty he had signed with the marechal; they had made up their minds to have a plain answer without delay. Such a way of speaking to him was so strange and unexpected, that Cavalier shrugged his shoulders and replied that such matters were no business of theirs, being too high for their intelligence; that it was his business to decide what course to take and theirs to take it; it had always been so in the past, and with the help of God and his own, Cavalier's, goodwill, it should still be so in future; and having so spoken, he told them to disperse. Ravanel upon this came forward, and in the name of all the others said they would not go away until they knew what orders Cavalier was about to give the troops, that they might consult among themselves whether they should obey them or not. This insubordination was too much for Cavalier's patience.

"The orders are," he said, "to put on the uniforms that are being made for you, and to follow me to Portugal."

The effect of such words on men who were expecting nothing less than the re-enactment of the Edict of Nantes, can be easily imagined; the words "coward" and "traitor" could be distinguished above the murmurs, as Cavalier noticed with increasing astonishment. Raising himself in his stirrups, and glancing round with that look before which

147

they had been used to tremble, he asked in a voice as calm as if all the demons of anger were not raging in his heart, "Who called Jean Cavalier traitor and coward?"

"I," said Ravanel, crossing his arms on his breast.

Cavalier drew a pistol from his holsters, and striking those near him with the butt end, opened a way towards his lieutenant, who drew his sword; but at this moment the commissary-general, Vincel, and Captain Cappon threw themselves between the two and asked the cause of the quarrel.

"The cause," said Ravanel, "is that the Cadets of the Cross, led by the 'Hermit,' have just knocked out the brains of two of our brethren, who were coming to join us, and are hindering others front attending our meetings to worship God: the conditions of the truce having been thus broken, is it likely they will keep those of the treaty? We refuse to accept the treaty."

"Sir," said Vincel, "if the 'Hermit' has done what you say, it is against the orders of the marachal, and the misdoer will be punished; besides, the large number of strangers at present in Calvisson ought to be sufficient proof that no attempt has been made to prevent the new converts from coming to the town, and it seems to me that you have been too easily led to believe everything that malicious people have told you."

"I believe what I choose to believe," said Ravanel impatiently; "but what I know and say is, that I shall never lay down arms till the king grants us full liberty of conscience, permission to rebuild our places of worship, and sends us back all prisoners and exiles."

"But, judging by your tone," said Cavalier, who had till now remained silent while toying with his pistol, "you seem to be in command here; have we changed, parts without my being aware?"

"It is possible," said Ravanel.

Cavalier burst out laughing.

"It seems to astonish you," said Ravanel, "but it is true. Make peace for yourself, lay down what conditions suit you, sell yourself for whatever you will bring; my only reply is, You are a coward and a traitor. But as to the troops, they will not lay down arms except on the conditions formulated by me."

Cavalier tried to get at Ravanel, but seeing from his paleness and his smile that terrible things would happen if he reached his lieutenant, Vincel and Cappon, backed by some Camisards, threw themselves before his horse. Just then the whole band shouted with one voice, "No peace! no peace! no reconciliation till our temples are restored!" Cavalier then saw for the first time that things were more serious than he had believed, but Vincel, Cappon, Berlie, and about twenty Camisards surrounded the young chief and forced him to enter a house; it was the house of Vincel.

They had hardly got indoors when the 'generale' was sounded: resisting all entreaties, Cavalier sprang to the door, but was detained by Berlie, who said that the first thing he ought to do was to write M. de Villars an account of what had happened, who would then take measures to put things straight.

"You are right," said Cavalier; "as I have so many enemies, the general might be told if I were killed that I had broken my word. Give me pen and ink."

Writing materials were brought, and he wrote to M. de Villars.

"Here," he said, giving the letter unsealed to Vincel, "set out for Nimes and give this to the marechal, and tell him, if I am killed in the attempt I am about to make, I died his humble servant."

With these words, he darted out of the house and mounted his horse, being met at the door by twelve to fifteen men who had remained faithful to him. He asked them where Ravanel and his troops were, not seeing a single Camisard in the streets; one of the soldiers answered that they were probably still in town, but that they were moving towards Les Garrigues de Calvisson. Cavalier set off at a gallop to overtake them.

In crossing the market-place he met Catinat, walking between two prophets, one called Moses and the other Daniel Guy; Catinat was just back from a visit to the mountains, so that he had taken no part in the scene of insubordination that had so lately been enacted.

Cavalier felt a ray of hope; he was sure he could depend on Catinat as on himself. He hurried to greet him, holding out his hand; but Catinat drew back his.

"What does this mean?" cried Cavalier, the blood mounting to his forehead.

"It means," answered Catinat, "that you are a traitor, and I cannot give my hand to a traitor."

150

Cavalier gave a cry of rage, and advancing on Catinat, raised his cane to strike him; but Moses and Daniel Guy threw themselves between, so that the blow aimed at Catinat fell on Moses. At the same moment Catinat, seeing Cavalier's gesture, drew a pistol from his belt. As it was at full cock, it went off in his hand, a bullet piercing Guy's hat, without, however, wounding him.

At the noise of the report shouts were heard about a hundred yards away. It was the Camisards, who had been on the point of leaving the town, but hearing the shot had turned back, believing that some of their brethren were being murdered. On seeing them appear, Cavalier forgot Catinat, and rode straight towards them. As soon as they caught sight of him they halted, and Ravanel advanced before them ready for every danger.

"Brethren," he cried, "the traitor has come once more to tempt us. Begone, Judas! You have no business here."

"But I have," exclaimed Cavalier. "I have to punish a scoundrel called Ravanel, if he has courage to follow me."

"Come on, then," cried Ravanel, darting down a small side-street, "and let us have done with it." The Camisards made a motion as if to follow them, but Ravanel turning towards them ordered them to remain where they were.

They obeyed, and thus Cavalier could see that, insubordinate as they had been towards him, they were ready to obey another.

Just at the moment as he turned into the narrow street where the dispute was to be settled once for all, Moses and Guy came up, and seizing the bridle of his horse stopped him, while the Camisards who were on the side of Cavalier surrounded Ravanel and forced him to return to his soldiers. The troops struck up a psalm, and resumed their march, while Cavalier was held back by force.

At last, however, the young Cevenol succeeded in breaking away from those who surrounded him, and as the street by which the Camisards had retired was blocked, he dashed down another. The two prophets suspecting his intention, hurried after the troops by the most direct route, and got up with them, just as Cavalier, who had made the circuit of the town, came galloping across the plain to intercept their passage. The troops halted, and Ravanel gave orders to fire. The first rank raised their muskets and took aim, thus indicating that they were ready to obey. But it was not a danger of this kind that could frighten Cavalier; he continued to advance. Then Moses seeing his peril, threw himself between the Camisards and him, stretching out his arms and shouting, "Stop! stop! misguided men! Are you going to kill Brother Cavalier like a highwayman and thief? You must pardon him, my brethren! you must pardon him! If he has done wrong in the past, he will do better in future."

Then those who had taken aim at Cavalier grounded their muskets, and Cavalier changing menace for entreaty, begged them not to break the promise that he had made in their name; whereupon the prophets struck up a psalm, and the rest of the soldiers joining in, his voice was completely drowned. Nevertheless, Cavalier did not lose heart, but accompanied them on their march to Saint-Esteve, about a league farther on, unable to relinquish all hope. On reaching Saint-Esteve the singing ceased for a moment, and he made another attempt to recall them to obedience. Seeing, however, that it was all in vain, he gave up hope, and calling out, "At least defend yourselves as well as you can, for the dragoons will soon be on you," he set his horse's head towards the town. Then turning to them for the last time, he said, "Brethren, let those who love me follow me!" He pronounced these words in tones so full of grief and affection that many were shaken in their resolution; but Ravanel and Moses seeing the effect he had produced, began to shout, "The sword of the Lord!" Immediately all the troops turned their back on Cavalier except about forty men who had joined him on his first appearance.

Cavalier went into a house near by, and wrote another letter to M. de Villars, in which he told him what had just taken place, the efforts he had made to win back his troops, and the conditions they demanded. He ended by assuring him that he would make still further efforts, and promised the marechal that he would keep him informed of everything that went on. He then withdrew to Cardet, not venturing to return to Calvisson.

Both Cavalier's letters reached M. de Villars at the same time; in the first impulse of anger aroused by this unexpected check, he issued the following order:

"Since coming to this province and taking over the government by order of the king, our sole thought has been how to put an end to the disorders we found existing here by gentle measures, and to restore peace and to preserve the property of those who had taken no part in the disturbances. To that end we obtained His Majesty's pardon for those rebels who had, by the persuasion of their chiefs, been induced to lay down their arms; the only condition exacted being that they should throw themselves on the king's clemency and beg his permission to expiate their crime by adventuring their lives in his service. But, being informed that instead of keeping the engagements they had made by signing petitions, by writing letters, and by speaking words expressing their intentions, some among them have been trying to delude the minds of the people with false hopes of full liberty for the exercise of this so-called Reformed religion, which there has never been any intention of granting, but which we have always declared as clearly as we could, to be contrary to the will of the king and likely to bring about great evils for which it would be difficult to find a remedy, it becomes necessary to prevent those who give belief to these falsehoods from expecting to escape from well-deserved chastisement. We therefore declare hereby that all religious assemblies are expressly forbidden under the penalties proclaimed in the edicts and ordinances of His Majesty, and that these will be more strictly enforced in the future than in the past.

"Furthermore, we order all the troops under our command to break up such assemblies by force, as having been always illegal, and we desire to impress on the new converts of this province that they are to give their obedience where it is due, and we forbid them to give any credence to the false reports which the enemies of their repose are spreading abroad. If they let themselves be led astray, they will soon find themselves involved in troubles and misfortunes, such as the loss of their lands, the ruin of their families, and the desolation of their country; and we shall take care that the true authors of these misfortunes shall receive punishment proportioned to their crime.

"MARECHAL DE VILLARS

"Given at Nimes the 27th day of May 1704"

This order, which put everything back upon the footing on which it had been in the time of M. de Montrevel, had hardly been issued than d'Aygaliers, in despair at seeing the result of so much labour destroyed in one day, set off for the mountains to try and find Cavalier. He found him at Cardet, whither, as we have said, he had retired after the day of Calvisson. Despite the resolution which Cavalier had taken never to show his face again to the marechal, the baron repeated to him so many times that M. de Villars was thoroughly convinced that what had happened had not been his fault, he having done everything that he could to prevent it, that the young chief began to feel his self-confidence and courage returning, and hearing that the marachal had expressed himself as very much pleased with his conduct, to which Vincel had borne high testimony, made up his mind to return to Nimes. They left Cardet at once, followed by the forty men who had remained true to Cavalier, ten on horse and thirty on foot, and arrived on the 31st May at Saint-Genies, whither M. de Villars had come to meet them.

The assurances of d'Aygaliers were justified. The marechal received Cavalier as if he were still the chief of a powerful party and able to negotiate with him on terms of equality. At Cavalier's request, in order to prove to him that he stood as high in his good opinion as ever, the marechal returned once more to gentle methods, and mitigated the

155

severity of his first proclamation by a second, granting an extension of the amnesty:

"The principal chiefs of the rebels, with the greater number of their followers, having surrendered, and having received the king's pardon, we declare that we give to all those who have taken up arms until next Thursday, the 5th instant inclusive, the opportunity of receiving the like pardon, by surrendering to us at Anduze, or to M. le Marquis de Lalande at Alais, or to M. de Menon at Saint Hippolyte, or to the commandants of Uzes, Nimes, and Lunel. But the fifth day passed, we shall lay a heavy hand on all rebels, pillaging and burning all the places which have given them refuge, provisions, or help of any kind; and that they may not plead ignorance of this proclamation, we order it to be publicly read and posted up in every suitable place.

"MARECHAL DE VILLARS

"At Saint-Genies, the 1st June 1704"

The next day, in order to leave no doubt as to his good intentions, the marechal had the gibbets and scaffolds taken down, which until then had been permanent erections.

At the same time all the Huguenots were ordered to make a last effort to induce the Camisard chiefs to accept the conditions offered them by M. de Villars. The towns of Alais, Anduze, Saint-Jean, Sauve, Saint-Hippolyte, and Lasalle, and the parishes of Cros, Saint-Roman, Manoblet, Saint-Felix, Lacadiere, Cesas, Cambo, Colognac, and Vabre were ordered to send deputies to Durfort to confer as to the best means of bringing about that peace which everyone desired. These deputies wrote at once to M. de Villars to beg him to send them M. d'Aygaliers, and to M. d'Aygaliers to request him to come.

Both consented to do as they were asked, and M. d'Aygaliers arrived at Durfort on the 3rd of June 1704.

The deputies having first thanked him for the trouble which he had taken to serve the common cause during the past year, resolved to divide their assembly into two parts, one of which, was to remain permanently sitting, while the other went to seek Roland and Ravanel to try and obtain a cessation of hostilities. The deputies charged with this task were ordered to make it quite clear to the two chiefs that if they did not accept the proposals made by M. de Villars, the Protestants in general would take up arms and hunt them down, and would cease to supply them with the means of subsistence.

On hearing this, Roland made reply that the deputies were to go back at once to those who sent them, and threatened, should they ever show him their faces again, to fire on them.

This answer put an end to the assembly, the deputies dispersed, and d'Aygaliers returned to the Marechal de Villars to make his report.

Hardly had he done this when a letter from Roland arrived, in which the Camisard chief asked M. de Villars to grant him an interview, such as he had granted to Cavalier. This letter was addressed to d'Aygaliers, who immediately communicated its contents to the marechal, from whom he received orders to set out at once to find Roland and to spare no pains to bring him round.

D'Aygaliers, who was always indefatigable when working for his country, started the same day, and went to a mountain about three-quarters of a league from Anduze, where Roland awaited him. After a conference of two hours, it was agreed that hostages should be exchanged and negotiations entered upon.

Consequently, M. de Villars on his side sent Roland M. de Montrevel, an officer commanding a battalion of marines, and M. de la Maison-Blanche, captain of the Froulay regiment; while Roland in return sent M. de Villars four of his principal officers with the title of plenipotentiaries.

Unskilled in diplomacy as these envoys were, and laughable as they appeared to contemporary historians, they received nevertheless the marechal's consent to the following conditions:

1. That Cavalier and Roland should each be placed in charge of a regiment serving abroad, and that each of them should be allowed a minister.
2. That all the prisoners should be released and the exiles recalled.
3. That the Protestants should be permitted to leave the kingdom, taking their effects with them.
4. That those Camisards who desired to remain might do so, on giving up their arms.
5. That those who were abroad might return.
6. That no one should be molested on account of his religion provided everyone remained quietly at home.

7. That indemnities should be borne by the whole province, and not exacted specially from the Protestants.
8. That a general amnesty should be granted to all without reserve.

These articles were laid before Roland and Ravanel by d'Aygaliers. Cavalier, who from the day he went back to Nimes had remained in the governor's suite, asked leave to return with the baron, and was permitted to do so. D'Aygaliers and he set out together in consequence for Anduze, and met Roland and Ravanel about a quarter of a league from the town, waiting to know the result of the negotiations. They were accompanied by MM. de Montbel and de Maison-Blanche, the Catholic hostages.

As soon as Cavalier and Roland met they burst out into recriminations and reproaches, but through the efforts of d'Aygaliers they soon became more friendly, and even embraced on parting.

But Ravanel was made of harder stuff: as soon as he caught sight of Cavalier he called him "traitor," saying that for his part he would never surrender till the Edict of Nantes was re-enacted; then, having warned them that the governor's promises were not to be trusted, and having predicted that a day would come when they would regret their too great confidence in him, he left the conference and rejoined his troops, which, with those of Roland, were drawn up on a mountain about three-quarters of a league distant.

The negotiators did not, however, despair. Ravanel had gone away, but Roland had debated with them at some length, so they determined to speak to "the brethren"—that is, to the troops under Roland and Ravanel, whose headquarters at the moment were at Leuzies, in order that they might know exactly what articles had been agreed on between Roland's envoys and the marechal. Those who made up their minds to take this step were, Cavalier, Roland, Moise, Saint-Paul, Laforet, Maille, and d'Aygaliers. We take the following account of what happened in consequence of this decision from d'Aygaliers' Memoirs:

"We had no sooner determined on this plan, than, anxious to carry it out, we set off. We followed a narrow mountain path on the face of the cliff which rose up to our right; to our left flowed the Gardon.

"Having gone about a league, we came in sight of the troops, about 3000 strong; an advanced post barred our way.

"Thinking it was placed there in our honour, I was advancing unsuspiciously, when suddenly we found our road cut off by Camisards to right and left, who threw themselves on Roland and forced him in among their troops. Maille and Malplach were dragged from their horses. As to Cavalier, who was somewhat behind, as soon as he saw people coming towards him with uplifted sabres and shouting Traitor! he put spurs to his horse and went off at full gallop, followed by some townspeople from Anduze who had come with us, and who, now that they saw the reception we met with, were ready to die with fear.

"I was too far forward to escape: five or six muskets rested on my breast and a pistol pressed each ear; so I made up my mind to be bold. I told the troopers to fire; I was willing to die in the service of my prince, my country, and my religion, as well as for themselves, whom I was trying to benefit by procuring them the king's goodwill.

"These words, which I repeated several times in the midst of the greatest uproar, gave them pause.

"They commanded me to retire, as they did not want to kill me. I said I should do nothing of the kind: I was going into the middle of the troops to defend Roland against the charge of treason, or be put to death myself, unless I could convince them that what I had proposed to him and Cavalier was for the good of the country, of our religion, and the brethren; and having thus expostulated at the top of my voice against thirty voices all trying to drown mine for about an hour, I offered to fight the man who had induced them to oppose us.

"At this offer they pointed their muskets at me once more; but Maille, Malplach, and some others threw themselves before me, and although they were unarmed, had enough influence to hinder my being insulted; I was forced, however, to retreat.

"In leaving, I warned them that they were about to bring great misfortunes on the province, whereupon a man named Claris stepped out from among the troops, and approaching me exclaimed, 'Go on, sir, and God bless you! We know that you mean well, and were the first to be taken in. But go on working for the good of the country, and God will bless you.'"

D'Aygaliers returned to the marechal, who, furious at the turn things had taken, resolved instantly to break off all negotiations and have recourse once more to measures of severity. However, before actually carrying out this determination, he wrote the following letter to the king:

"SIRE,—It is always my glory to execute faithfully your Majesty's orders, whatever those orders may be; but I should have been able, on many occasions since coming here, to display my zeal for your Majesty's service in other ways if I had not had to deal with madmen on whom no dependence could be placed. As soon as we were ready to attack them, they offered to submit, but a little later changed their minds again. Nothing could be a greater proof of madness than their hesitation to accept a pardon of which they were unworthy, and which was so generously offered by your Majesty. If they do not soon make up their minds, I shall bring them back to the paths of duty by force, and thus restore this province to that state of peace which has been disturbed by these fools."

The day after writing this letter to the king, Roland sent Maille to M. de Villars to beg him to wait till Saturday and Sunday the 7th and the 8th June were over, before resorting to severity, that being the end of the truce. He gave him a solemn promise that he would, in the interval, either bring in his troops to the last man, or would himself surrender along with a hundred and fifty followers. The marechal consented to wait till Saturday morning, but as soon as Saturday arrived he gave orders to attack the Camisards, and the next day led a considerable body of troops to Carnoulet, intending to take the Huguenots by surprise, as word had been brought that they were all gathered there. They, however, received intelligence of his plan, and evacuated the village during the night.

The village had to pay dearly for its sin of hospitality; it was pillaged and burnt down: the miquelets even murdered two women whom they found there, and d'Aygaliers failed to obtain any satisfaction for this crime. In this manner M. de Villars kept the fatal promise he had given, and internecine war raged once more.

Furious at having missed the Camisards, de Menon having heard from his scouts that Roland was to sleep next night at the chateau de Prade, went to M. de Villars and asked leave to conduct an expedition against the chief. He was almost sure of taking Roland by surprise, having procured a guide whose knowledge of the country was minute. The marechal gave him carte blanche. In the evening Menon set out with two hundred grenadiers. He had already put three-quarters of the way behind him without being discovered, when an Englishman met them by chance. This man was serving under Roland, but had been visiting his sweetheart in a neighbouring village, and was on his way home when he fell among Menon's grenadiers. Without a thought for his own safety, he fired off his gun, shouting, "Fly! fly! The royals are upon you!"

The sentinels took up the cry, Roland jumped out of bed, and, without staying for clothes or horse, ran off in his shirt, escaping by a postern gate which opened on the forest just as de Menon entered by another. He found Roland's bed still warm, and took possession of his clothes, finding in a coat pocket a purse containing thirty-five Louis, and in the stables three superb horses. The Camisards answered this beginning of hostilities by a murder. Four of them, thinking they had reasons for displeasure against one of M. de Baville's subordinates, named Daude, who was both mayor and magistrate; at Le Vigan, hid in a corn-field which he had to pass on his way back from La Valette, his country place. Their measures were successful: Daude came along just as was expected, and as he had not the slightest suspicion of the impending danger, he continued conversing with M. de Mondardier, a gentleman of the neighbourhood who had asked for the; hand of Daude's daughter in marriage that very day. Suddenly he found himself surrounded by four men, who, upbraiding him for his exactions and cruelties, shot him twice through the head with a pistol. They offered no violence to M. de Mondardier except to deprive him of his laced hat and sword. The day on which M. de Villars heard of its murder he set a price on the heads of Roland, Ravanel, and Catinat. Still the example set by Cavalier, joined to the resumption of hostilities, was not without influence on the Camisards; every day letters arrived from single troopers offering to lay down their arms, and in one day thirty rebels came in and put themselves into Lalande's hands, while twenty surrendered to Grandval; these were accorded not only pardon, but received a reward, in hopes that they might be able to induce others to do like them; and on the 15th June eight of the troops which had abandoned Cavalier at Calvisson made submission; while twelve others asked to be allowed to return to their old chief to follow him wherever he went. This request was at once granted: they were sent to Valabregues, where they found forty-two of their old comrades, amongst whom were Duplan and Cavalier's young brother, who had been ordered there a few days before. As they arrived they were given quarters in the barracks, and received good pay—the chiefs forty sous a day, and the privates ten. So they felt as happy as possible, being well fed and well lodged, and spent their time preaching, praying, and psalm-singing, in season and out of season. All this, says La Baume, was so disagreeable to the inhabitants of the place, who were Catholics, that if they had not been guarded by the king's soldiers they would have been pitched into the Rhone.

CHAPTER V

Meantime the date of Cavalier's departure drew near. A town was to be named in which he was to reside at a sufficient distance from the theatre of war to prevent the rebels from depending on him any more; in this town he was to organise his regiment, and as soon as it was complete it was to go, under his command, to Spain, and fight for the king. M. de Villars was still on the same friendly terms with him, treating him, not like a rebel, but according to his new rank in the French army. On the 21st June he told him that he was to get ready to leave the next day, and at the same time he handed him an advance on their future pay—fifty Louis for himself, thirty for Daniel Billard, who had been made lieutenant-colonel in the place of Ravanel, ten for each captain, five for each lieutenant, two for each sergeant, and one for each private. The number of his followers had then reached one hundred and fifty, only sixty of whom were armed. M. de Vassiniac, major in the Fimarcn regiment, accompanied them with fifty dragoons and fifty of the rank and file from Hainault.

All along the road Cavalier and his men met with a courteous reception; at Macon they found orders awaiting them to halt. Cavalier at once wrote to M. de Chamillard to tell him that he had things of importance to communicate to him, and the minister sent a courier of the Cabinet called Lavallee to bring Cavalier to Versailles. This message more than fulfilled all Cavalier's hopes: he knew that he had been greatly talked about at court, and in spite of his natural modesty the reception he had met with at Times had given him new ideas, if not of his own merit, at least of his own importance. Besides, he felt that his services to the king deserved some recognition.

The way in which Cavalier was received by Chamillard did not disturb these golden dreams: the minister welcomed the young colonel like a man whose worth he appreciated, and told him that the great lords and ladies of the court were not less favourably disposed towards him. The next day Chamillard announced to Cavalier that the king desired to see him, and that he was to keep himself prepared for a summons to court. Two days later, Cavalier received a letter from the minister telling him to be at the palace at four o'clock in the afternoon, and he would place him on the grand staircase, up which the king would pass.

Cavalier put on his handsomest clothes, for the first time in his life perhaps taking trouble with his toilet. He had fine features, to which his extreme youth, his long fair hair, and the gentle expression of his eyes lent much charm. Two years of warfare had given him a martial air; in short, even among the most elegant, he might pass as a beau cavalier.

At three o'clock he reached Versailles, and found Chamillard waiting for him; all the courtiers of every rank were in a state of great excitement, for they had learned that the great Louis had expressed a wish to meet the late Cevenol chief, whose name had been pronounced so loud and so often in the mountains of Languedoc that its echoes had resounded in the halls of Versailles. Cavalier had not been mistaken in thinking that everyone was curious to see him, only as no one yet knew in what light the king regarded him, the courtiers dared not accost him for fear of compromising their dignity; the manner of his reception by His Majesty would regulate the warmth of his reception by everyone else.

Met thus by looks of curiosity and affected silence, the young colonel felt some embarrassment, and this increased when Chamillard, who had accompanied him to his appointed place, left him to rejoin the king. However, in a few moments he did what embarrassed people so often do, hid his shyness under an air of disdain, and, leaning on the balustrade, crossed his legs and played with the feather of his hat.

When half an hour had passed in this manner, a great commotion was heard: Cavalier turned in the direction from which it came, and perceived the king just entering the vestibule. It was the first time he had seen him, but he recognized him at once. Cavalier's knees knocked together and his face flushed.

167

The king mounted the stairs step by step with his usual dignity, stopping from time to time to say a word or make a sign with head or hand. Behind him, two steps lower, came Chamillard, moving and stopping as the king moved and stopped, and answering the questions which His Majesty put to him in a respectful but formal and precise manner.

Reaching the level on which Cavalier stood, the king stopped under pretext of pointing out to Chamillard a new ceiling which Le Brun had just finished, but really to have a good look at the singular man who had maintained a struggle against two marshals of France and treated with a third on equal terms. When he had examined him quite at his ease, he turned to Chamillard, pretending he had only just caught sight of the stranger, and asked:

"Who is this young gentleman?"

"Sire," answered the minister, stepping forward to present him to the king, "this is Colonel Jean Cavalier."

"Ah yes," said the king contemptuously, "the former baker of Anduze!"

And shrugging his shoulders disdainfully, he passed on.

Cavalier on his side had, like Chamillard, taken a step forward, when the scornful answer of the great king changed him into a statue. For an instant he stood motionless and pale as death, then instinctively he laid his hand on his sword, but becoming conscious that he was lost if he remained an instant longer among these people, whom not one of his motions escaped, although they pretended to despise him too much to be aware of his presence, he dashed down the staircase and through the hall, upsetting two or three footmen who were in his way, hurried into the garden, ran across it at full speed, and regaining his room at the hotel, threw himself on the floor, where he rolled like a maniac, uttering cries of rage, and cursing the hour when, trusting to the promises of M. de Villars, he had abandoned the mountains where he was as much a king as Louis XIV at Versailles. The same evening he received orders to leave Paris and rejoin his regiment at Macon. He therefore set out the next morning, without seeing M. de Chamillard again.

Cavalier on arriving at Macon found that his comrades had had a visit from M. d'Aygaliers, who had come again to Paris, in the hope of obtaining more from the king than M. de Villars could or would grant.

Cavalier, without telling his comrades of the strange manner in which the king had received him, gave them to understand that he was beginning to fear that not only would the promises they had received be broken, but that some strange trick would be played upon them.

Thereupon these men, whose chief and oracle he had been for so long, asked him what they ought to do; Cavalier replied that if they would follow him, their best course and his would be to take the first opportunity of gaining the frontier and leaving the country. They all declared themselves ready to follow him anywhere. This caused Cavalier a new pang of regret, for he could not help recollecting that he had once had under his command fifteen hundred men like these.

The next day Cavalier and his comrades set out on their march without knowing whither they were being taken, not having been able to obtain any information as to their destination from their escort—a silence which confirmed

169

them in their resolution. As soon, therefore, as they reached Onnan, Cavalier declared that he considered that the looked-for opportunity had arrived, asking them if they were still in the same mind: they returned that they would do whatever he advised. Cavalier then ordered them to hold themselves in readiness, Daniel offered up a prayer, and the prayer ended, the whole company deserted in a body, and, crossing Mont Belliard, entered Porentruy, and took the road to Lausanne.

Meantime d'Aygaliers, in his turn, arrived at Versailles, with letters from M. de Villars for the Duke of Beauvilliers, president of the king's council, and for Chamillard. The evening of his arrival he delivered these letters to those to whom they were addressed, and both gentlemen promised to present him to the king.

Four days later, Chamillard sent word to d'Aygaliers that he was to be next day at the door of the king's chamber at the time when the council entered. D'Aygaliers was punctual, the king appeared at the usual hour, and as he paused before d'Aygaliers, Chamillard came forward and said:

"Baron d'Aygaliers, sire."

"I am very glad to see you, sir," said the king, "for I am very much pleased with the zeal you have displayed in Languedoc in my service—very much pleased indeed."

"Sire," answered d'Aygaliers, "I consider myself most unfortunate in that I have been able to accomplish nothing deserving of the gracious words which your Majesty deigns to address me, and I pray God of His grace to grant me in the future an opportunity of proving my zeal and loyalty in your Majesty's service more clearly than hitherto."

"Never mind, never mind," said the king. "I repeat, sir, that I am very much pleased with what you have done."

And he entered the room where the council was waiting.

D'Aygaliers went away only half satisfied: he had not come so far only to receive commendation from the king, but in the hope of obtaining some concession for his brethren; but with Louis XIV it was impossible either to intercede or complain, one could only wait.

The same evening Chamillard sent for the baron, and told him that as Marechal Villars had mentioned in his letter that the Camisards had great confidence in him, d'Aygaliers, he wished to ask him if he were willing to go once more to them and try and bring them back to the path of duty.

"Certainly I am willing; but I fear things have now got so far that there will be great difficulty in calming the general perturbation of mind."

"But what can these people want?" asked Chamillard, as if he had just heard them spoken of for the first time, "and by what means can we pacify them?"

"In my opinion," said the baron, "the king should allow to all his subjects the free exercise of their religion."

"What! legalise once more the exercise of the so-called Reformed religion!" exclaimed the minister. "Be sure you never mention such a thing again. The king would rather see his kingdom destroyed than consent to such a measure."

"Monseigneur," replied the baron, "if that is the case, then I must say with great regret that I know of no other way

171

to calm the discontent which will ultimately result in the ruin of one of the fairest provinces in France."

"But that is unheard-of obstinacy," said the minister, lost in astonishment; "these people will destroy themselves, and drag their country down with them. If they cannot conform to our religion, why do they not worship God in their own way at home? No one will disturb them as long as they don't insist on public worship."

"At first that was all they wanted, monseigneur; and I am convinced that if people had not been dragged to confession and communion by force, it would have been easy to keep them in that submissive frame of mind from which they were only driven by despair; but at present they say that it is not enough to pray at home, they want to be married, to have their children baptised and instructed, and to die and be buried according to the ordinances of their own faith."

"Where may you have seen anyone who was ever made to communicate by force?" asked Chamillard.

D'Aygaliers looked at the minister in surprise, thinking he spoke in joke; but seeing he was quite serious, he answered:

"Alas, monseigneur, my late father and my mother, who is still living, are both instances of people subjected to this indignity."

"Are you, then, not a Catholic?" asked Chamillard.

"No, monseigneur," replied d'Aygaliers.

"Then how did you manage to return to France?"

"To speak the truth, sir, I only came back to help my mother to escape; but she never could make up her mind to leave France, as such a step was surrounded by many difficulties which she feared she could never surmount. So she asked my other relations to persuade me to remain. I yielded to their importunities on condition that they would never interfere with my beliefs. To accomplish this end they got a priest with whom they were intimate to say that I had changed my views once more, and I did not contradict the report. It was a great sin on my part, and I deeply repent it. I must add, however, that whenever anyone has asked me the question your Excellency asked me just now I have always given the same reply."

The minister did not seem to take the baron's frankness in bad part; only he remarked, when dismissing him, that he hoped he would find out some way of ridding the kingdom of those who refused to think in religious matters as His Majesty commanded.

D'Aygaliers replied that it was a problem to which he had given much thought, but without ever being able to find a solution, but that he would think about it more earnestly in future. He then withdrew.

Some days later, Chamillard sent ward to d'Aygaliers that the king would graciously give him a farewell audience. The baron relates what took place at this second interview, as follows.

"His Majesty," says he, "received me in the council chamber, and was so good as to repeat once more in the presence of all his ministers that he was very much pleased with my services, but that there was one thing about me he should like to correct. I begged His Majesty to tell me what the fault was, and I should try to get rid of it at, the peril of my life."

"'It is your religion,' said the king. 'I should like to have you become a good Catholic, so that I might be able to grant you favours and enable you to serve me better.' His Majesty added that I ought to seek instruction, and that then I should one day recognise what a great benefit he desired to bring within my reach.

"I answered that I would esteem myself happy if at the cost of my life I could prove the burning zeal with which I was filled for the service of the greatest of earthly kings, but that I should be unworthy of the least of his favours if I obtained it by hypocrisy or by anything of which my conscience did not approve, but that I was grateful for the goodness which made him anxious for my salvation. I told him also that I had already taken every opportunity of receiving instruction, and had tried to put aside the prejudices arising from my birth, such as often hindered people from recognising the truth, with the result that I had at one time almost lost all sense of religion, until God, taking pity on me, had opened my eyes and brought me out of that deplorable condition, making me see that the faith in which I had been born was the only one for me. 'And I can assure your Majesty,' I added, 'that many of the Languedoc bishops who ought, it seems to me, to try to make us Catholics, are the instruments which Providence uses to prevent us from becoming so. For instead of attracting us by gentleness and good example, they ceaselessly subject us to all kinds of persecutions, as if to convince us that God is punishing us for our cowardice in giving up a religion which we know to be good, by delivering us up to pastors who, far from labouring to assure our salvation, use all their efforts to drive us to despair."

"At this the king shrugged his shoulders and said, 'Enough, do not say any more.' I asked for his blessing as the king and father of all his subjects. The king burst out laughing, and told me that M. de Chamillard would give me his orders."

In virtue of this intimation d'Aygaliers went next day to the minister's country house; for Chamillard had given him that address, and there he learned that the king had granted him a pension of 800 livres. The baron remarked that, not having worked for money, he had hoped for a better reward; as far as money was concerned, he desired only the reimbursement of the actual expenses of his journeys to and from, but Chamillard answered that the king expected all that he offered and whatever he offered to be accepted with gratitude. To this there was no possible reply, so the same evening d'Aygaliers set out on his return to Languedoc.

Three months later, Chamillard forwarded him an order to leave the kingdom, telling him that he was to receive a pension of four hundred crowns per annum, and enclosing the first quarter in advance.

As there was no means of evading this command, D'Aygaliers set out for Geneva, accompanied by thirty-three followers, arriving there on the 23rd of September. Once rid of him, Louis the Magnificent thought that he had done his part nobly and that he owed him nothing further, so that d'Aygaliers waited a whole year in vain for the second quarter of his pension.

At the end of this time, as his letters to Chamillard remained unanswered, and finding himself without resources in a foreign country, he believed himself justified in returning to France and taking up his residence on his family estate. Unfortunately, on his way through Lyons, the provost of merchants, hearing of his return, had him arrested, and sent word to the king, who ordered him to be taken to the chateau de Loches. After a year's imprisonment, d'Aygaliers, who had just entered on his thirty-fifth year, resolved to try and escape, preferring to die in the attempt rather than remain a prisoner for life. He succeeded in getting possession of a file with which he removed one of the bars of his window, and by means of knotting his sheets together, he got down, taking the loosened bar with him to serve, in case of need, as a weapon. A sentinel who was near cried, "Who goes there?" but d'Aygaliers stunned him with his bar. The cry, however, had given the alarm: a second sentinel saw a man flying, fired at him, and killed him on the spot.

Such was the reward of the devoted patriotism of Baron d'Aygaliers!

Meantime Roland's troops had increased greatly in number, having been joined by the main body of those who had once been commanded by Cavalier, so that he had, about eight hundred men at his disposal. Some distance away, another chief, named Joanny, had four hundred; Larose, to whom Castanet had transferred his command, found himself at the head of three hundred; Boizeau de Rochegude was followed by one hundred, Saltet de Soustel by two hundred, Louis Coste by fifty, and Catinat by forty, so that, in spite of the victory of Montrevel and the negotiations of M. de Villars, the Camisards still formed an effective force of eighteen hundred and ninety men, not to speak of many single troopers who owned no commander but acted each for himself, and were none the less mischievous for that. All these troops, except these latter, obeyed Roland, who since the defection of Cavalier had been recognised as generalissimo of the forces. M. de Villars thought if he could separate Roland from his troops as he had separated Cavalier, his plans would be more easy to carry out.

So he made use of every means within his reach to gain over Roland, and as soon as one plan failed he tried another. At one moment he was almost sure of obtaining his object by the help of a certain Jourdan de Mianet, a great friend of his, who offered his services as an intermediary, but who failed like all the others, receiving from Roland a positive refusal, so that it became evident that resort must be had to other means than those of persuasion. A sum of 100 Louis had already been set on Roland's head: this sum was now doubled.

Three days afterwards, a young man from Uzes, by name Malarte, in whom Roland had every confidence, wrote to M. de Paratte that the Camisard general intended to pass the night of the 14th of August at the chateau Castelnau.

De Paratte immediately made his dispositions, and ordered Lacoste-Badie, at the head of two companies of dragoons, and all the officers at Uzes who were well mounted, to hold themselves in readiness to start on an expedition at eight o'clock in the evening, but not revealing its object to them till the time came. At eight o'clock, having

177

been told what they had to do, they set off at such a pace that they came in sight of the chateau within an hour, and were obliged to halt and conceal themselves, lest they should appear too soon, before Roland had retired for the night. But they need not have been afraid; the Camisard chief, who was accustomed to rely on all his men as on himself, had gone to bed without any suspicion, having full confidence in the vigilance of one of his officers, named Grimaud, who had stationed himself as sentinel on the roof of the chateau. Led by Malarte, Lacoste-Badie and his dragoons took a narrow covered way, which led them to the foot of the walls, so that when Grimaud saw them it was already too late, the chateau being surrounded on all sides. Firing off his gun, he cried, "To arms!" Roland, roused by the cry and the shot, leaped out of bed, and taking his clothes in one hand and his sword in the other, ran out of his room. At the door he met Grimaud, who, instead of thinking of his own safety, had come to watch over that of his chief. They both ran to the stables to get horses, but three of their men—Marchand, Bourdalie, and Bayos—had been before them and had seized on the best ones, and riding them bare-backed had dashed through the front gates before the dragoons could stop them. The horses that were left were so wretched that Roland felt there was no chance of out-distancing the dragoons by their help, so he resolved to fly on foot, thus avoiding the open roads and being able to take refuge in every ravine and every bush as cover. He therefore hastened with Grimaud and four other officers who had gathered round him towards a small back gate which opened on the fields, but as there was, besides the troops which entered the chateau, a ring of dragoons round it, they fell at once into the hands of some men who had been placed in ambush. Seeing himself surrounded, Roland let fall the clothes which he had not yet had time to put on, placed his back against a tree, drew his sword, and challenged the boldest, whether officer or private, to approach. His features expressed such resolution, that when he thus, alone and half naked, defied them all, there was a moment's hesitation, during which no one ventured to take a forward step; but this pause was broken by the report of a gun: the arm which Roland had stretched out against his adversaries fell to his side, the sword with which he had threatened them escaped from his hand, his knees gave way, so that his body, which was only supported by the tree against which he leaned, after remaining an instant erect, gradually sank to the ground. Collecting all his strength, Roland raised his two hands to Heaven, as if to call down the vengeance of God upon his murderers, then, without having uttered a single word, he fell forward dead, shot through the heart. The name of the dragoon who killed him was Soubeyrand.

Maillie, Grimaud, Coutereau, Guerin, and Ressal, the five Camisard officers, seeing their chief dead, let themselves be taken as if they were children, without thinking of making any resistance.

The dead body of Roland was carried back in triumph to Uzes, and from there to Nimes, where it was put upon trial as if still alive. It was sentenced to be dragged on hurdles and then burnt. The execution of this sentence was carried out with such pomp as made it impossible for the one party to forget the punishment and for the other to forget the martyrdom. At the end the ashes of Roland were scattered to the four winds of heaven.

The execution of the five officers followed close on that of their chief's body; they were condemned to be broken on the wheel, and the sentence was carried out on all at once. But their death, instead of inspiring the Calvinists with terror, gave them rather fresh courage, for, as an eye-witness relates, the five Camisards bore their tortures not only with fortitude, but with a light-heartedness which surprised all present, especially those who had never seen a Camisard executed before.

Malarte received his 200 Louis, but to-day his name is coupled with that of Judas in the minds of his countrymen.

From this time on fortune ceased to smile on the Camisards. Genius had gone with Cavalier, and, faith with Roland. The very day of the death of the latter, one of their stores, containing more than eighty sacks of corn, had been taken at Toiras. The next day, Catinat, who, with a dozen men, was in hiding in a vineyard of La Vaunage, was surprised by a detachment of Soissonnais; eleven of his men were killed, the twelfth made prisoner, and he himself barely escaped with a severe wound. The 25th of the same month, a cavern near Sauve, which the rebels used as a store, and which contained one hundred and fifty sacks of fine wheat, was discovered; lastly, Chevalier de Froulay had found a third hiding-place near Mailet. In this, which had been used not only as a store but as a hospital, besides a quantity of salt beef, wine, and flour, six wounded Camisards were found, who were instantly shot as they lay.

The only band which remained unbroken was Ravanel's, but since the departure of Cavalier things had not gone well with his lieutenant.

In consequence of this, and also on account of the successive checks which the other bodies of Camisard troops had met with, Ravanel proclaimed a solemn fast, in order to intercede with God to protect the Huguenot cause. On Saturday, the 13th September, he led his entire force to the wood of St. Benazet, intending to pass the whole of the next day with them there in prayer. But treason was rife. Two peasants who knew of this plan gave information to M. Lenoir, mayor of Le Vigan, and he sent word to the marechal and M. de Saville, who were at Anduze.

Nothing could have been more welcome to the governor than this important information: he made the most careful disposition of his forces, hoping to destroy the rebellion at one blow. He ordered M. de Courten, a brigadier-colonel in command at Alais, to take a detachment of the troops under him and patrol the banks of the Gardon between Ners and Castagnols. He was of opinion that if the Camisards were attacked on the other side by a body of soldiers drawn from Anduze, which he had stationed during the night at Dommersargues, they would try to make good their retreat towards the river. The force at Dommersargues might almost be called a small army; for it was composed of a Swiss battalion, a battalion of the Hainault regiment, one from the Charolais regiment, and four companies of dragoons from Fimarcon and Saint-Sernin.

Everything took place as the peasants had said: on Saturday the 13th, the Camisards entered, as we have seen, the wood of St. Benazet, and passed the night there.

At break of day the royals from Dommersargues began their advance. The Camisard outposts soon perceived the movement, and warned Ravanel, who held his little council of war. Everyone was in favour of instant retreat, so they retired towards Ners, intending to cross the Gardon below that town: just as M. de Villars had foreseen, the Camisards did everything necessary for the success of his plans, and ended by walking right into the trap set for them.

On emerging from the wood of St. Benazet, they caught sight of a detachment of royals drawn up and waiting for them between Marvejols and a mill called the Moulin-du-Pont. Seeing the road closed in this direction, they turned sharp to the left, and gained a rocky valley which ran parallel to the Gardon. This they followed till they came out below Marvejols, where they crossed the river. They now thought themselves out of danger, thanks to this manoeuvre, but suddenly they saw another detachment of royals lying on the grass near the mill of La Scie. They at once halted again, and then, believing themselves undiscovered, turned back, moving as noiselessly as possible, intending to recross the river and make for Cardet. But they only avoided one trap to fall into another, for in this direction they were met by the Hainault battalion, which swooped down upon them. A few of these ill-fated men rallied at the sound of Ravanel's voice and made an effort to defend themselves in spite of the prevailing confusion; but the danger was so imminent, the foes so numerous, and their numbers decreased so rapidly under the fierce assault, that their example failed of effect, and flight became general: every man trusted to chance for guidance, and, caring nothing for the safety of others, thought only of his own.

Then it ceased to be a battle and become a massacre, for the royals were ten to one; and among those they encountered, only sixty had firearms, the rest, since the discovery of their various magazines, having been reduced to arm themselves with bad swords, pitchforks, and bayonets attached to sticks. Hardly a man survived the fray. Ravanel himself only succeeded in escaping by throwing himself into the river, where he remained under water between two rocks for seven hours, only coming to the surface to breathe. When night fell and the dragoons had retired, he also fled.

This was the last battle of the war, which had lasted four years. With Cavalier and Roland, those two mountain giants, the power of the rebels disappeared. As the news of the defeat spread, the Camisard chiefs and soldiers becoming convinced that the Lord had hidden His face from them, surrendered one by one. The first to set an example was Castanet. On September 6th, a week after the defeat of Ravanel, he surrendered to the marechal. On the 19th, Catinat and his lieutenant, Franqois Souvayre, tendered their submission; on the 22nd, Amet, Roland's brother, came in; on October 4th, Joanny; on the 9th, Larose, Valette, Salomon, Laforet, Moulieres, Salles, Abraham and Marion; on the 20th, Fidele; and on the 25th, Rochegude.

Each made what terms he could; in general the conditions were favourable. Most of those who submitted

183

received rewards of money, some more, some less; the smallest amount given being 200 livres. They all received passports, and were ordered to leave the kingdom, being sent, accompanied by an escort and at the king's expense, to Geneva. The following is the account given by Marion of the agreement he came to with the Marquis Lalande; probably all the others were of the same nature.

"I was deputed," he says, "to treat with this lieutenant-general in regard to the surrender of my own troops and those of Larose, and to arrange terms for the inhabitants of thirty-five parishes who had contributed to our support during the war. The result of the negotiations was that all the prisoners from our cantons should be set at liberty, and be reinstated in their possessions, along with all the others. The inhabitants of those parishes which had been ravaged by fire were to be exempt from land-tax for three years; and in no parish were the inhabitants to be taunted with the past, nor molested on the subject of religion, but were to be free to worship God in their own houses according to their consciences."

These agreements were fulfilled with such punctuality, that Larose was permitted to open the prison doors of St. Hippolyte to forty prisoners the very day he made submission.

As we have said, the Camisards, according as they came in, were sent off to Geneva. D'Aygaliers, whose fate we have anticipated, arrived there on September 23rd, accompanied by Cavalier's eldest brother, Malpach, Roland's secretary, and thirty-six Camisards. Catinat and Castanet arrived there on the 8th October, along with twenty-two other persons, while Larose, Laforet, Salomon, Moulieres, Salles, Marion, and Fidele reached it under the escort of forty dragoons from Fimarcon in the month of November.

Of all the chiefs who had turned Languedoc for four years into a vast arena, only Ravanel remained, but he refused either to surrender or to leave the country. On the 8th October the marechal issued an order declaring he had forfeited all right to the favour of an amnesty, and offering a reward of 150 Louis to whoever delivered him up living, and 2400 livres to whoever brought in his dead body, while any hamlet, village, or town which gave him refuge would be burnt to the ground and the inhabitants put to the sword.

The revolt seemed to be at an end and peace established. So the marechal was recalled to court, and left Nimes on January the 6th. Before his departure he received the States of Languedoc, who bestowed on him not only the praise which was his due for having tempered severity with mercy, but also a purse of 12,000 livres, while a sum of 8000 livres was presented to his wife. But all this was only a prelude to the favours awaiting him at court. On the day he returned to Paris the king decorated him with all the royal orders and created him a duke. On the following day he received him, and thus addressed him: "Sir, your past services lead me to expect much of those you will render me in the future. The affairs of my kingdom would be better conducted if I had several Villars at my disposal. Having only one, I must always send him where he is most needed. It was for that reason I sent you to Languedoc. You have, while there, restored tranquillity to my subjects, you must now

185

defend them against their enemies; for I shall send you to command my army on the Moselle in the next campaign."

The, Duke of Berwick arrived at Montpellier on the 17th March to replace Marechal Villars. His first care was to learn from M. de Baville the exact state of affairs. M. de Baville told him that they were not at all settled as they appeared to be on the surface. In fact, England and Holland, desiring nothing so much as that an intestine war should waste France, were making unceasing efforts to induce the exiles to return home, promising that this time they would really support them by lending arms, ammunition, and men, and it was said that some were already on their way back, among the number Castanet.

And indeed the late rebel chief, tired of inaction, had left Geneva in the end of February, and arrived safely at Vivarais. He had held a religious meeting in a cave near La Goree, and had drawn to his side Valette of Vals and Boyer of Valon. Just as the three had determined to penetrate into the Cevennes, they were denounced by some peasants before a Swiss officer named Muller, who was in command of a detachment of troops in the village of Riviere. Muller instantly mounted his horse, and guided by the informers made his way into the little wood in which the Camisards had taken refuge, and fell upon them quite unexpectedly. Boyer was killed in trying to escape; Castanet was taken and brought to the nearest prison, where he was joined the next day by Valette, who had also been betrayed by some peasants whom he had asked for assistance.

The first punishment inflicted on Castanet was, that he was compelled to carry in his hand the head of Boyer all the way from La Goree to Montpellier. He protested vehemently at first, but in vain: it was fastened to his wrist by the hair; whereupon he kissed it on both cheeks, and went through the ordeal as if it were a religious act, addressing words of prayer to the head as he might have done to a relic of a martyr.

Arrived at Montpellier, Castanet was examined, and at first persisted in saying that he had only returned from exile because he had not the wherewithal to live abroad. But when put to the torture he was made to endure such agony that, despite his courage and constancy, he confessed that he had formed a plan to introduce a band of Huguenot soldiers with their officers into the Cevennes by way of Dauphine or by water, and while waiting for their arrival he had sent on emissaries in advance to rouse the people to revolt; that he himself had also shared in this work; that Catinat was at the moment in Languedoc or Vivarais engaged in the same task, and provided with a considerable sum of money sent him by foreigners for distribution, and that several persons of still greater importance would soon cross the frontier and join him.

Castanet was condemned to be broken on the wheel. As he was about to be led to execution, Abbe Tremondy, the cure of Notre-Dame, and Abbe Plomet, canon of the cathedral, came to his cell to make a last effort to convert him, but he refused to speak. They therefore went on before, and awaited him on the scaffold. There they appeared to inspire Castanet with more horror than the instruments of torture, and while he addressed the executioner as "brother," he called out to the priests, "Go away out of my sight, imps from the bottomless pit! What are you doing here, you accursed tempters? I will die in the religion in which I was born. Leave me alone, ye hypocrites, leave me alone!" But the two abbes were unmoved, and Castanet expired cursing, not the executioner but the two priests, whose presence during his death-agony disturbed his soul, turning it away from things which should have filled it.

Valette was sentenced to be hanged, and was executed on the same day as Castanet.

In spite of the admissions wrung from Castanet in March, nearly a month passed without any sign of fresh intrigues or any attempt at rebellion. But on the 17th of April, about seven o'clock in the evening, M. de Baville received intelligence that several Camisards had lately returned from abroad, and were in hiding somewhere, though their retreat was not known. This information was laid before the Duke of Berwick, and he and M. de Baville ordered certain houses to be searched, whose owners were in their opinion likely to have given refuge to the malcontents. At midnight all the forces which they could collect were divided into twelve detachments, composed of archers and soldiers, and at the head of each detachment was placed a man that could be depended upon. Dumayne, the king's lieutenant, assigned to each the districts they were to search, and they all set out at once from the town hall, at half-past twelve, marching in silence, and separating at signs from their leaders, so anxious were they to make no noise. At first all their efforts were of no avail, several houses being searched without any result; but at length Jausserand, the diocesan provost, having entered one of the houses which he and Villa, captain of the town troops, had had assigned to them, they found three men sleeping on mattresses laid on the floor. The provost roused them by asking them who they were, whence they came, and what they were doing at Montpellier, and as they, still half asleep, did not reply quite promptly, he ordered them to dress and follow him.

These three men were Flessiere, Gaillard, and Jean-Louis. Flessiere was a deserter from the Fimarcon regiment: he it was who knew most about the plot. Gaillard had formerly served in the Hainault regiment; and Jean-Louis, commonly called "the Genevois," was a deserter from the Courten regiment.

Flessiere, who was the leader, felt that it would be a great disgrace to let themselves be taken without resistance; he therefore pretended to obey, but in lifting up his clothes, which lay upon a trunk, he managed to secure two pistols, which he cocked. At the noise made by the hammers the provost's suspicions were aroused, and throwing himself on Flessiere, he seized him round the waist from behind. Flessiere, unable to turn, raised his arm and fired over his shoulder. The shot missed the provost, merely burning a lock of his hair, but slightly wounded one of his servants, who was carrying a lantern. He then tried to fire a second shot, but Jausserand, seizing him by the wrist with one hand, blew out his brains with the other. While Jausserand and Flessiere were thus struggling, Gaillard threw himself on Villa, pinning his arms to his sides. As he had no weapons, he tried to push him to the wall, in order to stun him by knocking his head against it; but when the servant, being wounded, let the lantern fall, he took advantage of the

189

darkness to make a dash for the door, letting go his hold of his antagonist. Unfortunately for him, the doors, of which there were two, were guarded, and the guards, seeing a half-naked man running away at the top of his speed, ran after him, firing several shots. He received a wound which, though not dangerous, impeded his flight, so that he was boon overtaken and captured. They brought him back a prisoner to the town hall, where Flessiere's dead body already lay.

Meanwhile Jean-Louis had had better luck. While the two struggles as related above were going on, he slipped unnoticed to an open window and got out into the street. He ran round the corner of the house, and disappeared like a shadow in the darkness before the eyes of the guards. For a long time he wandered from street to street, running down one and up another, till chance brought him near La Poissonniere. Here he perceived a beggar propped against a post and fast asleep; he awoke him, and proposed that they should exchange clothes. As Jean-Louis' suit was new and the beggar's in rags, the latter thought at first it was a joke. Soon perceiving, however, that the offer was made in all seriousness, he agreed to the exchange, and the two separated, each delighted with his bargain. Jean-Louis approached one of the gates of the town, in order to be able to get out as soon as it was opened, and the beggar hastened off in another direction, in order to get away from the man who had let him have so good a bargain, before he had time to regret the exchange he had made.

But the night's adventures were far from being over. The beggar was taken a prisoner, Jean-Louis' coat being recognised, and brought to the town hall, where the mistake was discovered. The Genevois meantime got into a dark street, and lost his way. Seeing three men approach, one of whom carried a lantern, he went towards the light, in order to find out where he was, and saw, to his surprise, that one of the men was the servant whom Flessiere had wounded, and who was now going to have his wound dressed. The Genevois tried to draw back into the shade, but it was too late: the servant had recognised him. He then tried to fly; but the wounded man soon overtook him, and although one of his hands was disabled, he held him fast with the other, so that the two men who were with him ran up and easily secured him. He also was brought to the town hall, where he found the Duke of Berwick and M. de Baville, who were awaiting the result of the affray.

Hardly had the prisoner caught sight of them than, seeing himself already hanged, which was no wonder considering the marvellous celerity with which executions were conducted at that epoch, he threw himself on his knees, confessed who he was, and related for what reason he had joined the fanatics. He went on to say that as he had not joined them of his own free will, but had been forced to do so, he would, if they would spare his life, reveal important secrets to them, by means of which they could arrest the principal conspirators.

His offer was so tempting and his life of so little worth that the duke and de Baville did not long hesitate, but pledged their word to spare his life if the revelations he was about to make proved to be of real importance. The bargain being concluded, the Genevois made the following statement:

191

"That several letters having arrived from foreign countries containing promises of men and money, the discontented in the provinces had leagued together in order to provoke a fresh rebellion. By means of these letters and other documents which were scattered abroad, hopes were raised that M. de Miremont, the last Protestant prince of the house of Bourbon, would bring them reinforcements five or six thousand strong. These reinforcements were to come by sea and make a descent on Aigues-Mortes or Cette,—and two thousand Huguenots were to arrive at the same time by way of Dauphine and join the others as they disembarked.

"That in this hope Catinat, Clary, and Jonquet had left Geneva and returned to France, and having joined Ravanel had gone secretly through those parts of the country known to be infected with fanaticism, and made all necessary arrangements, such as amassing powder and lead, munitions of war, and stores of all kinds, as well as enrolling the names of all those who were of age to bear arms. Furthermore, they had made an estimate of what each city, town, and village ought to contribute in money or in kind to the—League of the Children of God, so that they could count on having eight or ten thousand men ready to rise at the first signal. They had furthermore resolved that there should be risings in several places at the same time, which places were already chosen, and each of those who were to take part in the movement knew his exact duty. At Montpellier a hundred of the most determined amongst the disaffected were to set fire in different quarters to the houses of the Catholics, killing all who attempted to extinguish the fires, and with the help of the Huguenot inhabitants were, to slaughter the garrison,

192

seize the citadel, and carry off the Duke of Berwick and M. de Baville. The same things were to be done at Nimes, Uzes, Alais, Anduze, Saint-Hippolyte, and Sommieres. Lastly, he said, this conspiracy had been going on for more than three months, and the conspirators, in order not to be found out, had only revealed their plans to those whom they knew to be ready to join them: they had not admitted a single woman to their confidence, or any man whom it was possible to suspect. Further, they had only met at night and a few persons at a time, in certain country houses, to which admittance was gained by means of a countersign; the 25th of April was the day fixed for the general rising and the execution of these projects."

As may be seen, the danger was imminent, as there was only six days' interval between the revelation and the expected outburst; so the Genevois was consulted, under renewed promises of safety for himself, as to the best means of seizing on the principal chiefs in the shortest possible time. He replied that he saw no other way but to accompany them himself to Nimes, where Catinat and Ravanel were in hiding, in a house of which he did not know the number and in a street of which he did not know the name, but which he was sure of recognising when he saw them. If this advice were to be of any avail, there was no time to be lost, for Ravanel and Catinat were to leave Nimes on the 20th or the 21st at latest; consequently, if they did not set off at once, the chiefs would no longer be there when they arrived. The advice seemed good, so the marechal and the intendant hastened to follow it: the informer was sent to Nimes guarded by six archers, the conduct of the expedition was given to Barnier, the provost's lieutenant, a man of intellect and common sense, and in whom the provost had full confidence. He carried letters for the Marquis of Sandricourt.

As they arrived late on the evening of the 19th, the Genevois was at once led up and down the streets of Nimes, and, as he had promised, he pointed out several houses in the district of Sainte-Eugenie. Sandricourt at once ordered the garrison officers, as well as those of the municipal and Courten regiments, to put all their soldiers under arms and to station them quietly throughout the town so as to surround that district. At ten o'clock, the Marquis of Sandricourt, having made certain that his instructions had been carefully carried out, gave orders to MM. de L'Estrade, Barnier, Joseph Martin, Eusebe, the major of the Swiss regiment, and several other officers, along with ten picked men, to repair to the house of one Alison, a silk merchant, this house having been specially pointed out by the prisoner. This they did, but seeing the door open, they had little hope of finding the chiefs of a conspiracy in a place so badly guarded; nevertheless, determined to obey their instructions, they glided softly into the hall. In a few moments, during which silence and darkness reigned, they heard people speaking rather loudly in an adjoining room, and by listening intently they caught the following words: "It is quite sure that in less than three weeks the king will be no longer master of Dauphine, Vivarais, and Languedoc. I am being sought for everywhere, and here I am in Nimes, with nothing to fear."

It was now quite clear to the listeners that close at hand were some at least of those for whom they were looking.

They ran to the door, which was ajar, and entered the room, sword in hand. They found Ravanel, Jonquet, and Villas talking together, one sitting on a table, another standing on the hearth, and the third lolling on a bed.

Jonquet was a young man from Sainte-Chatte, highly thought of among the Camisards. He had been, it may be remembered, one of Cavalier's principal officers. Villas was the son of a doctor in Saint-Hippolyte; he was still young, though he had seen ten years' service, having been cornet in England in the Galloway regiment. As to Ravanel, he is sufficiently known to our readers to make any words of introduction unnecessary.

De l'Estrade threw himself on the nearest of the three, and, without using his sword, struck him with his fist. Ravanel (for it was he) being half stunned, fell back a step and asked the reason of this violent assault; while Barnier exclaimed, "Hold him fast, M. de l'Estrade; it is Ravanel!" "Well, yes, I am Ravanel," said the Camisard, "but that is no reason for making so much noise." As he said these words he made an attempt to reach his weapons, but de l'Estrade and Barnier prevented him by throwing themselves on him, and succeeded in knocking him down after a fierce struggle. While, this was going on, his two companions were secured, and the three were removed to the fort, where their guard never left them night or day.

The Marquis of Sandricourt immediately sent off a courier to the Duke of Berwick and M. de Baville to inform them of the important capture he had made. They were so delighted at the news that they came next day to Nimes.

They found the town intensely excited, soldiers with fixed bayonets at every street corner, all the houses shut up, and the gates of the town closed, and no one allowed to leave without written permission from Sandricourt. On the 20th, and during the following night, more than fifty persons were arrested, amongst whom were Alison, the merchant in whose house Ravanel, Villas, and Jonquet were found; Delacroix, Alison's brother-in-law, who, on hearing the noise of the struggle, had hidden on the roof and was not discovered till next day; Jean Lauze, who was accused of having prepared Ravanel's supper; Lauze's mother, a widow; Tourelle, the maid-servant; the host of the Coupe d'Or, and a preacher named La Jeunesse.

Great, however, as was the joy felt by the duke, the marquis, and de Baville, it fell short of full perfection, for the most dangerous man among the rebels was still at large; in spite of every effort, Catinat's hiding-place had not till now been discovered.

Accordingly, the duke issued a proclamation offering a reward of one hundred Louis-d'or to whoever would take Catinat, or cause him to be taken prisoner, and granting a free pardon to anyone who had sheltered him, provided that he was denounced before the house-to-house visitation which was about to be made took place. After the search began, the master of the house in which he might be found would be hung at his own door, his family thrown into prison, his goods confiscated, his house razed to the ground, without any form of trial whatever.

This proclamation had the effect expected by the duke: whether the man in whose house Catinat was concealed grew frightened and asked him to leave, or whether Catinat thought his best course would be to try and get away from the town, instead of remaining shut up in it, he dressed himself one morning in suitable clothes, and went to a barber's, who shaved him, cut his hair, and made up his face so as to give him as much the appearance of a nobleman as possible; and then with wonderful assurance he went out into the streets, and pulling his hat over his eyes and holding a paper in his hand as if reading it, he crossed the town to the gate of St. Antoine. He was almost through when Charreau, the captain of the guard, having his attention directed to Catinat by a comrade to whom he was talking, stopped him, suspecting he was trying to escape. Catinat asked what he wanted with him, and Charreau replied that if he would enter the guard-house he would learn; as under such circumstances any examination was to be avoided, Catinat tried to force his way out; whereupon he was seized by Charreau and his brother-officer, and Catinat seeing that resistance would be not only useless but harmful, allowed himself to be taken to the guard-room.

He had been there about an hour without being recognised by any of those who, drawn by curiosity, came to look at him, when one of the visitors in going out said he bore a strong resemblance to Catinat; some children hearing these words, began to shout, "Catinat is taken! Catinat is taken!" This cry drew a large crowd to the guard-house, among others a man whose name was Anglejas, who, looking closely at the prisoner, recognised him and called him by name.

Instantly the guard was doubled, and Catinat searched: a psalm-book with a silver clasp and a letter addressed to "M. Maurel, called Catinat," were found on him, leaving no doubt as to his identity; while he himself, growing impatient, and desiring to end all these investigations, acknowledged that he was Catinat and no other.

He was at once taken to the palace, where the Presidial Court was sitting, M. de Baville and the president being occupied in trying Ravanel, Villas, and Jonquet. On hearing the news of this important capture, the intendant, hardly daring to believe his ears, rose and went out to meet the prisoner, in order to convince himself that it was really Catinat.

From the Presidial Court he was brought before the Duke of Berwick, who addressed several questions to him, which Catinat answered; he then told the duke he had something of importance to impart to him and to him alone. The duke was not very anxious for a tete-a-tete with Catinat; however, having ordered his hands to be securely bound, and telling Sandricourt not to go away, he consented to hear what the prisoner had to say.

Catinat then, in the presence of the duke and Sandricourt, proposed that an exchange of prisoners should be made, the Marechal de Tallard, who was a prisoner of war in England, being accepted in his place. Catinat added that if this offer was not accepted, the marechal would meet the same treatment from the English as might be meted out to him, Catinat, in France. The duke, full of the aristocratic ideas to which he was born, found the proposal insolent, and said,

"If that is all you have to propose, I can assure you that your hours are numbered."

Thereupon Catinat was promptly sent back to the palace, where truly his trial did not occupy much time. That of the three others was already finished, and soon his was also at an end, and it only remained to pronounce sentence on all four. Catinat and Ravanel, as the most guilty, were condemned to be burnt at the stake. Some of the councillors thought Catinat should have been torn apart by four horses, but the majority were for the stake, the agony lasting longer, being more violent and more exquisite than in the of other case.

Villars and Jonquet were sentenced to be broken on the wheel alive—the only difference between them being that Jonquet was to be to taken while still living and thrown into the fire lit round Catinat and Ravael. It was also ordered that the four condemned men before their execution should be put to the torture ordinary and extraordinary. Catinat, whose temper was fierce, suffered with courage, but cursed his torturers. Ravanel bore all the torments that could be inflicted on him with a fortitude that was more than human, so that the torturers were exhausted before he was. Jonquet spoke little, and the revelations he made were of slight importance. Villas confessed that the conspirators had the intention of carrying off the duke and M. de Baville when they were out walking or driving, and he added that this plot had been hatched at the house of a certain Boeton de Saint-Laurent-d'Aigozre, at Milhaud, in Rouergue.

Meanwhile all this torturing and questioning had taken so much time that when the stake and the scaffold were ready it was almost dark, so that the duke put off the executions until the next day, instead of carrying them out by torchlight. Brueys says that this was done in order that the most disaffected amongst the fanatics should not be able to say that it was not really Catinat, Ravanel, Villas, and Jonquet who had been executed but some other unknown men; but it is more probable that the duke and Baville were afraid of riots, as was proved by their ordering the scaffold and the stake to be erected at the end of the Cours and opposite the glacis of the fortress, so that the garrison might be at hand in case of any disturbance.

Catinat was placed in a cell apart, and could be, heard cursing and complaining all night through. Ravanel, Villas, and Jonquet were confined together, and passed the night singing and praying.

The next day, the 22nd April, 1705, they were taken from the prison and drawn to the place of execution in two carts, being unable to walk, on account of the severe torture to which they had been subjected, and which had crushed the bones of their legs. A single pile of wood had been prepared for Catinat and Ravanel, who were to be burnt together; they were in one cart, and Villas and Jonquet, for whom two wheels had been prepared, were in the other.

The first operation was to bind Catinat and Ravanel back to back to the same stake, care being taken to place Catinat with his face to windward, so that his agony might last longer, and then the pile was lit under Ravanel.

As had been foreseen, this precaution gave great pleasure to those people who took delight in witnessing executions. The wind being rather high, blew the flames away from Catinat, so that at first the fire burnt his legs only—a circumstance which, the author of the History of the Camisards tells us, aroused Catinat's impatience. Ravanel, however, bore everything to the end with the greatest heroism, only pausing in his singing to address words of encouragement to his companion in suffering, whom he could not see, but whose groans and curses he could hear; he would then return to his psalms, which he continued to sing until his voice was stifled in the flames. Just as he expired, Jonquet was removed from the wheel, and carried, his broken limbs dangling, to the burning pile, on which he was thrown. From the midst of the flames his voice was heard saying, "Courage, Catinat; we shall soon meet in heaven." A few moments later, the stake, being burnt through at the base, broke, and Catinat falling into the flames, was quickly suffocated. That this accident had not been forseen and prevented by proper precautions caused great displeasure to spectators who found that the three-quarter of an hour which the spectacle had lasted was much too brief a time.

Villas lived three hours longer on his wheel, and expired without having uttered a single complaint.

Two days later, there was another trial, at which six persons were condemned to death and one to the galleys; these were the two Alisons, in whose house Villas, Ravanel, and Jonquet had been found; Alegre, who was accused of having concealed Catinat, and of having been the Camisard treasurer; Rougier, an armourer who was found guilty of having repaired the muskets of the rebels; Jean Lauze, an innkeeper who had prepared meals for Ravanel; La Jeunesse, a preacher, convicted of having preached sermons and sung psalms; and young Delacroix, brother-in-law to one of the Alisons. The first three were condemned to be broken on the wheel, their houses demolished, and their goods confiscated. The next three were to be hanged. Jean Delacroix, partly because of his youth, but more because of the revelations he made, was only sent to the galleys. Several years later he was liberated and returned to Arles, and was carried off by the plague in 1720.

All these sentences were carried out with the utmost rigour.

Thus, as may be seen, the suppression of the revolt proceeded apace; only two young Camisard chiefs were still at large, both of whom had formerly served under Cavalier and Catinat. The name of the one was Brun and of the other Francezet. Although neither of them possessed the genius and influence of Catinat and Ravanel, yet they were both men to be feared, the one on account of his personal strength, the other for his skill and agility. Indeed, it was said of him that he never missed a shot, and that one day being pursued by dragoons he had escaped by jumping over the Gardon at a spot where it was twenty-two feet wide.

For a long time all search was in vain, but one day the wife of a miller named Semenil came into town ostensibly to buy provisions, but really to denounce them as being concealed, with two other Camisards, in her husband's house.

This information was received with an eager gratitude, which showed the importance which the governor of Nimes attached to their capture. The woman was promised a reward of fifty Louis if they were taken, and the Chevalier de la Valla, Grandidier, and fifty Swiss, the major of the Saint-Sernin regiment, a captain, and thirty dragoons, were sent off to make the capture. When they were within a quarter of a league of the mill, La Valla, who was in command of the expedition, made the woman give him all the necessary topographical information.

Having learned that besides the door by which they hoped to effect an entrance, the mill possessed only one other, which opened on a bridge over the Vistre, he despatched ten dragoons and five Swiss to occupy this bridge, whilst he and the rest of the troops bore down on the main entrance. As soon as the four Camisards perceived the approach of the soldiers, their first thought was to escape by the bridge, but one of them having gone up to the roof to make sure that the way was clear, came down exclaiming that the bridge was occupied. On hearing this, the four felt that they were lost, but nevertheless resolved to defend themselves as valiantly and to sell their lives as dearly as possible. As soon as the royals were within musket range of the mill, four shots were fired, and two dragoons, one Swiss, and one horse, fell. M. de Valla thereupon ordered the troops to charge at full gallop, but before the mill door was reached three other shots were heard, and two more men killed. Nevertheless, seeing they could not long hold out against such numbers, Francezet gave the signal for retreat, calling out, "Sauve qui petit!" at the same instant he jumped out of a lattice window twenty feet from the ground, followed by Brun. Neither of them being hurt, both set off across country, one trusting to his strength and the other to his fleetness of foot. The two other Camisards, who had tried to escape by the door, were captured.

The soldiers, horse and foot, being now free to give all their attention to Brun and Francezet, a wonderful race began; for the two fugitives, being strong and active, seemed to play with their pursuers, stopping every now and then, when they had gained sufficient headway, to shoot at the nearest soldiers; when Francezet, proving worthy of his reputation, never missed a single shot. Then, resuming their flight and loading their weapons as they ran, they leaped rivers and ditches, taking advantage of the less direct road which the troops were obliged to follow, to stop and take breath, instead of making for some cover where they might have found safety. Two or three times Brun was on the point of being caught, but each time the dragoon or Swiss who had got up to him fell, struck by Francezet's unerring bullet. The chase lasted four hours, during which time five officers, thirty dragoons, and fifty Swiss were baffled by two men, one of whom Francezet was almost a boy, being only twenty years old! Then the two Camisards, having exhausted their ammunition, gave each other the name of a village as a rendezvous, and each taking a different direction, bounded away with the lightness of a stag. Francezet ran in the direction of Milhaud with such rapidity that he gained on the dragoons, although they put their horses at full speed. He was within an inch of safety, when a peasant named La Bastide, who was hoeing in a field, whence he had watched the contest with interest from the moment he had first caught sight of it, seeing the fugitive make for an opening in a wall, ran along at the foot of the wall on the other side, and, just as Francezet dashed through the opening like a flash of lightning, struck him such a heavy blow on the head with his hoe that the skull was laid open, and he fell bathed in blood.

The dragoons, who had seen in the distance what had happened, now came up, and rescued Francezet from the hands of his assailant, who had continued to rain blows upon him, desiring to put an end to him. The unconscious Camisard was carried to Milhaud, where his wounds were bandaged, and himself revived by means of strong spirits forced into mouth and nostrils.

We now return to Brun. At first it seemed as if he were more fortunate than his comrade; for, meeting with no obstacle, he was soon not only out of reach, but out of sight of his enemies. He now, however, felt broken by fatigue, and taught caution by the treachery to which he had almost fallen a victim, he dared not ask for an asylum, so, throwing himself down in a ditch, he was soon fast asleep. The dragoons, who had not given up the search, presently came upon him, and falling on him as he lay, overpowered him before he was well awake.

When both Camisards met before the governor, Francezet replied to all interrogations that since the death of brother Catinat his sole desire had been to die a martyr's death like him; while Brun said that he was proud and happy to die in the cause of the Lord along with such a brave comrade as Francezet. This manner of defence led to the application of the question both ordinary and extraordinary, and to the stake; and our readers already know what such a double sentence meant. Francezet and Brun paid both penalties on the 30th of April, betraying no secrets and uttering no complaints.

Boeton, who had been denounced by Villas when under torture (and who thereby abridged his agony) as the person in whose house the plot to carry off the Duke of Berwick and de Baville had been arranged, still remained to be dealt with.

He was moderate in his religious views, but firm and full of faith; his principles resembled those of the Quakers in that he refused to carry arms; he was, however, willing to aid the good cause by all other means within his reach. He was at home waiting, with that calm which perfect trust in God gives, for the day to come which had been appointed for the execution of the plan, when suddenly his house was surrounded during the night by the royals. Faithful to his principles, he offered no resistance, but held out his hands to be bound. He was taken in triumph to Nimes, and from there to the citadel of Montpellier. On the way he encountered his wife and his son, who were going to the latter town to intercede for him. When they met him, they dismounted from their horse, for the mother was riding on a pillion behind the son, and kneeling on the highroad, asked for Boeton's blessing. Unfeeling though the soldiers were, they yet permitted their prisoner to stop an instant, while he, raising his fettered hands to heaven, gave the double blessing asked for. So touched was Baron Saint-Chatte by the scene (be it remarked in passing that the baron and Boeton were cousins by marriage) that he permitted them to embrace one another, so for a few moments they stood, the husband and father clasped to the hearts of his dear ones; then, on a sign from Boeton, they tore themselves away,

Boeton commanding them to pray for M. de Saint-Chatte, who had given them this consolation. As he resumed his march the prisoner set them the example by beginning to sing a psalm for the benefit of M. de Saint-Chatte.

The next day, despite the intercession of his wife and son, Boeton was condemned to torture both ordinary and extraordinary, and then to be broken on the wheel. On hearing this cruel sentence, he said that he was ready to suffer every ill that God might send him in order to prove the steadfastness of his faith.

And indeed he endured his torture with such firmness, that M. de Baville, who was present in the hope of obtaining a confession, became more impatient than the sufferer, and, forgetting his sacred office, the judge struck and insulted the prisoner. Upon this Baeton raised his eyes to heaven and cried, "Lord, Lord! how long shall the wicked triumph? How long shall innocent blood be shed? How long wilt Thou not judge and avenge our blood with cries to Thee? Remember Thy jealousy, O Lord, and Thy loving-kindness of old!" Then M. de Baville withdrew, giving orders that he was to be brought to the scaffold.

The scaffold was erected on the Esplanade: being, as was usual when this sort of death was to be inflicted, a wooden platform five or six feet high, on which was fastened flat a St. Andrew's cross, formed of two beams of wood in the form of an X. In each of the four arms two square pieces were cut out to about half the depth of the beam, and about a foot apart, so that when the victim was bound on the cross the outstretched limbs were easy to break by a blow at these points, having no support beneath. Lastly, near the cross, at one corner of the scaffold an upright wooden post was fixed, on which was fastened horizontally a small carriage wheel, as on a pivot, the projecting part of the nave being sawn off to make it flat. On this bed of pain the sufferer was laid, so that the spectators might enjoy the sight of his dying convulsions when, the executioner having accomplished his part, the turn of death arrived.

Boeton was carried to execution in a cart, and drums were beaten that his exhortations might not be heard. But above the roll of drums his voice rose unfalteringly, as he admonished his brethren to uphold their fellowship in Christ.

Half-way to the Esplanade a friend of the condemned man, who happened to be in the street, met the procession, and fearing that he could not support the sight, he took refuge in a shop. When Boeton was opposite the door, he stopped the cart and asked permission of the provost to speak to his friend. The request being granted, he called him out, and as he approached, bathed in tears, Boeton said, "Why do you run away from me? Is it because you see me covered with the tokens of Jesus Christ? Why do you weep because He has graciously called me to Himself, and all unworthy though I be, permits me to seal my faith with my blood?" Then, as the friend threw himself into Boeton's arms and some signs of sympathetic emotion appeared among the crowd; the procession was abruptly ordered to move on; but though the leave-taking was thus roughly broken short, no murmur passed the lips of Boeton.

In turning out of the first street, the scaffold came in sight; the condemned man raised his hands towards heaven,

208

and exclaimed in a cheerful voice, while a smile lit up his face, "Courage, my soul! I see thy place of triumph, whence, released from earthly bonds, thou shah take flight to heaven."

When he got to the foot of the scaffold, it was found he could not mount without assistance; for his limbs, crushed in the terrible "boot," could no longer sustain his weight. While they were preparing to carry him up, he exhorted and comforted the Protestants, who were all weeping round him. When he reached the platform he laid himself of his own accord on the cross; but hearing from the executioner that he must first be undressed, he raised himself again with a smile, so that the executioner's assistant could remove his doublet and small-clothes. As he wore no stockings, his legs being bandaged the man also unwound these bandages, and rolled up Boeton's shirts-sleeves to the elbow, and then ordered him to lay himself again on the cross. Boeton did so with unbroken calm. All his limbs were then bound to the beams with cords at every joint; this accomplished, the assistant retired, and the executioner came forward. He held in his hand a square bar of iron, an inch and a half thick, three feet long, and rounded at one end so as to form a handle.

When Boeton saw it he began singing a psalm, but almost immediately the melody was interrupted by a cry: the executioner had broken a bone of Boeton's right leg; but the singing was at once resumed, and continued without interruption till each limb had been broken in two places. Then the executioner unbound the formless but still living body from the cross, and while from its lips issued words of faith in God he laid it on the wheel, bending it back on the legs in such a manner that the heels and head met; and never once during the completion of this atrocious performance did the voice of the sufferer cease to sound forth the praises of the Lord.

No execution till then had ever produced such an effect on the crowd, so that Abbe Massilla, who was present, seeing the general emotion, hastened to call M. de Baville's attention to the fact that, far from Boeton's death inspiring the Protestants with terror, they were only encouraged to hold out, as was proved by their tears, and the praises they lavished on the dying man.

M de Baville, recognising the truth of this observation, ordered that Boeton should be put out of misery. This order being conveyed to the executioner, he approached the wheel to break in Boeton's chest with one last blow; but an archer standing on the scaffold threw himself before the sufferer, saying that the Huguenot had not yet suffered half enough. At this, Boeton, who had heard the dreadful dispute going on beside him, interrupted his prayers for an instant, and raising his head, which hung down over the edge of the wheel, said, "Friend, you think I suffer, and in truth I do; but He for whom I suffer is beside me and gives me strength to bear everything joyfully." Just then M. de Baville's order was repeated, and the archer, no longer daring to interfere, allowed the executioner to approach. Then Boeton, seeing his last moment had come, said, "My dear friends, may my death be an example to you, to incite you to preserve the gospel pure; bear faithful testimony that I died in the religion of Christ and His holy apostles." Hardly had these words passed his lips, than the death-blow was given and his chest crushed; a few inarticulate sounds, apparently prayers, were heard; the head fell back, the martyrdom was ended.

This execution ended the war in Languedoc. A few imprudent preachers still delivered belated sermons, to which the rebels listened trembling with fear, and for which the preachers paid on the wheel or gibbet. There were disturbances in Vivarais, aroused by Daniel Billard, during which a few Catholics were found murdered on the highway; there were a few fights, as for instance at Sainte-Pierre-Ville, where the Camisards, faithful to the old traditions which had come to them from Cavalier, Catinat, and Ravenal, fought one to twenty, but they were all without importance; they were only the last quiverings of the dying civil strife, the last shudderings of the earth when the eruption of the volcano is over.

Even Cavalier understood that the end had come, for he left Holland for England. There Queen Anne distinguished him by a cordial welcome; she invited him to enter her service, an offer which he accepted, and he was placed in command of a regiment of refugees; so that he actually received in England the grade of colonel, which he had been offered in France. At the battle of Almanza the regiment commanded by Cavalier found itself opposed by a French regiment. The old enemies recognised each other, and with a howl of rage, without waiting for the word of command or executing any military evolutions, they hurled themselves at each other with such fury that, if we may believe the Duke of Berwick, who was present, they almost annihilated each other in the conflict. Cavalier, however, survived the

211

slaughter, in which he had performed his part with energy; and for his courage was made general and governor of the island of Jersey. He died at Chelsea in May 1740, aged sixty years. "I must confess," says Malesherbes, "that this soldier, who without training became a great general by means of his natural gifts; this Camisard, who dared in the face of fierce troopers to punish a crime similar to those by which the troopers existed; this rude peasant, who, admitted into the best society; adopted its manners and gained its esteem and love; this man, who though accustomed to an adventurous life, and who might justly have been puffed up by success, had yet enough philosophy to lead for thirty-five years a tranquil private existence, appears to me to be one of the rarest characters to be met with in the pages of history."

CHAPTER VI

At length Louis XIV, bowed beneath the weight of a reign of sixty years, was summoned in his turn to appear before God, from whom, as some said, he looked for reward, and others for pardon. But Nimes, that city with the heart of fire, was quiet; like the wounded who have lost the best part of their blood, she thought only, with the egotism of a convalescent, of being left in peace to regain the strength which had become exhausted through the terrible wounds which Montrevel and the Duke of Berwick had dealt her. For sixty years petty ambition had taken the place of sublime self-sacrifice, and disputes about etiquette succeeded mortal combats. Then the philosophic era dawned, and the sarcasms of the encyclopedists withered the monarchical intolerance of Louis XIV and Charles IX. Thereupon the Protestants resumed their preaching, baptized their children and buried their dead, commerce flourished once more, and the two religions lived side by side, one concealing under a peaceful exterior the memory of its martyrs, the other the memory of its triumphs. Such was the mood on which the blood-red orb of the sun of '89 rose. The Protestants greeted it with cries of joy, and indeed the promised liberty gave them back their country, their civil rights, and the status of French citizens.

Nevertheless, whatever were the hopes of one party or the fears of the other, nothing had as yet occurred to disturb the prevailing tranquillity, when, on the 19th and 20th of July, 1789, a body of troops was formed in the capital of La Gard which was to bear the name of the Nimes Militia: the resolution which authorised this act was passed by the citizens of the three orders sitting in the hall of the palace.

It was as follows:—

"Article 10. The Nimes Legion shall consist of a colonel, a lieutenant-colonel, a major, a lieutenant-major, an adjutant, twenty-four captains, twenty-four lieutenants, seventy-two sergeants, seventy-two corporals, and eleven hundred and fifty-two privates—in all, thirteen hundred and forty-nine men, forming eighty companies.

"Article 11. The place of general assembly shall be, the Esplanade.

"Article 12. The eighty companies shall be attached to the four quarters of the town mentioned below—viz., place de l'Hotel-de-Ville, place de la Maison-Carree, place Saint-Jean, and place du Chateau.

"Article 13. The companies as they are formed by the permanent council shall each choose its own captain, lieutenant, sergeants and corporals, and from the date of his nomination the captain shall have a seat on the permanent council."

The Nimes Militia was deliberately formed upon certain lines which brought Catholics and Protestants closely together as allies, with weapons in their hands; but they stood over a mine which was bound to explode some day, as the slightest friction between the two parties would produce a spark.

This state of concealed enmity lasted for nearly a year, being augmented by political antipathies; for the Protestants almost to man were Republicans, and the Catholics Royalists.

In the interval—that is to say, towards January, 1790—a Catholic called Francois Froment was entrusted by the Marquis de Foucault with the task of raising, organising, and commanding a Royalist party in the South. This we learn from one of his own letters to the marquis, which was printed in Paris in 1817. He describes his mode of action in the following words:—

It is not difficult to understand that being faithful to my religion and my king, and shocked at the seditious ideas which were disseminated on all sides, I should try to inspire others with the same spirit with which I myself was animated, so, during the year 1789, I published several articles in which I exposed the dangers which threatened altar and throne. Struck with the justice of my criticisms, my countrymen displayed the most zealous ardor in their efforts to restore to the king the full exercise of all his rights. Being anxious to take advantage of this favourable state of feeling, and thinking that it would be dangerous to hold communication with the ministers of Louis XVI, who were watched by the conspirators, I went secretly to Turin to solicit the approbation and support of the French princes there. At a consultation which was held just after my arrival, I showed them that if they would arm not only the partisans of the throne, but those of the altar, and advance the interests of religion while advancing the interests of royalty, it would be easy to save both.

"My plan had for sole object to bind a party together, and give it as far as I was able breadth and stability.

"As the revolutionists placed their chief dependence on force, I felt that they could only be met by force; for then as now I was convinced of this great truth, that one strong passion can only be overcome by another stronger, and that therefore republican fanaticism could only be driven out by religious zeal.

"The princes being convinced of the correctness of my reasoning and the efficacy of my remedies, promised me the arms and supplies necessary to stem the tide of faction, and the Comte d'Artois gave me letters of recommendation to the chief nobles in Upper Languedoc, that I might concert measures with them; for the nobles in that part of the country had assembled at Toulouse to deliberate on the best way of inducing the other Orders to unite in restoring to the

Catholic religion its useful influence, to the laws their power, and to the king his liberty and authority.

"On my return to Languedoc, I went from town to town in order to meet those gentlemen to whom the Comte d'Artois had written, among whom were many of the most influential Royalists and some members of the States of Parliament. Having decided on a general plan, and agreed on a method of carrying on secret correspondence with each other, I went to Nimes to wait for the assistance which I had been promised from Turin, but which I never received. While waiting, I devoted myself to awakening and sustaining the zeal of the inhabitants, who at my suggestion, on the 20th April, passed a resolution, which was signed by 5,000 inhabitants."

This resolution, which was at once a religious and political manifesto, was drafted by Viala, M. Froment's secretary, and it lay for signature in his office. Many of the Catholics signed it without even reading it, for there was a short paragraph prefixed to the document which contained all the information they seemed to desire.

"GENTLEMEN,—The aspirations of a great number of our Catholic and patriotic fellow-citizens are expressed in the resolution which we have the honour of laying before you. They felt that under present circumstances such a resolution was necessary, and they feel convinced that if you give it your support, as they do not doubt you will, knowing your patriotism, your religious zeal, and your love for our august sovereign, it will conduce to the happiness of France, the maintenance of the true religion, and the rightful authority of the king.

"We are, gentlemen, with respect, your very humble and obedient servants, the President and Commissioners of the Catholic Assembly of Nimes.

"(Signed):
"FROMENT, Commissioner
LAPIERRE, President
FOLACHER, "
LEVELUT, Commissioner
FAURE,
MELCHIOND, "
ROBIN, "
VIGNE, " "

At the same time a number of pamphlets, entitled Pierre Roman to the Catholics of Nines, were distributed to the people in the streets, containing among other attacks on the Protestants the following passages:

"If the door to high positions and civil and military honours were closed to the Protestants, and a powerful tribunal established at Nimes to see that this rule were strictly kept, you would soon see Protestantism disappear.

"The Protestants demand to share all the privileges which you enjoy, but if you grant them this, their one thought will then be to dispossess you entirely, and they will soon succeed.

"Like ungrateful vipers, who in a torpid state were harmless, they will when warmed by your benefits turn and kill you.

"They are your born enemies: your fathers only escaped as by a miracle from their blood-stained hands. Have you not often heard of the cruelties practised on them? It was a slight thing when the Protestants inflicted death alone, unaccompanied by the most horrible tortures. Such as they were such they are."

It may easily be imagined that such attacks soon embittered minds already disposed to find new causes for the old hatred, and besides the Catholics did not long confine themselves to resolutions and pamphlets. Froment, who had already got himself appointed Receiver-General of the Chapter and captain of one of the Catholic companies, insisted on being present at the installation of the Town Council, and brought his company with him armed with pitchforks, in spite of the express prohibition of the colonel of the legion. These forks were terrible weapons, and had been fabricated in a particular form for the Catholics of Nimes, Uzes, and Alais. But Froment and his company paid no attention to the prohibition, and this disobedience made a great impression on the Protestants, who began to divine the hostility of their adversaries, and it is very possible that if the new Town Council had not shut their eyes to this act of insubordination, civil war might have burst forth in Nimes that very day.

The next day, at roll-call, a sergeant of another company, one Allien, a cooper by trade, taunted one of the men with having carried a pitchfork the day before, in disobedience to orders. He replied that the mayor had permitted him to carry it; Allien not believing this, proposed to some of the men to go with him to the mayor's and ask if it were true. When they saw M. Marguerite, he said that he had permitted nothing of the kind, and sent the delinquent to

218

prison. Half an hour later, however, he gave orders for his release.

As soon as he was free he set off to find his comrades, and told them what had occurred: they, considering that an insult to one was an insult to the whole company, determined on having satisfaction at once, so about eleven o'clock P.M. they went to the cooper's house, carrying with them a gallows and ropes ready greased. But quietly as they approached, Allien heard them, for his door being bolted from within had to be forced. Looking out of the window, he saw a great crowd, and as he suspected that his life was in danger, he got out of a back window into the yard and so escaped. The militia being thus disappointed, wreaked their vengeance on some passing Protestants, whose unlucky stars had led them that way; these they knocked about, and even stabbed one of them three times with a knife.

On the 22nd April, 1790, the royalists—that is to say, the Catholics—assumed the white cockade, although it was no longer the national emblem, and on the 1st May some of the militia who had planted a maypole at the mayor's door were invited to lunch with him. On the 2nd, the company which was on guard at the mayor's official residence shouted several times during the day, "Long live the king! Up with the Cross and down with the black throats!" (This was the name which they had given to the Calvinists.) "Three cheers for the white cockade! Before we are done, it will be red with the blood of the Protestants!" However, on the 5th of May they ceased to wear it, replacing it by a scarlet tuft, which in their patois they called the red pouf, which was immediately adopted as the Catholic emblem.

219

Each day as it passed brought forth fresh brawls and provocations: libels were invented by the Capuchins, and spread abroad by three of their number. Meetings were held every day, and at last became so numerous that the town authorities called in the aid of the militia-dragoons to disperse them. Now these gatherings consisted chiefly of those tillers of the soil who are called cebets, from a Provencal word cebe, which means "onion," and they could easily be recognised as Catholics by their red pouf, which they wore both in and out of uniform. On the other hand, the dragoons were all Protestants.

However, these latter were so very gentle in their admonitions, that although the two parties found themselves, so to speak, constantly face to face and armed, for several days the meetings were dispersed without bloodshed. But this was exactly what the cebets did not want, so they began to insult the dragoons and turn them into ridicule. Consequently, one morning they gathered together in great numbers, mounted on asses, and with drawn swords began to patrol the city.

At the same time, the lower classes, who were nearly all Catholics, joined the burlesque patrols in complaining loudly of the dragoons, some saying that their horses had trampled on their children, and others that they had frightened their wives.

The Protestants contradicted them, both parties grew angry, swords were half drawn, when the municipal authorities came on the scene, and instead of apprehending the ringleaders, forbade the dragoons to patrol the town any more, ordering them in future to do nothing more than send twenty men every day to mount guard at the episcopal palace and to undertake no other duty except at the express request of the Town Council. Although it was expected that the dragoons would revolt against such a humiliation, they submitted, which was a great disappointment to the cebets, who had been longing for a chance to indulge in new outrages. For all that, the Catholics did not consider themselves beaten; they felt sure of being able to find some other way of driving their quarry to bay.

Sunday, the 13th of June, arrived. This day had been selected by the Catholics for a great demonstration. Towards ten o'clock in the morning, some companies wearing the red tuft, under pretext of going to mass, marched through the city armed and uttering threats. The few dragoons, on the other hand, who were on guard at the palace, had not even a sentinel posted, and had only five muskets in the guard-house. At two o'clock P.M. there was a meeting held in the Jacobin church, consisting almost exclusively of militia wearing the red tuft. The mayor pronounced a panegyric on those who wore it, and was followed by Pierre Froment, who explained his mission in much the same words as those quoted above. He then ordered a cask of wine to be broached and distributed among the cebets, and told them to walk about the streets in threes, and to disarm all the dragoons whom they might meet away from their post. About six o'clock in the evening a red-tuft volunteer presented himself at the gate of the palace, and ordered the porter to sweep the courtyard, saying that the volunteers were going to get up a ball for the dragoons. After this piece of bravado he went

221

away, and in a few moments a note arrived, couched in the following terms:

"The bishop's porter is warned to let no dragoon on horse or on foot enter or leave the palace this evening, on pain of death.

"13th June 1790."

This note being brought to the lieutenant, he came out, and reminded the volunteer that nobody but the town authorities could give orders to the servants at the palace. The volunteer gave an insolent answer, the lieutenant advised him to go away quietly, threatening if he did not to put him out by force. This altercation attracted a great many of the red-tufts from outside, while the dragoons, hearing the noise, came down into the yard; the quarrel became more lively, stones were thrown, the call to arms was heard, and in a few moments about forty cebets, who were prowling around in the neighbourhood of the palace, rushed into the yard carrying guns and swords. The lieutenant, who had only about a dozen dragoons at his back, ordered the bugle to sound, to recall those who had gone out; the volunteers threw themselves upon the bugler, dragged his instrument from his hands, and broke it to pieces. Then several shots were fired by the militia, the dragoons returned them, and a regular battle began. The lieutenant soon saw that this was no mere street row, but a deliberate rising planned beforehand, and realising that very serious consequences were likely to ensue, he sent a dragoon to the town hall by a back way to give notice to the authorities.

M de Saint-Pons, major of the Nimes legion, hearing some noise outside, opened his window, and found the whole city in a tumult: people were running in every direction, and shouting as they ran that the dragoons were being killed at the palace. The major rushed out into the streets at once, gathered together a dozen to fifteen patriotic citizens without weapons, and hurried to the town hall: There he found two officials of the town, and begged them to go at once to the place de l'Eveche, escorted by the first company, which was on guard at the town hall. They agreed, and set off. On the way several shots were fired at them, but no one was hit. When they arrived at the square, the cebets fired a volley at them with the same negative result. Up the three principal streets which led to the palace numerous red-tufts were hurrying; the first company took possession of the ends of the streets, and being fired at returned the fire, repulsing the assailants and clearing the square, with the loss of one of their men, while several of the retreating cebets were wounded.

While this struggle was going on at the palace, the spirit of murder broke loose in the town.

At the gate of the Madeleine, M. de Jalabert's house was broken into by the red-tufts; the unfortunate old man came out to meet them and asked what they wanted. "Your life and the lives of all the other dogs of Protestants!" was the reply. Whereupon he was seized and dragged through the streets, fifteen insurgents hacking at him with their swords.

At last he managed to escape from their hands, but died two days later of his wounds.

Another old man named Astruc, who was bowed beneath the weight of seventy-two years and whose white hair covered his shoulders, was met as he was on his way to the gate of Carmes. Being recognised as a Protestant, he received five wounds from some of the famous pitchforks belonging to the company of Froment. He fell, but the assassins picked him up, and throwing him into the moat, amused themselves by flinging stones at him, till one of them, with more humanity than his fellows, put a bullet through his head.

Three electors—M. Massador from near Beaucaire, M. Vialla from the canton of Lasalle, and M. Puech of the same place-were attacked by red-tufts on their way home, and all three seriously wounded. The captain who had been in command of the detachment on guard at the Electoral Assembly was returning to his quarters, accompanied by a sergeant and three volunteers of his own company, when they were stopped on the Petit-Cours by Froment, commonly called Damblay, who, pressing the barrel of a pistol to the captain's breast, said, "Stand, you rascal, and give up your arms." At the same time the red-tufts, seizing the captain from behind by the hair, pulled him down. Froment fired his pistol, but missed. As he fell the captain drew his sword, but it was torn from his hands, and he received a cut from Froment's sword. Upon this the captain made a great effort, and getting one of his arms free, drew a pistol from his pocket, drove back his assassins, fired at Froment, and missed him. One of the men by his side was wounded and disarmed.

A patrol of the regiment of Guienne, attached to which was M. Boudon, a dragoon officer, was passing the Calquieres. M. Boudon was attacked by a band of red-tufts and his casque and his musket carried off. Several shots

224

were fired at him, but none of them hit him; the patrol surrounded him to save him, but as he had received two bayonet wounds, he desired revenge, and, breaking through his protectors, darted forward to regain possession of his musket, and was killed in a moment. One of his fingers was cut off to get at a diamond ring which he wore, his pockets were rifled of his purse and watch, and his body was thrown into the moat.

Meantime the place-des-Recollets, the Cours, the place-des-Carmes, the Grand-Rue, and rue de Notre Dame-de-l'Esplanade were filled with men armed with guns, pitchforks, and swords. They had all come from Froment's house, which overlooked that part of Nimes called Les Calquieres, and the entrance to which was on the ramparts near the Dominican Towers. The three leaders of the insurrection—Froment. Folacher, and Descombiez—took possession of these towers, which formed a part of the old castle; from this position the Catholics could sweep the entire quay of Les Calquieres and the steps of the Salle de Spectacle with their guns, and if it should turn out that the insurrection they had excited did not attain the dimensions they expected nor gain such enthusiastic adherents, it would be quite feasible for them to defend themselves in such a position until relief came.

These arrangements were either the result of long meditation or were the inspiration of some clever strategist. The fact is that everything leads one to believe that it was a plan which had been formed with great care, for the rapidity with which all the approaches to the fortress were lined with a double row of militiamen all wearing the red tuft, the care

225

which was taken to place the most eager next the barracks in which the park of artillery was stationed, and lastly, the manner in which the approach to the citadel was barred by an entire company (this being the only place where the patriots could procure arms), combine to prove that this plan was the result of much forethought; for, while it appeared to be only defensive, it enabled the insurrectionists to attack without much, danger; it caused others to believe that they had been first attacked. It was successfully carried out before the citizens were armed, and until then only a part of the foot guard and the twelve dragoons at the palace had offered any resistance to the conspirators.

The red flag round which, in case of civil war, all good citizens were expected to gather, and which was kept at the town hall, and which should have been brought out at the first shot, was now loudly called for. The Abbe de Belmont, a canon, vicar-general, and municipal official, was persuaded, almost forced, to become standard-bearer, as being the most likely on account of his ecclesiastical position to awe rebels who had taken up arms in the name of religion. The abbe himself gives the following account of the manner in which he fulfilled this mandate:

"About seven o'clock in the evening I was engaged with MM. Porthier and Ferrand in auditing accounts, when we heard a noise in the court, and going out on the lobby, we saw several dragoons coming upstairs, amongst whom was M. Paris. They told us that fighting was going on in the place de-l'Eveche, because some one or other had brought a note to the porter ordering him to admit no more dragoons to the palace on pain of death. At this point I interrupted their story by asking why the gates had not been closed and the bearer of the letter arrested, but they replied to me that it had not been possible; thereupon MM. Ferrand and Ponthier put on their scarfs and went out.

"A few instants later several dragoons, amongst whom I recognised none but MM. Lezan du Pontet, Paris junior, and Boudon, accompanied by a great number of the militia, entered, demanding that the red flag should be brought out. They tried to open the door of the council hall, and finding it locked, they called upon me for the key. I asked that one of the attendants should be sent for, but they were all out; then I went to the hall-porter to see if he knew where the key was. He said M. Berding had taken it. Meanwhile, just as the volunteers were about to force an entrance, someone ran up with the key. The door was opened, and the red flag seized and forced into my hands. I was then dragged down into the courtyard, and from thence to the square.

"It was all in vain to tell them that they ought first to get authority, and to represent to them that I was no suitable standard-bearer on account of my profession; but they would not listen to any objection, saying that my life depended upon my obedience, and that my profession would overawe the disturbers of the public peace. So I went on, followed by a detachment of the Guienne regiment, part of the first company of the legion, and several dragoons; a young man with fixed bayonet kept always at my side. Rage was depicted on the faces of all those who accompanied me, and they indulged in oaths and threats, to which I paid no attention.

227

"In passing through the rue des Greffes they complained that I did not carry the red flag high enough nor unfurl it fully. When we got to the guardhouse at the Crown Gate, the guard turned out, and the officer was commanded to follow us with his men. He replied that he could not do that without a written order from a member of the Town Council. Thereupon those around me told me I must write such an order, but I asked for a pen and ink; everybody was furious because I had none with me. So offensive were the remarks indulged in by the volunteers and some soldiers of the Guienne regiment, and so threatening their gestures, that I grew alarmed. I was hustled and even received several blows; but at length M. de Boudon brought me paper and a pen, and I wrote:—'I require the troops to assist us to maintain order by force if necessary.' Upon this, the officer consented to accompany us. We had hardly taken half a dozen steps when they all began to ask what had become of the order I had just written, for it could not be found. They surrounded me, saying that I had not written it at all, and I was on the point of being trampled underfoot, when a militiaman found it all crumpled up in his pocket. The threats grew louder, and once more it was because I did not carry the flag high enough, everyone insisting that I was quite tall enough to display it to better advantage.

"However, at this point the militiamen with the red tufts made their appearance, a few armed with muskets but the greater number with swords; shots were exchanged, and the soldiers of the line and the National Guard arranged themselves in battle order, in a kind of recess, and desired me to go forward alone, which I refused to do, because I should have been between two fires.

"Upon this, curses, threats, and blows reached their height. I was dragged out before the troops and struck with the butt ends of their muskets and the flat of their swords until I advanced. One blow that I received between the shoulders filled my mouth with blood.

"All this time those of the opposite party were coming nearer, and those with whom I was continued to yell at me to go on. I went on until I met them. I besought them to retire, even throwing myself at their feet. But all persuasion was in vain; they swept me along with them, making me enter by the Carmelite Gate, where they took the flag from me and allowed me to enter the house of a woman whose name I have never known. I was spitting such a quantity of blood that she took pity on me and brought me everything she could think of as likely to do me good, and as soon as I was a little revived I asked to be shown the way to M. Ponthier's."

While Abbe de Belmont was carrying the red flag the militia forced the Town Councillors to proclaim martial law. This had just been done when word was brought that the first red flag had been carried off, so M. Ferrand de Missol got out another, and, followed by a considerable escort, took the same road as his colleague, Abbe de Belmont. When he arrived at the Calquieres, the red-tufts, who still adorned the ramparts and towers, began to fire upon the procession, and one of the militia was disabled; the escort retreated, but M. Ferrand advanced alone to the Carmelite Gate, like M. de Belmont, and like him, he too, was taken prisoner.

He was brought to the tower, where he found Froment in a fury, declaring that the Council had not kept its promise, having sent no relief, and having delayed to give up the citadel to him.

The escort, however, had only retreated in order to seek help; they rushed tumultuously to the barracks, and finding the regiment of Guienne drawn up in marching order in command of Lieutenant-Colonel Bonne, they asked him to follow them, but he refused without a written order from a Town Councillor. Upon this an old corporal shouted, "Brave soldiers of Guienne! the country is in danger, let us not delay to do our duty." "Yes, yes," cried the soldiers; "let us march" The lieutenant colonel no longer daring to resist, gave the word of command, and they set off for the Esplanade.

As they came near the rampart with drums beating, the firing ceased, but as night was coming on the new-comers did not dare to risk attacking, and moreover the silence of the guns led them to think that the rebels had given up their enterprise. Having remained an hour in the square, the troops returned to their quarters, and the patriots went to pass the night in an inclosure on the Montpellier road.

It almost seemed as if the Catholics were beginning to recognise the futility of their plot; for although they had appealed to fanaticism, forced the Town Council to do their will, scattered gold lavishly and made wine flow, out of eighteen companies only three had joined them. "Fifteen companies," said M. Alquier in his report to the National Assembly, "although they had adopted the red tuft, took no part in the struggle, and did not add to the number of crimes committed either on that day or during the days that followed. But although the Catholics gained few partisans among their fellow-citizens, they felt certain that people from the country would rally to their aid; but about ten o'clock in the evening the rebel ringleaders, seeing that no help arrived from that quarter either, resolved to apply a stimulus to those without. Consequently, Froment wrote the following letter to M. de Bonzols, under-commandant of the province of Languedoc, who was living at Lunel:

"SIR, Up to the present all my demands, that the Catholic companies should be put under arms, have been of no avail. In spite of the order that you gave at my request, the officials of the municipality were of opinion that it would be more prudent to delay the distribution of the muskets until after the meeting of the Electoral Assembly. This day the Protestant dragoons have attacked and killed several of our unarmed Catholics, and you may imagine the confusion and alarm that prevail in the town. As a good citizen and a true patriot, I entreat you to send an order to the regiment of royal dragoons to repair at once to Nimes to restore tranquillity and put down all who break the peace. The Town Council does not meet, none of them dares to leave his house; and if you receive no requisition from them just now, it is because they go in terror of their lives and fear to appear openly. Two red flags have been carried about the streets, and municipal officers without guards have been obliged to take refuge in patriotic houses. Although I am only a private citizen, I take the liberty of asking for aid from you, knowing that the Protestants have sent to La Vannage and La Gardonninque to ask you for reinforcements, and the arrival of fanatics from these districts would expose all good

231

patriots to slaughter. Knowing as I do of your kindness and justice, I have full trust that my prayer will receive your favourable attention.

"FROMENT, Captain of Company No. 39

"June 13, 1790, 11 o'c. p.m."

Unfortunately for the Catholic party, Dupre and Lieutaud, to whom this letter was entrusted for delivery, and for whom passports were made out as being employed on business connected with the king and the State, were arrested at Vehaud, and their despatches laid before the Electoral Assembly. Many other letters of the same kind were also intercepted, and the red-tufts went about the town saying that the Catholics of Nimes were being massacred.

The priest of Courbessac, among others, was shown a letter saying that a Capuchin monk had been murdered, and that the Catholics were in need of help. The agents who brought this letter to him wanted him to put his name to it that they might show it everywhere, but were met by a positive refusal.

At Bouillargues and Manduel the tocsin was sounded: the two villages joined forces, and with weapons in their hands marched along the road from Beaucaire to Nimes. At the bridge of Quart the villagers of Redressan and Marguerite joined them. Thus reinforced, they were able to bar the way to all who passed and subject them to examination; if a man could show he was a Catholic, he was allowed to proceed, but the Protestants were murdered then and there. We may remind our readers that the "Cadets de la Croix" pursued the same method in 1704.

Meantime Descombiez, Froment, and Folacher remained masters of the ramparts and the tower, and when very early one morning their forces were augmented by the insurgents from the villages (about two hundred men), they took advantage of their strength to force a way into the house of a certain Therond, from which it was easy to effect an entrance to the Jacobin monastery, and from there to the tower adjoining, so that their line now extended from the gate at the bridge of Calquieres to that at the end of College Street. From daylight to dusk all the patriots who came within range were fired at whether they were armed or not.

On the 14th June, at four o'clock in the morning, that part of the legion which was against the Catholics gathered together in the square of the Esplanade, where they were joined by the patriots from the adjacent towns and villages, who came in in small parties till they formed quite an army. At five A.M. M. de St. Pons, knowing that the windows of the Capuchin monastery commanded the position taken up by the patriots, went there with a company and searched the house thoroughly, and also the Amphitheatre, but found nothing suspicious in either.

Immediately after, news was heard of the massacres that had taken place during the night.

The country-house belonging to M. and Mme. Noguies had been broken into, the furniture destroyed, the owners killed in their beds, and an old man of seventy who lived with them cut to pieces with a scythe.

A young fellow of fifteen, named Payre, in passing near the guard placed at the Pont des files, had been asked by a red-tuft if he were Catholic or Protestant. On his replying he was Protestant, he was shot dead on the spot. "That was like killing a lamb," said a comrade to the murderer. "Pooh!" said he, "I have taken a vow to kill four Protestants, and he may pass for one."

M Maigre, an old man of eighty-two, head of one of the most respected families in the neighbourhood, tried to escape from his house along with his son, his daughter-in-law, two grandchildren, and two servants; but the carriage was stopped, and while the rebels were murdering him and his son, the mother and her two children succeeded in escaping to an inn, whither the assassins pursued them, Fortunately, however, the two fugitives having a start, reached the inn a few minutes before their pursuers, and the innkeeper had enough presence of mind to conceal them and open the garden gate by which he said they had escaped. The Catholics, believing him, scattered over the country to look for them, and during their absence the mother and children were rescued by the mounted patrol.

The exasperation of the Protestants rose higher and higher as reports of these murders came in one by one, till at last the desire for vengeance could no longer be repressed, and they were clamorously insisting on being led against the ramparts and the towers, when without warning a heavy fusillade began from the windows and the clock tower of the Capuchin monastery. M. Massin, a municipal officer, was killed on the spot, a sapper fatally wounded, and twenty-five of the National Guard wounded more or less severely. The Protestants immediately rushed towards the monastery in a disorderly mass; but the superior, instead of ordering the gates to be opened, appeared at a window above the

234

entrance, and addressing the assailants as the vilest of the vile, asked them what they wanted at the monastery. "We want to destroy it, we want to pull it down till not one stone rests upon another," they replied. Upon this, the reverend father ordered the alarm bells to be rung, and from the mouths of bronze issued the call for help; but before it could arrive, the door was burst in with hatchets, and five Capuchins and several of the militia who wore the red tuft were killed, while all the other occupants of the monastery ran away, taking refuge in the house of a Protestant called Paulhan. During this attack the church was respected; a man from Sornmieres, however, stole a pyx which he found in the sacristy, but as soon as his comrades perceived this he was arrested and sent to prison.

In the monastery itself, however, the doors were broken in, the furniture smashed, the library and the dispensary wrecked. The sacristy itself was not spared, its presses being broken into, its chests destroyed, and two monstrances broken; but nothing further was touched. The storehouses and the small cloth-factory connected with the monastery remained intact, like the church.

But still the towers held out, and it was round them that the real fighting took place, the resistance offered from within being all the more obstinate that the besieged expected relief from moment to moment, not knowing that their letters had been intercepted by the enemy. On every side the rattling of shot was heard, from the Esplanade, from the windows, from the roofs; but very little effect was produced by the Protestants, for Descombiez had told his men to put their caps with the red tufts on the top of the wall, to attract the bullets, while they fired from the side. Meantime the conspirators, in order to get a better command of the besiegers, reopened a passage which had been long walled up between the tower Du Poids and the tower of the Dominicans. Descombiez, accompanied by thirty men, came to the door of the monastery nearest the fortifications and demanded the key of another door which led to that part of the ramparts which was opposite the place des Carmes, where the National Guards were stationed. In spite of the remonstrances of the monks, who saw that it would expose them to great danger, the doors were opened, and Froment hastened to occupy every post of vantage, and the battle began in that quarter, too, becoming fiercer as the conspirators remarked that every minute brought the Protestants reinforcements from Gardonninque and La Vaunage. The firing began at ten o'clock in the morning, and at four o'clock in the afternoon it was going on with unabated fury.

At four o'clock, however, a servant carrying a flag of truce appeared; he brought a letter from Descombiez, Fremont, and Folacher, who styled themselves "Captains commanding the towers of the Castle." It was couched in the following words:—

"To the Commandant of the troops of the line, with the request that the contents be communicated to the militia stationed in the Esplanade.

"SIR,—We have just been informed that you are anxious for peace. We also desire it, and have never done anything to break it. If those who have caused the frightful confusion which at present prevails in the city are willing to bring it to an end, we offer to forget the past and to live with them as brothers.

"We remain, with all the frankness and loyalty of patriots and Frenchmen, your humble servants,

"The Captains of the Legion of Nimes, in command of the towers of the Castle,

"FROMENT, DESCOMBIEZ, FOLACHER NIMES, the 14th June 1790, 4.00 P.M."

On the receipt of this letter, the city herald was sent to the towers to offer the rebels terms of capitulation. The three "captains in command" came out to discuss the terms with the commissioners of the electoral body; they were armed and followed by a great number of adherents. However, as the negotiators desired peace before all things, they proposed that the three chiefs should surrender and place themselves in the hands of the Electoral Assembly. This offer being refused, the electoral commissioners withdrew, and the rebels retired behind their fortifications. About five o'clock in the evening, just as the negotiations were broken off, M. Aubry, an artillery captain who had been sent with two hundred men to the depot of field artillery in the country, returned with six pieces of ordnance, determined to make a breach in the tower occupied by the conspirators, and from which they were firing in safety at the soldiers, who had no cover. At six o'clock, the guns being mounted, their thunder began, first drowning the noise of the musketry and then silencing it altogether; for the cannon balls did their work quickly, and before long the tower threatened to fall. Thereupon the electoral commissioners ordered the firing to cease for a moment, in the hope that now the danger had become so imminent the leaders would accept the conditions which they had refused one hour before; and not desiring to drive them to desperation, the commissioners advanced again down College Street, preceded by a bugler, and the captains were once more summoned to a parley. Froment and Descombiez came out to meet them, and seeing the condition of the tower, they agreed to lay down their arms and send them for the palace, while they themselves would proceed to the Electoral Assembly and place themselves under its protection. These proposals being accepted, the commissioners waved their hats as a sign that the treaty was concluded.

At that instant three shots were fired from the ramparts, and cries of "Treachery! treachery!" were heard on every side. The Catholic chiefs returned to the tower, while the Protestants, believing that the commissioners were being assassinated, reopened the cannonade; but finding that it took too long to complete the breach, ladders were brought, the walls scaled, and the towers carried by assault. Some of the Catholics were killed, the others gained Froment's house, where, encouraged by him, they tried to organise a resistance; but the assailants, despite the oncoming darkness, attacked the place with such fury that doors and windows were shattered in an instant. Froment and his brother Pierre tried to escape by a narrow staircase which led to the roof, but before they reached it Pierre was wounded in the hip and fell; but Froment reached the roof, and sprang upon an adjacent housetop, and climbing from roof to roof, reached the college, and getting into it by a garret window, took refuge in a large room which was

238

always unoccupied at night, being used during the day as a study.

Froment remained hidden there until eleven o'clock. It being then completely dark, he got out of the window, crossed the city, gained the open country, and walking all night, concealed himself during the day in the house of a Catholic. The next night he set off again, and reached the coast, where he embarked on board a vessel for Italy, in order to report to those who had sent him the disastrous result of his enterprise.

For three whole days the carnage lasted. The Protestants losing all control over themselves, carried on the work of death not only without pity but with refined cruelty. More than five hundred Catholics lost their lives before the 17th, when peace was restored.

For a long time recriminations went on between Catholics and Protestants, each party trying to fix on the other the responsibility for those dreadful three days; but at last Franqois Froment put an end to all doubt on the subject, by publishing a work from which are set forth many of the details just laid before our readers, as well as the reward he met with when he reached Turin. At a meeting of the French nobles in exile, a resolution was passed in favour of M. Pierre Froment and his children, inhabitants of Nimes.

We give a literal reproduction of this historic document:

"We the undersigned, French nobles, being convinced that our Order was instituted that it might become the prize of valour and the encouragement of virtue, do declare that the Chevalier de Guer having given us proof of the devotion to their king and the love of their country which have been displayed by M. Pierre Froment, receiver of the clergy, and his three sons, Mathieu Froment citizen, Jacques Froment canon, Francois Froment advocate, inhabitants of Nimes, we shall henceforward regard them and their descendants as nobles and worthy to enjoy all the distinctions which belong to the true nobility. Brave citizens, who perform such distinguished actions as fighting for the restoration of the monarchy, ought to be considered as the equals of those French chevaliers whose ancestors helped to found it. Furthermore, we do declare that as soon as circumstances permit we shall join together to petition His Majesty to grant to this family, so illustrious through its virtue, all the honours and prerogatives which belong to those born noble.

"We depute the Marquis de Meran, Comte d'Espinchal, the Marquis d'Escars, Vicomte de Pons, Chevalier de Guer, and the Marquis de la Feronniere to go to Mgr. le Comte d'Artois, Mgr. le Duc d'Angouleme, Mgr. le Duc de Berry, Mgr. le Prince de Conde, Mgr. le Due de Bourbon, and Mgr. le Duc d'Enghien, to beg them to put themselves at our head when we request His Majesty to grant to MM. Froment all the distinctions and advantages reserved for the true nobility.

"At TURIN, 12th September 1790."

The nobility of Languedoc learned of the honours conferred on their countryman, M. Froment, and addressed the following letter to him:

"LORCH, July 7, 1792

"MONSIEUR, The nobles of Languedoc hasten to confirm the resolution adopted in your favour by the nobles assembled at Turin. They appreciate the zeal and the courage which have distinguished your conduct and that of

240

your family; they have therefore instructed us to assure you of the pleasure with which they will welcome you among those nobles who are under the orders of Marshal de Castries, and that you are at liberty to repair to Lorch to assume your proper rank in one of the companies.

"We have the honour to be, monsieur, your humble and obedient servants,

"COMTE DE TOULOUSE-LAUTREC

"MARQUIS DE LA JONQUIERE "ETC."

CHAPTER VII

The Protestants, as we have said, hailed the golden dawn of the revolution with delight; then came the Terror, which struck at all without distinction of creed. A hundred and thirty-eight heads fell on the scaffold, condemned by the revolutionary tribunal of the Gard. Ninety-one of those executed were Catholic, and forty-seven Protestants, so that it looked as if the executioners in their desire for impartiality had taken a census of the population.

Then came the Consulate: the Protestants being mostly tradesmen and manufacturers, were therefore richer than the Catholics, and had more to lose; they seemed to see more chance of stability in this form of government than in those preceding it, and it was evident that it had a more powerful genius at its head, so they rallied round it with confidence and sincerity. The Empire followed, with its inclination to absolutism, its Continental system, and its increased taxation; and the Protestants drew back somewhat, for it was towards them who had hoped so much from him that Napoleon in not keeping the promises of Bonaparte was most perjured.

The first Restoration, therefore, was greeted at Nimes with a universal shout of joy; and a superficial-observer might have thought that all trace of the old religious leaven had disappeared. In fact, for seventeen years the two faiths had lived side by side in perfect peace and mutual good-will; for seventeen years men met either for business or for social purposes without inquiring about each other's religion, so that Nimes on the surface might have been held up as an example of union and fraternity.

When Monsieur arrived at Nimes, his guard of honour was drawn from the city guard, which still retained its organisation of 1812, being composed of citizens without distinction of creed. Six decorations were conferred on it—three on Catholics, and three on Protestants. At the same time, M. Daunant, M. Olivier Desmonts, and M. de Seine, the first the mayor, the second the president of the Consistory, and the third a member of the Prefecture, all three belonging to the Reformed religion, received the same favour.

Such impartiality on the part of Monsieur almost betrayed a preference, and this offended the Catholics. They muttered to one another that in the past there had been a time when the fathers of those who had just been decorated by the hand of the prince had fought against his faithful adherents. Hardly had Monsieur left the town, therefore, than it became apparent that perfect harmony no longer existed.

The Catholics had a favorite cafe, which during the whole time the Empire lasted was also frequented by Protestants without a single dispute caused by the difference of religion ever arising. But from this time forth the Catholics began to hold themselves aloof from the Protestants; the latter perceiving this, gave up the cafe by degrees to the Catholics, being determined to keep the peace whatever it might cost, and went to a cafe which had been just opened under the sign of the "Isle of Elba." The name was enough to cause them to be regarded as Bonapartists, and as to Bonapartists the cry "Long live the king!" was supposed to be offensive, they were saluted at every turn with these words, pronounced in a tone which became every day more menacing. At first they gave back the same cry, "Long live the king!" but then they were called cowards who expressed with their lips a sentiment which did not come from their hearts. Feeling that this accusation had some truth in it, they were silent, but then they were accused of hating the royal family, till at length the cry which at first had issued from full hearts in a universal chorus grew to be nothing but an expression of party hatred, so that on the 21st February, 1815, M. Daunant the mayor, by a decree, prohibited the public from using it, as it had become a means of exciting sedition. Party feeling had reached this height at Nimes when, on the 4th March, the news of the landing of Napoleon arrived.

Deep as was the impression produced, the city remained calm, but somewhat sullen; in any case, the report

243

wanted confirmation. Napoleon, who knew of the sympathy that the mountaineers felt for him, went at once into the Alps, and his eagle did not as yet take so high a flight that it could be seen hovering above Mount Geneve.

On the 12th, the Duc d'Angouleme arrived: two proclamations calling the citizens to arms signalised his presence. The citizens answered the call with true Southern ardour: an army was formed; but although Protestants and Catholics presented themselves for enrolment with equal alacrity, the Protestants were excluded, the Catholics denying the right of defending their legitimate sovereign to any but themselves.

This species of selection apparently went on without the knowledge of the Duc d'Angouleme. During his stay in Nimes he received Protestants and Catholics with equal cordiality, and they set at his table side by side. It happened once, on a Friday, at dinner, that a Protestant general took fish and a Catholic general helped himself to fowl. The duke being amused, drew attention to this anomaly, whereupon the Catholic general replied, "Better more chicken and less treason." This attack was so direct, that although the Protestant general felt that as far as he was concerned it had no point, he rose from table and left the room. It was the brave General Gilly who was treated in this cruel manner.

Meanwhile the news became more disastrous every day: Napoleon was moving about with the rapidity of his eagles. On the 24th March it was reported in Nimes that Louis XVIII had left Paris on the 19th and that Napoleon had entered on the 20th. This report was traced to its source, and it was found that it had been spread abroad by M.

Vincent de Saint-Laurent, a councillor of the Prefecture and one of the most respected men in Nimes. He was summoned at once before the authorities and asked whence he had this information; he replied, "From a letter received from M. Bragueres," producing the letter. But convincing as was this proof, it availed him nothing: he was escorted from brigade to brigade till he reached the Chateau d'If. The Protestants sided with M. Vincent de Saint-Laurent, the Catholics took the part of the authorities who were persecuting him, and thus the two factions which had been so long quiescent found themselves once more face to face, and their dormant hatred awoke to new life. For the moment, however, there was no explosion, although the city was at fever heat, and everyone felt that a crisis was at hand.

On the 22nd March two battalions of Catholic volunteers had already been enlisted at Nimes, and had formed part of the eighteen hundred men who were sent to Saint-Esprit. Just before their departure fleurs-de-lys had been distributed amongst them, made of red cloth; this change in the colour of the monarchical emblem was a threat which the Protestants well understood.

The prince left Nimes in due course, taking with him the rest of the royal volunteers, and leaving the Protestants practically masters of Nimes during the absence of so many Catholics. The city, however, continued calm, and when provocations began, strange to say they came from the weaker party.

On the 27th March six men met in a barn; dined together, and then agreed to make the circuit of the town. These men were Jacques Dupont, who later acquired such terrible celebrity under the name of Trestaillons, Truphemy the butcher, Morenet the dog shearer, Hours, Servant, and Gilles. They got opposite the cafe "Isle of Elba," the name of which indicated the opinion of those who frequented it. This cafe was faced by a guard-house which was occupied by soldiers of the 67th Regiment. The six made a halt, and in the most insulting tones raised the cry of "Long live the king!" The disturbance that ensued was so slight that we only mention it in order to give an idea of the tolerance of the Protestants, and to bring upon the stage the men mentioned above, who were three months later to play such a terrible part.

On April 1st the mayor summoned to a meeting at his official residence the municipal council, the members of all the variously constituted administrative bodies in Nimes, the officers of the city guards, the priests, the Protestant pastors, and the chief citizens. At this meeting, M. Trinquelague, advocate of the Royal Courts, read a powerful address, expressing the love, of the citizens for their king and country, and exhorting them to union and peace. This address was unanimously adopted and signed by all present, and amongst the signatures were those of the principal Protestants of Nimes. But this was not all: the next day it was printed and published, and copies sent to all the communes in the department over which the white flag still floated. And all this happened, as we have said, on April and, eleven days after Napoleon's return to Paris.

The same day word arrived that the Imperial Government had been proclaimed at Montpellier.

The next day, April 3rd, all the officers on half-pay assembled at the fountain to be reviewed by a general and a sub-inspector, and as these officers were late, the order of the, day issued by General Ambert, recognising the Imperial Government, was produced and passed along the ranks, causing such excitement that one of the officers drew his sword and cried, "Long live the emperor!" These magic words were re-echoed from every side, and they all hastened to the barracks of the 63rd Regiment, which at once joined the officers. At this juncture Marshal Pelissier arrived, and did not appear to welcome the turn things had taken; he made an effort to restrain the enthusiasm of the crowd, but was immediately arrested by his own soldiers. The officers repaired in a body to the headquarters of General Briche, commandant of the garrison, and asked for the official copy of the order of the day. He replied that he had received none, and when questioned as to which side he was on he refused to answer. The officers upon this took him prisoner. Just as they had consigned him to the barracks for confinement, a post-office official arrived bringing a despatch from General Ambert. Learning that General Briche was a prisoner, the messenger carried his packet to the colonel of the 63rd Regiment, who was the next in seniority after the general. In opening it, it was found to contain the order of the day.

Instantly the colonel ordered the 'gineyale' to sound: the town guards assumed arms, the troops left the barracks and formed in line, the National Guards in the rear of the regular troops, and when they were all thus drawn up; the order of the day was read; it was then snatched out of the colonel's hands, printed on large placards, and in less time

247

than seemed possible it was posted up in every street and at every street corner; the tricolour replaced the white cockade, everyone being obliged to wear the national emblem or none at all, the city was proclaimed in a state of seige, and the military officers formed a vigilance committee and a police force.

While the Duc d'Angouleme had been staying at Nimes, General Gilly had applied for a command in that prince's army, but in spite of all his efforts obtained nothing; so immediately after the dinner at which he was insulted he had withdrawn to Avernede, his place in the country. He was awoke in the night of the 5th-6th April by a courier from General Ambert, who sent to offer him the command of the 2nd Subdivision. On the 6th, General Gilly went to Nimes, and sent in his acceptance, whereby the departments of the Gard, the Lozere, and Ardeche passed under his authority.

Next day General Gilly received further despatches from General Ambert, from which he learned that it was the general's intention, in order to avoid the danger of a civil war, to separate the Duc d'Angouleme's army from the departments which sympathised with the royal cause; he had therefore decided to make Pont-Saint-Esprit a military post, and had ordered the 10th Regiment of mounted chasseurs, the 13th artillery, and a battalion of infantry to move towards this point by forced marches. These troops were commanded by Colonel Saint-Laurent, but General Ambert was anxious that if it could be done without danger, General Gilly should leave Nimes, taking with him part of the 63rd Regiment, and joining the other forces under the command of Colonel Saint-Laurent, should assume the chief

248

command. As the city was quite tranquil, General Gilly did not hesitate to obey this order: he set out from Nimes on the 7th, passed the night at Uzes, and finding that town abandoned by the magistrates, declared it in a state of siege, lest disturbances should arise in the absence of authority. Having placed M. de Bresson in command, a retired chief of battalion who was born in Uzes, and who usually lived there, he continued his march on the morning of the 8th.

Beyond the village of Conans, General Gilly met an orderly sent to him by Colonel Saint-Laurent to inform him that he, the colonel, had occupied Pont Saint-Esprit, and that the Duc d'Angouleme, finding himself thus caught between two fires, had just sent General d'Aultanne, chief of staff in the royal army, to him, to enter into negotiations for a surrender. Upon this, General Gilly quickened his advance, and on reaching Pont-Saint-Esprit found General d'Aultanne and Colonel Saint-Laurent conferring together at the Hotel de la Poste.

As Colonel Saint-Laurent had received his instructions directly from the commander-in-chief, several points relating to the capitulation had already been agreed upon; of these General Gilly slightly altered some, and approved of the others, and the same day the following convention was signed:

"Convention concluded between General Gilly and Baron de Damas

"S.A.R. Mgr. le Duc d'Angouleme, Commander-in-Chief of the royal army in the South, and Baron de Gilly, General of Division and Commander-in-Chief of the first corps of the Imperial Army, being most anxiously desirous to prevent any further effusion of French blood, have given plenary powers to arrange the terms of a convention to S.A.R. M. le Baron de Damas, Field-Marshal and Under-Chief of Staff, and General de Gilly and Adjutant Lefevre, Chevalier of the Legion of Honour, and Chief of the Staff of the first Army Corps; who, having shown each other their respective credentials, have agreed on the following terms:—

"Art. 1. The royal army is to be disbanded; and the National Guards which are enrolled in it, under whatever name they may have been levied, will return to their homes, after laying down their arms. Safe conducts will be provided, and the general of division commanding-in-chief guarantees that they shall never be molested for anything they may have said or done in connection with the events preceding the present convention.

"The officers will retain their swords; the troops of the line who form part of this army will repair to such garrisons as may be assigned to them.

"Art. 2. The general officers, superior staff officers and others of all branches of the service, and the chiefs and subordinates of the administrative departments, of whose names a list will be furnished to the general-in-chief, will retire to their homes and there await the orders of His Majesty the Emperor.

"Art. 3. Officers of every rank who wish to resign their commissions are competent to do so. They will receive passports for their homes.

"Art. 4. The funds of the army and the lists of the paymaster-general will be handed over at once to commissioners appointed for that purpose by the commander-in-chief.

"Art. 5. The above articles apply to the corps commanded by Mgr. le Duc d'Angouleme in person, and also to those who act separately but under his orders, and as forming part of the royal army of the South.

"Art. 6. H.R.H. will post to Cette, where the vessels necessary for him and his suite will be waiting to take him wherever he may desire. Detachments of the Imperial Army will be placed at all the relays on the road to protect His Royal Highness during the journey, and the honours due to his rank will be everywhere paid him, if he so desire.

"Art. 7. All the officers and other persons of His Royal Highness' suite who desire to follow him will be permitted to do so, and they may either embark with him at once or later, should their private affairs need time for arrangement.

"Art. 8. The present treaty will be kept secret until His Royal Highness have quitted the limits of the empire.

"Executed in duplicate and agreed upon between the above-mentioned plenipotentiaries the 8th day of April in the year 1815, with the approval of the general commanding-in-chief, and signed,

"At the headquarters at Pont-Saint-Esprit on the day and year above written.

"(Signed) LEFEVRE Adjutant and Chief of Staff of the First Corps of the Imperial Army of the South

"(Signed) BARON DE DAMAS Field-Marshal and Under-Chief of Staff

"The present convention is approved of by the General of Division Commanding-in-Chief the Imperial Army of the South.

"(Signed) GILLY"

After some discussion between General Gilly and General Grouchy, the capitulation was carried into effect. On the 16th April, at eight o'clock in the morning, the Duc d'Angouleme arrived at Cette, and went on board the Swedish vessel Scandinavia, which, taking advantage of a favourable wind, set sail the same day.

Early in the morning of the 9th an officer of high rank had been sent to La Palud to issue safe-conducts to the troops, who according to Article I of the capitulation were to return home "after laying down their arms." But during the preceding day and night some of the royal volunteers had evaded this article by withdrawing with their arms and baggage. As this infraction of the terms led to serious consequences, we propose, in order to establish the fact, to cite the depositions of three royal volunteers who afterwards gave evidence.

"On leaving the army of the Duc d'Angouleme after the capitulation," says Jean Saunier, "I went with my officers and my corps to Saint-Jean-des-Anels. From there we marched towards Uzes. In the middle of a forest, near a village, the name of which I have forgotten, our General M. de Vogue told us that we were all to return to our own homes. We asked him where we should deposit the flag. Just then Commandant Magne detached it from the staff and put it in his pocket. We then asked the general where we should deposit our arms; he replied, that we had better keep them, as we should probably find use for them before long, and also to take our ammunition with us, to ensure our safety on the road.

"From that time on we all did what we thought best: sixty-four of us remained together, and took a guide to enable us to avoid Uzes."

Nicholas Marie, labourer, deposed as follows:

"On leaving the army of the Duc d'Angouleme after the capitulation, I went with my officers and my corps to Saint-Jean-des-Anels. We marched towards Uzes, but when we were in the middle of a forest, near a village the name of which I have forgotten, our general, M. de Vogue, told us that we were to go to our own homes as soon as we liked. We saw Commandant Magne loose the flag from its staff, roll it up and put it in his pocket. We asked the general what we were to do with our arms; he replied that we were to keep both them and our ammunition, as we should find them of use. Upon this, our chiefs left us, and we all got away as best we could."

"After the capitulation of the Duc d'Angouleme I found myself," deposes Paul Lambert, lace-maker of Nimes, "in one of several detachments under the orders of Commandant Magne and General Vogue. In the middle of a forest near a village, the name of which I do not know, M. de Vogue and the other officer, told us we might go home. The flag was folded up, and M. Magne put it in his pocket. We asked our chiefs what we were to do with our arms. M. de Vogue told us that we had better keep them, as we should need them before very long; and in any case it would be well to have

253

them with us on the road, lest anything should happen to us."

The three depositions are too much alike to leave room for any doubt. The royal volunteers contravened Article I of the convention.

Being thus abandoned by their chiefs, without general and without flag, M. de Vogue's soldiers asked no further counsel of anyone but themselves, and, as one of them has already told us, sixty-four of them joined together to hire a guide who was to show them how to get by Uzes without going through it, for they were afraid of meeting with insult there. The guide brought them as far as Montarem without anyone opposing their passage or taking notice of their arms.

Suddenly a coachman named Bertrand, a confidential servant of Abbe Rafin, former Grand-Vicar of Alais, and of Baroness Arnaud-Wurmeser (for the abbe administered the estate of Aureillac in his own name and that of the baroness), galloped into the village of Arpaillargues, which was almost entirely Protestant and consequently Napoleonist, announcing that the miquelets (for after one hundred and ten years the old name given to the royal troops was revived) were on the way from Montarem, pillaging houses, murdering magistrates, outraging women, and then throwing them out of the windows. It is easy to understand the effect of such a story. The people gathered together in groups; the mayor and his assistant being absent, Bertrand was taken before a certain Boucarut, who on receiving his report ordered the generale to be beaten and the tocsin to be rung. Then the consternation became general: the men seized their muskets, the women and children stones and pitchforks, and everyone made ready to face a danger which only existed in the imagination of Bertrand, for there was not a shadow of foundation for the story he had told.

While the village was in this state of feverish excitement the royal volunteers came in sight. Hardly were they seen than the cry, "There they are! There they are!" arose on all sides, the streets were barricaded with carts, the tocsin rang out with redoubled frenzy, and everyone capable of carrying arms rushed to the entrance of the village.

The volunteers, hearing the uproar and seeing the hostile preparations, halted, and to show that their intentions were peaceful, put their shakos on their musket stocks and waved them above their heads, shouting that no one need fear, for they would do no harm to anyone. But alarmed as they were by the terrible stories told by Bertrand, the villagers shouted back that they could not trust to such assurances, and that if they wanted to pass through the village they must first give up their weapons. It may easily be imagined that men who had broken the convention in order to keep their weapons were not likely to give them up to these villagers—in fact, they obstinately refused to let them out of their hands, and by doing so increased the suspicions of the people. A parley of a very excited character took place between M. Fournier for the royal guards and M. Boucarut, who was chosen spokesman by the villagers. From words they came to deeds: the miquelets tried to force their way through, some shots were fired, and two miquelets, Calvet and Fournier, fell. The others scattered, followed by a lively discharge, and two more miquelets were slightly wounded. Thereupon they all took to flight through the fields on either side of the road, pursued for a short distance by the villagers, but soon returned to examine the two wounded men, and a report was drawn up by Antoine Robin, advocate and magistrate of the canton of Uzes, of the events just related.

This accident was almost the only one of its kind which happened during the Hundred Days: the two parties remained face to face, threatening but self-controlled. But let there be no mistake: there was no peace; they were simply awaiting a declaration of war. When the calm was broken, it was from Marseilles that the provocation came. We shall efface ourselves for a time and let an eye-witness speak, who being a Catholic cannot be suspected of partiality for the Protestants.

"I was living in Marseilles at the time of Napoleon's landing, and I was a witness of the impression which the news produced upon everyone. There was one great cry; the enthusiasm was universal; the National Guard wanted to join him to the last man, but Marshal Massena did not give his consent until it was too late, for Napoleon had already reached the mountains, and was moving with such swiftness that it would have been impossible to overtake him. Next we heard of his triumphal entry into Lyons, and of his arrival in Paris during the night. Marseilles submitted like the rest of France; Prince d'Essling was recalled to the capital, and Marshal Brune, who commanded the 6th corps of observation, fixed his headquarters at Marseilles.

"With quite incomprehensible fickleness, Marseilles, whose name during the Terror had been, as one may say, the symbol of the most advanced opinions, had become almost entirely Royalist in 1815. Nevertheless, its inhabitants saw without a murmur the tricolour flag after a year's absence floating once more above the walls. No arbitrary interference on the part of the authorities, no threats, and no brawling between the citizens and the soldiers, troubled the peace of old Phocea; no revolution ever took place with such quietness and facility.

"It must, however, be said, that Marshal Brune was just the man to accomplish such a transformation without friction; in him the frankness and loyalty of an old soldier were combined with other qualities more solid than brilliant. Tacitus in hand, he looked on at modern revolutions as they passed, and only interfered when the, voice of his country called him to her defence. The conqueror of Harlem and Bakkun had been for four years forgotten in retirement, or rather in exile, when the same voice which sent him away recalled him, and at the summons Cincinnatus left his plough and grasped his weapons. Physically he was at this period a man of about fifty-five, with a frank and open face framed by large whiskers; his head was bald except for a little grizzled hair at the temples; he was tall and active, and had a remarkably soldierly bearing.

"I had been brought into contact with him by a report which one of my friends and I had drawn up on the opinions of the people of the South, and of which he had asked to have a copy. In a long conversation with us, he discussed the subject with the impartiality of a man who brings an open mind to a debate, and he invited us to come often to see him.

We enjoyed ourselves so much in his society that we got into the habit of going to his house nearly every evening.

"On his arrival in the South an old calumny which had formerly pursued him again made its appearance, quite rejuvenated by its long sleep. A writer whose name I have forgotten, in describing the Massacres of the Second of September and the death of the unfortunate Princesse de Lamballe, had said, 'Some people thought they recognised in the man who carried her head impaled on a pike, General Brune in disguise,' and this accusation; which had been caught up with eagerness under the Consulate, still followed him so relentlessly in 1815, that hardly a day passed without his receiving an anonymous letter, threatening him with the same fate which had overtaken the princess. One evening while we were with him such a letter arrived, and having read it he passed it on to us. It was as follows:

"'Wretch,—We are acquainted with all your crimes, for which you will soon receive the chastisement you well deserve. It was you who during the revolution brought about the death of the Princesse de Lamballe; it was you who carried her head on a pike, but your head will be impaled on something longer. If you are so rash as to be present at the review of the Allies it is all up with you, and your head will be stuck on the steeple of the Accoules. Farewell, SCOUNDREL!'

"We advised him to trace this calumny to its source, and then to take signal vengeance on the authors. He paused an instant to reflect, and then lit the letter at a candle, and looking at it thoughtfully as it turned to ashes in his hand, said,—Vengeance! Yes, perhaps by seeking that I could silence the authors of these slanders and preserve the public tranquillity which they constantly imperil. But I prefer persuasion to severity. My principle is, that it is better to bring men's heads back to a right way of thinking than to cut them off, and to be regarded as a weak man rather than as a bloodthirsty one.'

"The essence of Marshal Brune's character was contained in these words.

"Public tranquillity was indeed twice endangered at Marseilles during the Hundred Days, and both times in the same manner. The garrison officers used to gather at a coffee-house in the place Necker, and sing songs suggested by passing events. This caused an attack by the townspeople, who broke the windows by throwing stones, some of which struck the officers. These rushed out, crying, 'To arms!' The townspeople were not slow to respond, but the commandant ordered the 'geneydle' to beat, sent out numerous patrols, and succeeded in calming the excitement and restoring quietness without any casualties.

"The day of the Champ du Mai orders for a general illumination were given, and that the tricolour flag should be displayed from the windows. The greater number of the inhabitants paid no attention to the desires of the authorities, and the officers being annoyed at this neglect, indulged in reprehensible excesses, which, however, resulted in nothing mare serious than some broken windows belonging to houses which had not illuminated, and in some of the householders being forced to illuminate according to order.

"In Marseilles as in the rest of France, people began to despair of the success of the royal cause, and those who represented this cause, who were very numerous at Marseilles, gave up annoying the military and seemed to resign themselves to their fate. Marshal Brune had left the city to take up his post on the frontier, without any of the dangers with which he was threatened having come across his path.

"The 25th of June arrived, and the news of the successes obtained at Fleurus and at Ligny seemed to justify the hopes of the soldiers, when, in the middle of the day, muttered reports began to spread in the town, the distant reverberations of the cannon of Waterloo. The silence of the leaders, the uneasiness of the soldiers, the delight of the Royalists, foretold the outbreak of a new struggle, the, results of which it was easy to anticipate. About four o'clock in the afternoon, a man, who had probably got earlier information than his fellow-townspeople, tore off his tricoloured cockade and trampled it under foot, crying, "Long live the king!" The angry soldiers seized him and were about to drag him to the guard-house, but the National Guards prevented them, and their interference led to a fight. Shouts were heard on all sides, a large ring was formed round the soldiers, a few musket shots heard, others answered, three or four men fell, and lay there weltering in their blood. Out of this confused uproar the word "Waterloo" emerged distinct; and with this unfamiliar name pronounced for the first time in the resounding voice of history, the news of the defeat of the French army and the triumph of the Allies spread apace. Then General Verdier, who held the chief command in the absence of Marshal Brune, tried to harangue the people, but his voice was drowned by the shouts of the mob who had gathered round a coffee-house where stood a bust of the emperor, which they insisted should be given up to them. Verdier, hoping to calm, what he took to be a simple street row, gave orders that the bust should be brought out, and this concession, so significant on the part of a general commanding in the emperor's name, convinced the crowd that his cause was lost. The fury of the populace grew greater now that they felt that they could indulge it with impunity; they ran to the Town Hall, and tearing down and burning the tricoloured, raised the white flag. The roll of the generale, the clang of the tocsin were heard, the neighbouring villages poured in their populations and increased the throng in the streets; single acts of violence began to occur, wholesale massacres were approaching. I had arrived in the town with my friend M___ the very beginning of the tumult, so we had seen the dangerous agitation and excitement grow under our eyes, but we were still ignorant of its true cause, when, in the rue de Noailles, we met an acquaintance, who, although his political opinions did not coincide with ours, had always shown himself very friendly to us. 'Well,' said I, 'what news?' 'Good for me and bad for you,' he answered;' I advise you to go away at once.' Surprised and somewhat alarmed at these words, we begged him to explain. 'Listen,' said he; 'there are going to be riots in the town; it is well known that you used to go to Brune's nearly every evening, and that you are in consequence no favourite with your neighbours; seek safety in the country.' I addressed some further question to him,

261

but, turning his back on me, he left me without another word.

"M_____ and I were still looking at each other in stupefaction, when the increasing uproar aroused us to a sense that if we desired to follow the advice just given we had not a moment to lose. We hastened to my house, which was situated in the Allees de Meilhan. My wife was just going out, but I stopped her.

"'We are not safe here,' I said; 'we must get away into the country.'

"'But where can we go?'

"'Wherever luck takes us. Let us start.'

"She was going to put on her bonnet, but I told her to leave it behind; for it was most important that no one should think we suspected anything, but were merely going for a stroll. This precaution saved us, for we learned the next day that if our intention to fly had been suspected we should have been stopped.

"We walked at random, while behind us we heard musket shots from every part of the town. We met a company of soldiers who were hurrying to the relief of their comrades, but heard later that they had not been allowed to pass the gate.

"We recollected an old officer of our acquaintance who had quitted the service and withdrawn from the world some years before, and had taken a place in the country near the village of Saint-Just; we directed our course towards his house.

"'Captain,' said I to him, 'they are murdering each other in the town, we are pursued and without asylum, so we

262

come to you.' 'That's right, my children,' said he; 'come in and welcome. I have never meddled with political affairs, and no one can have anything against me. No one will think of looking for you here.'

"The captain had friends in the town, who, one after another, reached his house, and brought us news of all that went on during that dreadful day. Many soldiers had been killed, and the Mamelukes had been annihilated. A negress who had been in the service of these unfortunates had been taken on the quay. 'Cry "Long live the king!" shouted the mob. 'No,' she replied. 'To Napoleon I owe my daily bread; long live Napoleon!' A bayonet-thrust in the abdomen was the answer. 'Villains!' said she, covering the wound with her hand to keep back the protruding entrails. 'Long live Napoleon!' A push sent her into the water; she sank, but rose again to the surface, and waving her hand, she cried for the last time, 'Long live Napoleon!' a bullet shot putting an end to her life.

"Several of the townspeople had met with shocking deaths. For instance, M. Angles, a neighbour of mine, an old man and no inconsiderable scholar, having unfortunately, when at the palace some days before, given utterance before witnesses to the sentiment that Napoleon was a great man, learned that for this crime he was about to be arrested. Yielding to the prayers of his family, he disguised himself, and, getting into a waggon, set off to seek safety in the country. He was, however, recognised and brought a prisoner to the place du Chapitre, where, after being buffeted about and insulted for an hour by the populace, he was at last murdered.

263

"It may easily be imagined that although no one came to disturb us we did not sleep much that night. The ladies rested on sofas or in arm-chairs without undressing, while our host, M____ and myself took turns in guarding the door, gun in hand.

"As soon as it was light we consulted what course we should take: I was of the opinion that we ought to try to reach Aix by unfrequented paths; having friends there, we should be able to procure a carriage and get to Nimes, where my family lived. But my wife did not agree with me. 'I must go back to town for our things,' said she; 'we have no clothes but those on our backs. Let us send to the village to ask if Marseilles is quieter to-day than yesterday.' So we sent off a messenger.

"The news he brought back was favourable; order was completely restored. I could not quite believe this, and still refused to let my wife return to the town unless I accompanied her. But in that everyone was against me: my presence would give rise to dangers which without me had no existence. Where were the miscreants cowardly enough to murder a woman of eighteen who belonged to no-party and had never injured anyone? As for me, my opinions were well known. Moreover, my mother-in-law offered to accompany her daughter, and both joined in persuading me that there was no danger. At last I was forced to consent, but only on one condition.

"'I cannot say,' I observed, 'whether there is any foundation for the reassuring tidings we have heard, but of one thing you may be sure: it is now seven o'clock in the morning, you can get to Marseilles in an hour, pack your trunks in another hour, and return in a third; let us allow one hour more for unforeseen delays. If you are not back by eleven o'clock, I shall believe something has happened, and take steps accordingly.' 'Very well,' said my wife; 'if I am not back by then, you may think me dead, and do whatever you think best.' And so she and her mother left me.

"An hour later, quite different news came to hand. Fugitives, seeking like ourselves safety in the country, told us that the rioting, far from ceasing, had increased; the streets were encumbered with corpses, and two people had been murdered with unheard-of cruelty.

"An old man named Bessieres, who had led a simple and blameless life, and whose only crime was that he had served under the Usurper, anticipating that under existing circumstances this would be regarded as a capital crime, made his will, which was afterwards found among his papers. It began with the following words:

"'As it is possible that during this revolution I may meet my death, as a partisan of Napoleon, although I have never loved him, I give and bequeath, etc., etc.

"The day before, his brother-in-law, knowing he had private enemies, had come to the house and spent the night trying to induce him to flee, but all in vain. But the next morning, his house being attacked, he yielded, and tried to escape by the back door. He was stopped by some of the National Guard, and placed himself under their protection.

"They took him to the Cours St. Louis, where, being hustled by the crowd and very ineffectually defended by the Guards, he tried to enter the Cafe Mercantier, but the door was shut in his face. Being broken by fatigue, breathless, and covered with dust and sweat, he threw himself on one of the benches placed against the wall, outside the house. Here he was wounded by a musket bullet, but not killed. At the sight of his blood shrieks of joy were heard, and then a young man with a pistol in each hand forced his way through the throng and killed the old man by two shots fired point blank in his face.

"Another still more atrocious murder took place in the course of the same morning. A father and son, bound back to back, were delivered over to the tender mercies of the mob. Stoned and beaten and covered with each other's blood, for two long hours their death-agony endured, and all the while those who could not get near enough to strike were dancing round them.

"Our time passed listening to such stories; suddenly I saw a friend running towards the house. I went to meet him. He was so pale that I hardly dared to question him. He came from the city, and had been at my house to see what had become of me. There was no one in it, but across the door lay two corpses wrapped in a blood-stained sheet which he had not dared to lift.

"At these terrible words nothing could hold me back. I set off for Marseilles. M____ who would not consent to let me return alone, accompanied me. In passing through the village of Saint-Just we encountered a crowd of armed peasants in the main street who appeared to belong to the free companies. Although this circumstance was rather alarming, it would have been dangerous to turn back, so we continued our way as if we were not in the least uneasy. They examined our bearing and our dress narrowly, and then exchanged some sentences in a low, voice, of which we only caught the word austaniers. This was the name by which the Bonapartists were called by the peasants, and means 'eaters of chestnuts,' this article of food being brought from Corsica to France. However, we were not molested in any way, for as we were going towards the city they did not think we could be fugitives. A hundred yards beyond the village we came up with a crowd of peasants, who were, like us, on the way to Marseilles. It was plain to see that they had just been pillaging some country house, for they were laden with rich stuffs, chandeliers and jewels. It proved to be that of M. R___, inspector of reviews. Several carried muskets. I pointed out to my companion a stain of blood on the trousers of one of the men, who began to laugh when he saw what we were looking at. Two hundred yards outside the city I met a woman who had formerly been a servant in my house. She was very much astonished to see me, and said, 'Go away at once; the massacre is horrible, much worse than yesterday.'

"'But my wife,' I cried, 'do you know anything about her?'

"'No, sir,' she replied; 'I was going to knock at the door, but some people asked me in a threatening manner if I could tell them where the friend of that rascal Brine was, as they were going to take away his appetite for bread. So take my advice,' she continued, 'and go back to where you came from.'

"This advice was the last I could make up my mind to follow, so we went on, but found a strong guard at the gate, and saw that it would be impossible to get through without being recognised. At the same time, the cries and the reports of firearms from within were coming nearer; it would therefore have been to court certain death to advance, so we retraced our steps. In passing again through the village of Saint-Just we met once more our armed peasants. But this time they burst out into threats on seeing us, shouting, 'Let us kill them! Let us kill them!' Instead of running away, we approached them, assuring them that we were Royalists. Our coolness was so convincing that we got through safe and sound.

"On getting back to the captain's I threw myself on the sofa, quite overcome by the thought that only that morning my wife had been beside me under my protection, and that I had let her go back to the town to a cruel and inevitable death. I felt as if my heart would break, and nothing that our host and my friend could say gave me the slightest comfort. I was like a madman, unconscious of everything round me.

"M____ went out to try to pick up some news, but in an instant we heard him running back, and he dashed into the room, calling out:

"'They are coming! There they are!'

"'Who are coming?' we asked.

"'The assassins!'

"My first feeling, I confess, was one of joy. I pounced upon a pair of double-barrelled pistols, resolved not to let myself be slaughtered like a sheep. Through the window I could see some men climbing over the wall and getting down into the garden. We had just sufficient time to escape by a back staircase which led to a door, through which we passed, shutting it behind us. We found ourselves on a road, at the other side of which was a vineyard. We crossed the road and crept under the vines, which completely concealed us.

"As we learned later, the captain's house had been denounced as a Bonapartist nest, and the assassins had hoped to take it by surprise; and, indeed, if they had come a little sooner we had been lost, for before we had been five minutes in our hiding-place the murderers rushed out on the road, looking for us in every direction, without the slightest suspicion that we were not six yards distant. Though they did not see us I could see them, and I held my pistols ready cocked, quite determined to kill the first who came near. However, in a short time they went away.

"As soon as they were out of hearing we began to consider our situation and weigh our chances. There was no use in going back to the captain's, for he was no longer there, having also succeeded in getting away. If we were to wander about the country we should be recognised as fugitives, and the fate that awaited us as such was at that moment brought home to us, for a few yards away we suddenly heard the shrieks of a man who was being murdered. They were the first cries of agony I had ever heard, and for a few moments, I confess, I was frozen with terror. But soon a violent reaction took place within me, and I felt that it would be better to march straight to meet peril than to await its coming, and although I knew the danger of trying to go through Saint-Just again, I resolved to risk it, and to get to Marseilles at all costs. So, turning to M____, I said:

"'You can remain here without danger until the evening, but I am going to Marseilles at once; for I cannot endure this uncertainty any longer. If I find Saint-Just clear, I shall come back and rejoin you, but if not I shall get away as best I can alone.'

"Knowing the danger that we were running, and how little chance there was that we should ever see each other again, he held out his hand to me, but I threw myself into his arms and gave him a last embrace.

"I started at once: when I reached Saint-Just I found the freebooters still there; so I walked up to them, trolling a melody, but one of them seized me by the collar and two others took aim at me with their muskets.

"If ever in my life I shouted 'Long live the king!' with less enthusiasm than the cry deserves, it was then: to assume a rollicking air, to laugh with cool carelessness when there is nothing between you and death but the more or less strong pressure of a highwayman's finger on the trigger of a musket, is no easy task; but all this I accomplished, and once more got through the village with a whole skin indeed, but with the unalterable resolution to blow my brains out rather than again try such an experiment.

"Having now a village behind me which I had vowed never to re-enter, and there being no road available by which I could hope to get round Marseilles, the only course open to me was to make my way into the city. At that moment this was a thing of difficulty, for many small bodies of troops, wearing the white cockade, infested the approaches. I soon perceived that the danger of getting in was as great as ever, so I determined to walk up and down till night, hoping the darkness would come to my aid; but one of the patrols soon gave me to understand that my prowling about had aroused suspicion, and ordered me either to go on to the city, in which by all accounts there was small chance of safety for me, or back to the village; where certain death awaited me. A happy inspiration flashed across my mind, I would get some refreshment, and seeing an inn near by, I went in and ordered a mug of beer, sitting down near the window, faintly hoping that before the necessity for a final decision arrived, someone who knew me would pass by. After waiting half an hour, I did indeed see an acquaintance—no other than M＿＿, whom I had left in the vineyard. I beckoned him, and he joined me. He told me that, being too impatient to await my return, he had soon made up his mind to follow me, and by joining a band of pillagers was lucky enough to get safely through Saint-Just. We consulted together as to what we had better do next, and having applied to our host, found he could supply us with a trusty messenger, who would carry the news of our whereabouts to my brother-in-law. After an anxious wait of three hours, we saw him coming. I was about to run out to meet him, but M＿＿ held me back, pointing out the danger of such a step; so we sat still our eyes fixed on the approaching figure. But when my brother-in-law reached the inn, I could restrain my impatience no longer, but rushing out of the room met him on the stairs.

"'My wife?' I cried. 'Have you seen my wife?'

"'She is at my house,' was the reply, and with a cry of joy I threw myself into his arms.

"My wife, who had been threatened, insulted, and roughly treated because of my opinions, had indeed found safety at my brother-in-law's.

"Night was coming on. My brother-in-law, who wore the uniform of the National Guard, which was at that moment a safeguard, took us each by an arm, and we passed the barrier without anyone asking us who we were. Choosing quiet streets, we reached his house unmolested; but in fact the whole city was quiet, for the carnage was practically at an end.

"My wife safe! this thought filled my heart with joy almost too great to bear.

"Her adventures were the following:

"My wife and her mother had gone to our house, as agreed upon, to pack our trunks. As they left their rooms, having accomplished their task, they found the landlady waiting on the staircase, who at once overwhelmed my wife with a torrent of abuse.

"The husband, who until then had known nothing of their tenant's return, hearing the noise, came out of his room, and, seizing his wife by the arm, pulled her in and shut the door. She, however, rushed to the window, and just as my wife and her mother reached the street, shouted to a free band who were on guard across the way, 'Fire! they are Bonapartists!' Fortunately the men, more merciful than the woman, seeing two ladies quite alone, did not hinder their passage, and as just then my brother-in-law came by, whose opinions were well known and whose uniform was respected, he was allowed to take them under his protection and conduct them to his house in safety.

"A young man, employed at the Prefecture, who had called at my house the day before, I having promised to help him in editing the Journal des Bouches-du-Rhone, was not so

272

lucky. His occupation and his visit to me laid him under suspicion of possessing dangerous opinions, and his friends urged him to fly; but it was too late. He was attacked at the corner of the rue de Noailles, and fell wounded by a stab from a dagger. Happily, however, he ultimately recovered.

"The whole day was passed in the commission of deeds still more bloody than those of the day before; the sewers ran blood, and every hundred yards a dead body was to be met. But this sight, instead of satiating the thirst for blood of the assassins, only seemed to awaken a general feeling of gaiety. In the evening the streets resounded with song and roundelay, and for many a year to come that which we looked back on as 'the day of the massacre' lived in the memory of the Royalists as 'the day of the farce.'

"As we felt we could not live any longer in the midst of such scenes, even though, as far as we were concerned, all danger was over, we set out for Nimes that same evening, having been offered the use of a carriage.

"Nothing worthy of note happened on the road to Orgon, which we reached next day; but the isolated detachments of troops which we passed from time to time reminded us that the tranquillity was nowhere perfect. As we neared the town we saw three men going about arm in arm; this friendliness seemed strange to us after our recent experiences, for one of them wore a white cockade, the second a tricolour, and the third none at all, and yet they went about on the most brotherly terms, each awaiting under a different banner the outcome of events. Their wisdom impressed me much, and feeling I had nothing to fear from such philosophers, I went up to them and questioned them, and they explained their hopes to me with the greatest innocence, and above all, their firm determination to belong to what ever party got the upper hand. As we drove into Orgon we saw at a glance that the whole town was simmering with excitement. Everybody's face expressed anxiety. A man who, we were told, was the mayor, was haranguing a group. As everyone was listening, with the greatest attention, we drew near and asked them the cause of the excitement.

"'Gentlemen,' said he, 'you ought to know the news: the king is in his capital, and we have once more hoisted the white flag, and there has not been a single dispute to mar the tranquillity of the day; one party has triumphed without violence, and the other has submitted with resignation. But I have just learned that a band of vagabonds, numbering about three hundred, have assembled on the bridge over the Durance, and are preparing to raid our little town to-night, intending by pillage or extortion to get at what we possess. I have a few guns left which I am about to distribute, and each man will watch over the safety of all.'

"Although he had not enough arms to go round, he offered to supply us, but as I had my double-barrelled pistols I did not deprive him of his weapons. I made the ladies go to bed, and, sitting at their door, tried to sleep as well as I could, a pistol in each hand. But at every instant the noise of a false alarm sounded through the town, and when day dawned my only consolation was that no one else in Orgon had slept any better than I.

"The next day we continued our journey to Tarascon, where new excitements awaited us. As we got near the town

274

we heard the tocsin clanging and drums beating the generale. We were getting so accustomed to the uproar that we were not very much astonished. However, when we got in we asked what was going on, and we were told that twelve thousand troops from Nimes had marched on Beaucaire and laid it waste with fire and sword. I insinuated that twelve thousand men was rather a large number for one town to furnish, but was told that that included troops from the Gardonninque and the Cevennes. Nimes still clung to the tricolour, but Beaucaire had hoisted the white flag, and it was for the purpose of pulling it down and scattering the Royalists who were assembling in numbers at Beaucaire that Nimes had sent forth her troops on this expedition. Seeing that Tarascon and Beaucaire are only separated by the Rhone, it struck me as peculiar that such quiet should prevail on one bank, while such fierce conflict was raging on the other. I did not doubt that something had happened, but not an event of such gravity as was reported. We therefore decided to push on to Beaucaire, and when we got there we found the town in the most perfect order. The expedition of twelve thousand men was reduced to one of two hundred, which had been easily repulsed, with the result that of the assailants one had been wounded and one made prisoner. Proud of this success, the people of Beaucaire entrusted us with a thousand objurgations to deliver to their inveterate enemies the citizens of Nimes.

"If any journey could give a correct idea of the preparations for civil war and the confusion which already prevailed in the South, I should think that without contradiction it would be that which we took that day. Along

275

the four leagues which lie between Beaucaire and Nimes were posted at frequent intervals detachments of troops displaying alternately the white and the tricoloured cockade. Every village upon our route except those just outside of Nimes had definitely joined either one party or the other, and the soldiers, who were stationed at equal distances along the road, were now Royalist and now Bonapartist. Before leaving Beaucaire we had all provided ourselves, taking example by the men we had seen at Orgon, with two cockades, one white, and one tricoloured, and by peeping out from carriage windows we were able to see which was worn by the troops we were approaching in time to attach a similar one to our hats before we got up to them, whilst we hid the other in our shoes; then as we were passing we stuck our heads, decorated according to circumstances, out of the windows, and shouted vigorously, 'Long live the king!' or 'Long live the emperor!' as the case demanded. Thanks to this concession to political opinions on the highway, and in no less degree to the money which we gave by way of tips to everybody everywhere, we arrived at length at the barriers of Nimes, where we came up with the National Guards who had been repulsed by the townspeople of Beaucaire.

"This is what had taken place just before we arrived in the city:

"The National Guard of Nimes and the troops of which the garrison was composed had resolved to unite in giving a banquet on Sunday, the 28th of June, to celebrate the success of the French army. The news of the battle of Waterloo travelled much more quickly to Marseilles than to Nimes, so the banquet took place without interruption. A bust of

276

Napoleon was carried in procession all over the town, and then the regular soldiers and the National Guard devoted the rest of the day to rejoicings, which were followed by no excess.

"But the day was not quite finished before news came that numerous meetings were taking place at Beaucaire, so although the news of the defeat at Waterloo reached Nimes on the following Tuesday, the troops which we had seen returning at the gates of the city had been despatched on Wednesday to disperse these assemblies. Meantime the Bonapartists, under the command of General Gilly, amongst whom was a regiment of chasseurs, beginning to despair of the success of their cause, felt that their situation was becoming very critical, especially as they learnt that the forces at Beaucaire had assumed the offensive and were about to march upon Nimes. As I had had no connection with anything that had taken place in the capital of the Gard, I personally had nothing to fear; but having learned by experience how easily suspicions arise, I was afraid that the ill-luck which had not spared either my friends or my family might lead to their being accused of having received a refugee from Marseilles, a word which in itself had small significance, but which in the mouth of an enemy might be fatal. Fears for the future being thus aroused by my recollections of the past, I decided to give up the contemplation of a drama which might become redoubtable, asked to bury myself in the country with the firm intention of coming back to Nimes as soon as the white flag should once more float from its towers.

"An old castle in the Cevennes, which from the days when the Albigenses were burnt, down to the massacre of La Bagarre, had witnessed many a revolution and counter revolution, became the asylum of my wife, my mother, M____, and myself. As the peaceful tranquillity of our life there was unbroken by any event of interest, I shall not pause to dwell on it. But at length we grew weary, for such is man, of our life of calm, and being left once for nearly a week without any news from outside, we made that an excuse for returning to Nimes in order to see with our own eyes how things were going on.

"When we were about two leagues on our way we met the carriage of a friend, a rich landed proprietor from the city; seeing that he was in it, I alighted to ask him what was happening at Nimes. 'I hope you do not think of going there,' said he, 'especially at this moment; the excitement is intense, blood has already flowed, and a catastrophe is imminent.' So back we went to our mountain castle, but in a few days became again a prey to the same restlessness, and, not being able to overcome it, decided to go at all risks and see for ourselves the condition of affairs; and this time, neither advice nor warning having any effect, we not only set out, but we arrived at our destination the same evening.

"We had not been misinformed, frays having already taken place in the streets which had heated public opinion. One man had been killed on the Esplanade by a musket shot, and it seemed as if his death would be only the forerunner of many. The Catholics were awaiting with impatience the arrival of those doughty warriors from Beaucaire on whom they placed their chief reliance. The Protestants went about in painful silence, and fear blanched every face. At length the white flag was hoisted and the king proclaimed without any of the disorders which had been dreaded taking place, but it was plainly visible that this calm was only a pause before a struggle, and that on the slightest pretext the pent-up passions would break loose again.

"Just at this time the memory of our quiet life in the mountains inspired us with a happy idea. We had learned that the obstinate resolution of Marshal Brune never to acknowledge Louis XVIII as king had been softened, and that the marshal had been induced to hoist the white flag at Toulon, while with a cockade in his hat he had formally resigned the command of that place into the hands of the royal authorities.

"Henceforward in all Provence there was no spot where he could live unmarked. His ultimate intentions were unknown to us, indeed his movements seemed to show great hesitation on his part, so it occurred to us to offer him our little country house as a refuge where he could await the arrival of more peaceful times. We decided that M___ and another friend of ours who had just arrived from Paris should go to him and make the offer, which he would at once accept all the more readily because it came from the hearts which were deeply devoted to him. They set out, but to my great surprise returned the same day. They brought us word that Marshal Brune had been assassinated at Avignon.

"At first we could not believe the dreadful news, and took it for one of those ghastly rumours which circulate with such rapidity during periods of civil strife; but we were not left long in uncertainty, for the details of the catastrophe arrived all too soon."

CHAPTER VIII

For some days Avignon had its assassins, as Marseilles had had them, and as Nimes was about to have them; for some days all Avignon shuddered at the names of five men— Pointu, Farges, Roquefort, Naudaud, and Magnan.

Pointu was a perfect type of the men of the South, olive-skinned and eagle-eyed, with a hook nose, and teeth of ivory. Although he was hardly above middle height, and his back was bent from bearing heavy burdens, his legs bowed by the pressure of the enormous masses which he daily carried, he was yet possessed of extraordinary strength and dexterity. He could throw over the Loulle gate a 48-pound cannon ball as easily as a child could throw its ball. He could fling a stone from one bank of the Rhone to the other where it was two hundred yards wide. And lastly, he could throw a knife backwards while running at full speed with such strength and precision of aim that this new kind of Parthian arrow would go whistling through the air to hide two inches of its iron head in a tree trunk no thicker than a man's thigh. When to these accomplishments are added an equal skill with the musket, the pistol, and the quarter-staff, a good deal of mother wit, a deep hatred for Republicans, against whom he had vowed vengeance at the foot of the scaffold on which his father and mother had perished, an idea can be formed of the terrible chief of the assassins of Avignon, who had for his lieutenants, Farges the silk-weaver, Roquefort the porter, Naudaud the baker, and Magnan the secondhand clothes dealer.

Avignon was entirely in the power of these five men, whose brutal conduct the civil and military authorities would not or could not repress, when word came that Marshal Brune, who was at Luc in command of six thousand troops, had been summoned to Paris to give an account of his conduct to the new Government.

The marshal, knowing the state of intense excitement which prevailed in the South, and foreseeing the perils likely to meet him on the road, asked permission to travel by water, but met with an official refusal, and the Duc de Riviere, governor of Marseilles, furnished him with a safe-conduct. The cut-throats bellowed with joy when they learned that a Republican of '89, who had risen to the rank of marshal under the Usurper, was about to pass through Avignon. At the same time sinister reports began to run from mouth to mouth, the harbingers of death. Once more the infamous slander which a hundred times had been proved to be false, raised its voice with dogged persistence, asserting that Brune, who did not arrive at Paris until the 5th of September, 1792, had on the 2nd, when still at Lyons, carried the head of the Princesse de Lamballe impaled on a pike. Soon the news came that the marshal had just escaped assassination at Aix, indeed he owed his safety to the fleetness of his horses. Pointu, Forges, and Roquefort swore that they would manage things better at Avignon.

By the route which the marshal had chosen there were only two ways open by which he could reach Lyons: he must either pass through Avignon, or avoid it by taking a cross-road, which branched off the Pointet highway, two leagues outside the town. The assassins thought he would take the latter course, and on the 2nd of August, the day on which the marshal was expected, Pointu, Magnan, and Naudaud, with four of their creatures, took a carriage at six o'clock in the morning, and, setting out from the Rhone bridge, hid themselves by the side of the high road to Pointet.

When the marshal reached the point where the road divided, having been warned of the hostile feelings so rife in Avignon, he decided to take the cross-road upon which Pointu and his men were awaiting him; but the postillion obstinately refused to drive in this direction, saying that he always changed horses at Avignon, and not at Pointet. One of the marshal's aides-de-camp tried, pistol in hand, to force him to obey; but the marshal would permit no violence to be offered him, and gave him orders to go on to Avignon.

The marshal reached the town at nine o'clock in the morning, and alighted at the Hotel du Palais Royal, which was also the post-house. While fresh horses were being put to and the passports and safe-conduct examined at the Loulle gate, the marshal entered the hotel to take a plate of soup. In less than five minutes a crowd gathered round the door, and M. Moulin the proprietor noticing the sinister and threatening expression many of the faces bore, went to the marshal's room and urged him to leave instantly without waiting for his papers, pledging his word that he would send a man on horseback after him, who would overtake him two or three leagues beyond the town, and bring him his own safe-conduct and the passports of his aides-de-camp. The marshal came downstairs, and finding the horses ready, got into the carriage, on which loud murmurs arose from the populace, amongst which could be distinguished the terrible word 'zaou!' that excited cry of the Provencal, which according to the tone in which it is uttered expresses every shade of threat, and which means at once in a single syllable, "Bite, rend, kill, murder!"

The marshal set out at a gallop, and passed the town gates unmolested, except by the howlings of the populace, who, however, made no attempt to stop him. He thought he had left all his enemies behind, but when he reached the Rhone bridge he found a group of men armed with muskets waiting there, led by Farges and Roquefort. They all raised their guns and took aim at the marshal, who thereupon ordered the postillion to drive back. The order was obeyed, but when the carriage had gone about fifty yards it was met by the crowd from the "Palais Royal," which had followed it, so the postillion stopped. In a moment the traces were cut, whereupon the marshal, opening the door, alighted, followed by his valet, and passing on foot through the Loulle gate, followed by a second carriage in which were his aides-de-camp, he regained the "Palais Royal," the doors of which were opened to him and his suite, and immediately secured against all others.

The marshal asked to be shown to a room, and M. Moulin gave him No. 1, to the front. In ten minutes three thousand people filled the square; it was as if the population sprang up from the ground. Just then the carriage, which the marshal had left behind, came up, the postillion having tied the traces, and a second time the great yard gates were opened, and in spite of the press closed again and barricaded by the porter Vernet, and M. Moulin himself, both of whom were men of colossal strength. The aides-de-camp, who had remained in the carriage until then, now alighted, and asked to be shown to the marshal; but Moulin ordered the porter to conceal them in an outhouse. Vernet taking one in each hand, dragged them off despite their struggles, and pushing them behind some empty barrels, over which he threw an old piece of carpet, said to them in a voice as solemn as if he were a prophet, "If you move, you are dead men," and left them. The aides-de-camp remained there motionless and silent.

At that moment M. de Saint-Chamans, prefect of Avignon, who had arrived in town at five o'clock in the morning, came out into the courtyard. By this time the crowd was smashing the windows and breaking in the street door. The square was full to overflowing, everywhere threatening cries were heard, and above all the terrible zaou, which from moment to moment became more full of menace. M. Moulin saw that if they could not hold out until the troops under Major Lambot arrived, all was lost; he therefore told Vernet to settle the business of those who were breaking in the door, while he would take charge of those who were trying to get in at the window. Thus these two men, moved by a common impulse and of equal courage, undertook to dispute with a howling mob the possession of the blood for which it thirsted.

Both dashed to their posts, one in the hall, the other in the dining-room, and found door and windows already smashed, and several men in the house. At the sight of Vernet, with whose immense strength they were acquainted, those in the hall drew back a step, and Vernet, taking advantage of this movement, succeeded in ejecting them and in securing the door once more. Meantime M. Moulin, seizing his double-barrelled gun, which stood in the chimney-corner, pointed it at five men who had got into the dining-room, and threatened to fire if they did not instantly get out again. Four obeyed, but one refused to budge; whereupon Moulin, finding himself no longer outnumbered, laid aside his gun, and, seizing his adversary round the waist, lifted him as if he were a child and flung him out of the window. The man died three weeks later, not from the fall but from the squeeze.

Moulin then dashed to the window to secure it, but as he laid his hand on it he felt his head seized from behind and pressed violently down on his left shoulder; at the same instant a pane was broken into splinters, and the head of a hatchet struck his right shoulder. M. de Saint-Chamans, who had followed him into the room, had seen the weapon thrown at Moulin's head, and not being able to turn aside the iron, had turned aside the object at which it was aimed. Moulin seized the hatchet by the handle and tore it out of the hands of him who had delivered the blow, which fortunately had missed its aim. He then finished closing the window, and secured it by making fast the inside shutters, and went upstairs to see after the marshal.

Him he found striding up and down his room, his handsome and noble face as calm as if the voices of all those shouting men outside were not demanding his death. Moulin made him leave No. 1 for No. 3, which, being a back room and looking out on the courtyard, seemed to offer more chances of safety than the other. The marshal asked for writing materials, which Moulin brought, whereupon the marshal sat down at a little table and began to write.

Just then the cries outside became still more uproarious. M. de Saint-Chamans had gone out and ordered the crowd to disperse, whereupon a thousand people had answered him with one voice, asking who he was that he should give such an order. He announced his rank and authority, to which the answer was, "We only know the prefect by his clothes." Now it had unfortunately happened that M. de Chamans having sent his trunks by diligence they had not yet arrived, and being dressed in a green coat; nankeen trousers, and a pique vest, it could hardly be expected that in such a suit he should overawe the people under the circumstances; so, when he got up on a bench to harangue the populace, cries arose of "Down with the green coat! We have enough of charlatans like that!" and he was forced to get down again. As Vernet opened the door to let him in, several men took advantage of the circumstance to push in along with him; but Vernet let his fist fall three times, and three men rolled at his feet like bulls struck by a club. The others withdrew. A dozen champions such as Vernet would have saved the marshal. Yet it must not be forgotten that this man was a Royalist, and held the same opinions as those against whom he fought; for him as for them the

286

marshal was a mortal enemy, but he had a noble heart, and if the marshal were guilty he desired a trial and not a murder. Meantime a certain onlooker had heard what had been said to M. de Chamans about his unofficial costume, and had gone to put on his uniform. This was M. de Puy, a handsome and venerable old man, with white hair, pleasant expression, and winning voice. He soon came back in his mayor's robes, wearing his scarf and his double cross of St. Louis and the Legion of Honour. But neither his age nor his dignity made the slightest impression on these people; they did not even allow him to get back to the hotel door, but knocked him down and trampled him under foot, so that he hardly escaped with torn clothes and his white hair covered with dust and blood. The fury of the mob had now reached its height.

At this juncture the garrison of Avignon came in sight; it was composed of four hundred volunteers, who formed a battalion known as the Royal Angouleme. It was commanded by a man who had assumed the title of Lieutenant-General of the Emancipating Army of Vaucluse. These forces drew up under the windows of the "Palais Royal." They were composed almost entirely of Provenceaux, and spoke the same dialect as the people of the lower orders. The crowd asked the soldiers for what they had come, why they did not leave them to accomplish an act of justice in peace, and if they intended to interfere. "Quite the contrary," said one of the soldiers; "pitch him out of the window, and we will catch him on the points of our bayonets." Brutal cries of joy greeted this answer, succeeded by a short silence, but it was easy to see that under the apparent calm the crowd was in a state of eager expectation. Soon new shouts were heard, but this time from the interior of the hotel; a small band of men led by Forges and Roquefort had separated themselves from the throng, and by the help of ladders had scaled the walls and got on the roof of the house, and, gliding down the other side, had dropped into the balcony outside the windows of the rooms where the marshal was writing.

Some of these dashed through the windows without waiting to open them, others rushed in at the open door. The marshal, thus taken by surprise, rose, and not wishing that the letter he was writing to the Austrian commandant to claim his protection should fall into the hands of these wretches, he tore it to pieces. Then a man who belonged to a better class than the others, and who wears to-day the Cross of the Legion of Honour, granted to him perhaps for his conduct on this occasion, advanced towards the marshal, sword in hand, and told him if he had any last arrangements to make, he should make them at once, for he had only ten minutes to live.

"What are you thinking of?" exclaimed Forges. "Ten minutes! Did he give the Princesse de Lamballe ten minutes?" and he pointed his pistol at the marshal's breast; but the marshal striking up the weapon, the shot missed its aim and buried itself in the ceiling.

"Clumsy fellow!" said the marshal, shrugging his shoulders, "not to be able to kill a man at such close range."

"That's true," replied Roquefort in his patois. "I'll show you how to do it"; and, receding a step, he took aim with his carbine at his victim, whose back was partly towards him. A report was heard, and the marshal fell dead on the spot, the bullet which entered at the shoulder going right through his body and striking the opposite wall.

The two shots, which had been heard in the street, made the howling mob dance for joy. One cowardly fellow, called Cadillan, rushed out on one of the balconies which looked on the square, and, holding a loaded pistol in each hand, which he had not dared to discharge even into the dead body of the murdered man, he cut a caper, and, holding up the innocent weapons, called out, "These have done the business!" But he lied, the braggart, and boasted of a crime which was committed by braver cutthroats than he.

Behind him came the general of the "Emancipating Army of Vaucluse," who, graciously saluting the crowd, said, "The marshal has carried out an act of justice by taking his own life." Shouts of mingled joy, revenge, and hatred rose from the crowd, and the king's attorney and the examining magistrate set about drawing up a report of the suicide.

Now that all was over and there was no longer any question of saving the marshal, M. Moulin desired at least to save the valuables which he had in his carriage. He found in a cash box 40,000 francs, in the pockets a snuff-box set with diamonds, and a pair of pistols and two swords; the hilt of one of these latter was studded with precious stones, a gift from the ill-starred Selim. M. Moulin returned across the court, carrying these things. The Damascus blade was wrenched from his hands, and the robber kept it five years as a trophy, and it was not until the year 1820 that he was forced to give it up to the representative of the marshal's widow. Yet this man was an officer, and kept his rank all through the Restoration, and was not dismissed the army till

1830. When M. Moulin had placed the other objects in safety, he requested the magistrate to have the corpse removed, as he wished the crowds to disperse, that he might look after the aides-de camp. While they were undressing the marshal, in order to certify the cause of death, a leathern belt was found on him containing 5536 francs. The body was carried downstairs by the grave-diggers without any opposition being offered, but hardly had they advanced ten yards into the square when shouts of "To the Rhone! to the Rhone!" resounded on all sides. A police officer who tried to interfere was knocked down, the bearers were ordered to turn round; they obeyed, and the crowd carried them off towards the wooden bridge. When the fourteenth arch was reached, the bier was torn from the bearers' hands, and the corpse was flung into the river. "Military honours!" shouted some one, and all who had guns fired at the dead body, which was twice struck. "Tomb of Marshal Brune" was then written on the arch, and the crowd withdrew, and passed the rest of the day in holiday-making.

Meanwhile the Rhone, refusing to be an accomplice in such a crime, bore away the corpse, which the assassins believed had been swallowed up for ever. Next day it was found on the sandy shore at Tarascon, but the news of the murder had preceded it, and it was recognised by the wounds, and pushed back again into the waters, which bore it towards the sea.

Three leagues farther on it stopped again, this time by a grassy bank, and was found by a man of forty and another of eighteen. They also recognised it, but instead of shoving it back into the current, they drew it up gently on the bank and carried it to a small property belonging to one of them, where they reverently interred it. The elder of the two was M. de Chartruse, the younger M. Amedee Pichot.

The body was exhumed by order of the marshal's widow, and brought to her castle of Saint-Just, in Champagne; she had it embalmed, and placed in a bedroom adjoining her own, where it remained, covered only by a veil, until the memory of the deceased was cleansed from the accusation of suicide by a solemn public trial and judgment. Then only it was finally interred, along with the parchment containing the decision of the Court of Riom.

The ruffians who killed Marshal Brune, although they evaded the justice of men, did not escape the vengeance of God: nearly every one of them came to a miserable end. Roquefort and Farges were attacked by strange and hitherto unknown diseases, recalling the plagues sent by God on the peoples whom He desired to punish in bygone ages. In the case of Farges, his skin dried up and became horny, causing him such intense irritation, that as the only means of allaying it he had to be kept buried up to the neck while still alive. The disease under which Roquefort suffered seemed to have its seat in the marrow, for his bones by degrees lost all solidity and power of resistance, so that his limbs refused to bear his weight, and he went about the streets crawling like a serpent. Both died in such dreadful torture that they regretted having escaped the scaffold, which would have spared them such prolonged agony.

Pointu was condemned to death, in his absence, at the Assizes Court of La Drome, for having murdered five people, and was cast off by his own faction. For some time his wife, who was infirm and deformed, might be seen going from house to house asking alms for him, who had been for two months the arbiter of civil war and assassination. Then came a day when she ceased her quest, and was seen sitting, her head covered by a black rag: Pointu was dead, but it was never known where or how. In some corner, probably, in the crevice of a rock or in the heart of the forest, like an old tiger whose talons have been clipped and his teeth drawn.

Naudaud and Magnan were sentenced to the galleys for ten years. Naudaud died there, but Magnan finished his time and then became a scavenger, and, faithful to his vocation as a dealer of death, a poisoner of stray dogs.

Some of these cut-throats are still living, and fill good positions, wearing crosses and epaulets, and, rejoicing in their impunity, imagine they have escaped the eye of God.

We shall wait and see!

CHAPTER IX

It was on Saturday that the white flag was hoisted at Nimes. The next day a crowd of Catholic peasants from the environs marched into the city, to await the arrival of the Royalist army from Beaucaire. Excitement was at fever heat, the desire of revenge filled every breast, the hereditary hatred which had slumbered during the Empire again awoke stronger than ever. Here I may pause to say that in the account which follows of the events which took place about this time, I can only guarantee the facts and not the dates: I relate everything as it happened; but the day on which it happened may sometimes have escaped my memory, for it is easier to recollect a murder to which one has been an eye-witness, than to recall the exact date on which it happened.

The garrison of Nimes was composed of one battalion of the 13th Regiment of the line, and another battalion of the 79th Regiment, which not being up to its full war-strength had been sent to Nimes to complete its numbers by enlistment. But after the battle of Waterloo the citizens had tried to induce the soldiers to desert, so that of the two battalions, even counting the officers, only about two hundred men remained.

When the news of the proclamation of Napoleon II reached Nimes, Brigadier-General Malmont, commandant of the department, had him proclaimed in the city without any disturbance being caused thereby. It was not until some days later that a report began to be circulated that a royal army was gathering at Beaucaire, and that the populace would take advantage of its arrival to indulge in excesses. In the face of this two-fold danger, General Malmont had ordered the regular troops, and a part of the National Guard of the Hundred Days, to be drawn up under arms in the rear of the barracks upon an eminence on which he had mounted five pieces of ordnance. This disposition was maintained for two days and a night, but as the populace remained quiet, the troops returned to the barracks and the Guards to their homes.

But on Monday a concourse of people, who had heard that the army from Beaucaire would arrive the next day, made a hostile demonstration before the barracks, demanding with shouts and threats that the five cannons should be handed over to them. The general and the officers who were quartered in the town, hearing of the tumult, repaired at once to the barracks, but soon came out again, and approaching the crowd tried to persuade it to disperse, to which the only answer they received was a shower of bullets. Convinced by this, as he was well acquainted with the character of the people with whom he had to deal, that the struggle had begun in earnest and must be fought out to the bitter end, the general retreated with his officers, step by step, to the barracks, and having got inside the gates, closed and bolted them.

He then decided that it was his duty to repulse force by force, for everyone was determined to defend, at no matter what cost, a position which, from the first moment of revolt, was fraught with such peril. So, without waiting for orders, the soldiers, seeing that some of their windows had been broken by shots from without, returned the fire, and, being better marksmen than the townspeople, soon laid many low. Upon this the alarmed crowd retired out of musket range, and entrenched themselves in some neighbouring houses.

About nine o'clock in the evening, a man bearing something resembling a white flag approached the walls and asked to speak to the general. He brought a message inquiring on what terms the troops would consent to evacuate Nimes. The general sent back word that the conditions were, that the troops should be allowed to march out fully armed and with all their baggage; the five guns alone would be left behind. When the forces reached a certain valley outside the city they would halt, that the men might be supplied with means sufficient to enable them either to rejoin the regiments to which they belonged, or to return to their own homes.

At two o'clock A. M. the same envoy returned, and announced to the general that the conditions had been accepted with one alteration, which was that the troops, before marching out, should lay down their arms. The messenger also intimated that if the offer he had brought were not quickly accepted—say within two hours—the time for capitulation would have gone by, and that he would not be answerable for what the people might then do in their fury. The general accepted the conditions as amended, and the envoy disappeared.

When the troops heard of the agreement, that they should be disarmed before being allowed to leave the town, their first impulse was to refuse to lay down their weapons before a rabble which had run away from a few musket shots; but the general succeeded in soothing their sense of humiliation and winning their consent by representing to them that there could be nothing dishonourable in an action which prevented the children of a common fatherland from shedding each other's blood.

The gendarmerie, according to one article of the treaty, were to close in at, the rear of the evacuating column; and thus hinder the populace from molesting the troops of which it was composed. This was the only concession obtained in return for the abandoned arms, and the farce in question was already drawn up in field order, apparently waiting to escort the troops out of the city.

At four o'clock P.M. the troops got ready, each company stacking its arms in the courtyard before: marching out; but hardly had forty or fifty men passed the gates than fire was opened on them at such close range that half of them were killed or disabled at the first volley. Upon this, those who were still within the walls closed the courtyard gates, thus cutting off all chance of retreat from their comrades. In the event; however, it turned out that several of the latter contrived to escape with their lives and that they lost nothing through being prevented from returning; for as soon as the mob saw that ten or twelve of their victims had slipped through their hands they made a furious attack on the barracks, burst in the gates, and scaled the walls with such rapidity, that the soldiers had no time to repossess themselves of their muskets, and even had they succeeded in seizing them they would have been of little use, as ammunition was totally wanting. The barracks being thus carried by assault, a horrible massacre ensued, which lasted for three hours. Some of the wretched men, being hunted from room to room, jumped out of the first window they could reach, without stopping to measure its height from the ground, and were either impaled on the bayonets held in readiness below, or, falling on the pavement, broke their limbs and were pitilessly despatched.

The gendarmes, who had really been called out to protect the retreat of the garrison, seemed to imagine they were there to witness a judicial execution, and stood immovable and impassive while these horrid deeds went on before their eyes. But the penalty of this indifference was swiftly exacted, for as soon as the soldiers were all done with, the mob, finding their thirst for blood still unslacked, turned on the gendarmes, the greater number of whom were wounded, while all lost their horses, and some their lives.

The populace was still engaged at its bloody task when news came that the army from Beaucaire was within sight of the town, and the murderers, hastening to despatch some of the wounded who still showed signs of life, went forth to meet the long expected reinforcements.

Only those who saw the advancing army with their own eyes can form any idea of its condition and appearance, the first corps excepted. This corps was commanded by M. de Barre, who had put himself at its head with the noble purpose of preventing, as far as he could, massacre and pillage. In this he was seconded by the officers under him, who were actuated by the same philanthropic motives as their general in identifying themselves with the corps. Owing to their exertions, the men advanced in fairly regular order, and good discipline was maintained. All the men carried muskets.

But the first corps was only a kind of vanguard to the second, which was the real army, and a wonderful thing to see and hear. Never were brought together before or since so many different kinds of howl, so many threats of death, so many rags; so many odd weapons, from the matchlock of the time of the Michelade to the steel-tipped goad of the bullock drovers of La Camargue, so that when the Nimes mob; which in all conscience was howling and ragged enough, rushed out to offer a brotherly welcome to the strangers, its first feeling was one of astonishment and dismay as it caught sight of the motley crew which held out to it the right hand of fellowship.

The new-comers soon showed that it was through necessity and not choice that their outer man presented such a disreputable appearance; for they were hardly well within the gates before demanding that the houses of the members of the old Protestant National Guard should be pointed out to them.

This being done, they promptly proceeded to exact from each household a musket, a coat, a complete kit, or a sum of money, according to their humour, so that before evening those who had arrived naked and penniless were provided with complete uniforms and had money in their pockets. These exactions were levied under the name of a contribution, but before the day was ended naked and undisguised pillage began.

Someone asserted that during the assault on the barracks a certain individual had fired out of a certain house on the assailants. The indignant people now rushed to the house indicated, and soon left nothing of it in existence but its walls. A little later it was clearly proved that the individual accused was quite innocent of the crime laid to his charge.

The house of a rich merchant lay in the path of the advancing army. A cry arose that the owner was a Bonapartist, and nothing more was needed. The house was broken into and pillaged, and the furniture thrown out of the windows.

Two days later it turned out that not only was the merchant no Bonapartist, but that his son had been one of those who had accompanied the Duc d'Angouleme to Cette when he left the country. The pillagers excused themselves by saying they had been misled by a resemblance between two names, and this excuse, as far as appears, was accepted as valid by the authorities.

It was not long before the populace of Nimes began to think they might as well follow the example set them by their brothers from Beaucaire. In twenty-four hours free companies were formed, headed by Trestaillons, Trupheny, Graffan, and Morinet. These bands arrogated to themselves the title of National Guard, and then what took place at Marseilles in the excitement of the moment was repeated at Nimes with deliberation and method, inspired by hate and the desire of vengeance. A revolt broke out which followed the ordinary course: first pillage, then fire, then murder, laid waste the city.

M V_____'s house, which stood in the middle of the town, was sacked and then burnt to the ground, without a hand being raised to prevent the crime.

M T_____'s house, on the road to Montpellier, was sacked and wrecked and a bonfire made of the furniture, round which the crowd danced; as if it had been an occasion of public rejoicing. Then cries were raised for the proprietor, that he might be killed, and as he could not be found the baffled fury of the mob vented itself on the dead. A child three months buried was dragged from its grave, drawn by the feet through the sewers and wayside puddles, and then flung on a dung-heap; and, strange to say, while incendiarism and sacrilege thus ran riot, the mayor of the place slept so sound that when he awoke he was "quite astonished," to use his own expression, to hear what had taken place during the night.

This expedition completed, the same company which had brought this expedition to a successful issue next turned their attention to a small country house occupied by a widow, whom I had often begged to take refuge with us. But, secure in her insignificance, she had always declined our offers, preferring to live solitary and retired in her own home. But the freebooters sought her out, burst in her doors, drove her away with blows and insults, destroyed her house and burnt her furniture. They then proceeded to the vault in which lay the remains of her family, dragged them out of their coffins and scattered them about the fields. The next day the poor woman-ventured back, collected the desecrated remains with pious care, and replaced them in the vault. But this was counted to her as a crime; the company returned, once more cast forth the contents of the coffins, and threatened to kill her should she dare to touch them again. She was often seen in the days that followed shedding bitter tears and watching over the sacred relics as they lay exposed on the ground.

The name of this widow was Pepin, and the scene of the sacrilege was a small enclosure on the hill of the Moulins-a-Vent.

Meantime the people in the Faubourg des Bourgades had invented a new sort of game, or rather, had resolved to vary the serious business of the drama that was being enacted by the introduction of comic scenes. They had possessed themselves of a number of beetles such as washerwomen use, and hammered in long nails, the points of which projected an inch on the other side in the form of a fleur-de-lis. Every Protestant who fell into their hands, no matter what his age or rank, was stamped with the bloody emblem, serious wounds being inflicted in many cases.

Murders were now becoming common. Amongst other names of victims mentioned were Loriol, Bigot, Dumas, Lhermet, Heritier, Domaison, Combe, Clairon, Begomet, Poujas, Imbert, Vigal, Pourchet, Vignole. Details more or less shocking came to light as to the manner in which the murderers went to work. A man called Dalbos was in the custody of two armed men; some others came to consult with them. Dalbos appealed for mercy to the new-comers. It was granted, but as he turned to go he was shot dead. Another of the name of Rambert tried to escape by disguising himself as a woman, but was recognised and shot down a few yards outside his own door. A gunner called Saussine was walking in all security along the road to Uzes, pipe in mouth, when he was met by five men belonging to Trestaillon's company, who surrounded him and stabbed him to the heart with their knives. The elder of two brothers named Chivas ran across some fields to take shelter in a country house called Rouviere, which, unknown to him, had been occupied by some of the new National Guard. These met him on the threshold and shot him dead.

Rant was seized in his own house and shot. Clos was met by a company, and seeing Trestaillons, with whom he had always been friends, in its ranks, he went up to him and held out his hand; whereupon Trestaillons drew a pistol from his belt and blew his brains out. Calandre being chased down the rue des Soeurs-Grises, sought shelter in a tavern, but was forced to come out, and was killed with sabres. Courbet was sent to prison under the escort of some men, but these changed their minds on the way as to his punishment, halted, and shot him dead in the middle of the street.

A wine merchant called Cabanot, who was flying from Trestaillons, ran into a house in which there was a venerable priest called Cure Bonhomme. When the cut-throat rushed in, all covered with blood, the priest advanced and stopped him, crying:

"What will happen, unhappy man, when you come to the confessional with blood-stained hands?"

"Pooh!" replied Trestaillons, "you must put on your wide gown; the sleeves are large enough to let everything pass."

To the short account given above of so many murders I will add the narrative of one to which I was an eye-witness, and which made the most terrible impression on me of, anything in my experience.

It was midnight. I was working beside my wife's bed; she was just becoming drowsy, when a noise in the distance caught our attention. It gradually became more distinct, and drums began to beat the 'generale' in every direction. Hiding my own alarm for fear of increasing hers, I answered my wife, who was asking what new thing was about to happen, that it was probably troops marching in or out of garrison. But soon reports of firearms, accompanied by an uproar with which we were so familiar that we could no longer mistake its meaning, were heard outside. Opening my window, I heard bloodcurdling imprecations, mixed with cries of "Long live the king!" going on. Not being able to remain any longer in this uncertainty, I woke a captain who lived in the same house. He rose, took his arms, and we went out together, directing our course towards the point whence the shouts seemed to come. The moon shone so bright that we could see everything almost as distinctly as in broad daylight.

A concourse of people was hurrying towards the Cours yelling like madmen; the greater number of them, half naked, armed with muskets, swords, knives, and clubs, and swearing to exterminate everything, waved their weapons above the heads of men who had evidently been torn from their houses and brought to the square to be put to death. The rest of the crowd had, like ourselves, been drawn thither by curiosity, and were asking what was going on. "Murder is abroad," was the answer; "several people have been killed in the environs, and the patrol has been fired on." While this questioning was going on the noise continued to increase. As I had really no business to be on a spot where such things were going on, and feeling that my place was at my wife's side, to reassure her for the present and to watch over her should the rioters come our way, I said good-bye to the captain, who went on to the barracks, and took the road back to the suburb in which I lived.

I was not more than fifty steps from our house when I heard loud talking behind me, and, turning, saw gun barrels glittering in the moonlight. As the speakers seemed to be rapidly approaching me, I kept close in the shadow of the houses till I reached my own door, which I laid softly to behind me, leaving myself a chink by which I could peep out and watch the movements of the group which was drawing near. Suddenly I felt something touch my hand; it was a great

303

Corsican dog, which was turned loose at night, and was so fierce that it was a great protection to our house. I felt glad to have it at my side, for in case of a struggle it would be no despicable ally.

Those approaching turned out to be three armed men leading a fourth, disarmed and a prisoner. They all stopped just opposite my door, which I gently closed and locked, but as I still wished to see what they were about, I slipped into the garden, which lay towards the street, still followed by my dog. Contrary to his habit, and as if he understood the danger, he gave a low whine instead of his usual savage growl. I climbed into a fig tree the branches of which overhung the street, and, hidden by the leaves, and resting my hands on the top of the wall, I leaned far enough forward to see what the men were about.

They were still on the same spot, but there was a change in their positions. The prisoner was now kneeling with clasped hands before the cut-throats, begging for his life for the sake of his wife and children, in heartrending accents, to which his executioners replied in mocking tones, "We have got you at last into our hands, have we? You dog of a Bonapartist, why do you not call on your emperor to come and help you out of this scrape?" The unfortunate man's entreaties became more pitiful and their mocking replies more pitiless. They levelled their muskets at him several times, and then lowered them, saying; "Devil take it, we won't shoot yet; let us give him time to see death coming," till at last the poor wretch, seeing there was no hope of mercy, begged to be put out of his misery.

Drops of sweat stood on my forehead. I felt my pockets to see if I had nothing on me which I could use as a weapon, but I had not even a knife. I looked at my dog; he was lying flat at the foot of the tree, and appeared to be a prey to the most abject terror. The prisoner continued his supplications, and the assassins their threats and mockery. I climbed quietly down out of the fig tree, intending to fetch my pistols. My dog followed me with his eyes, which seemed to be the only living things about him. Just as my foot touched the ground a double report rang out, and my dog gave a plaintive and prolonged howl. Feeling that all was over, and that no weapons could be of any use, I climbed up again into my perch and looked out. The poor wretch was lying face downwards writhing in his blood; the assassins were reloading their muskets as they walked away.

Being anxious to see if it was too late to help the man whom I had not been able to save, I went out into the street and bent over him. He was bloody, disfigured, dying, but was yet alive, uttering dismal groans. I tried to lift him up, but soon saw that the wounds which he had received from bullets fired at close range were both mortal, one being in the head, and the other in the loins. Just then a patrol, of the National Guard turned round the corner of the street. This, instead of being a relief, awoke me to a sense of my danger, and feeling I could do nothing for the wounded man, for the death rattle had already begun, I entered my house, half shut the door, and listened.

"Qui vive?" asked the corporal.

"Idiot!" said someone else, "to ask 'Qui vive?' of a dead man!"

305

"He is not dead," said a third voice; "listen to him singing"; and indeed the poor fellow in his agony was giving utterance to dreadful groans.

"Someone has tickled him well," said a fourth, "but what does it matter? We had better finish the job."

Five or six musket shots followed, and the groans ceased.

The name of the man who had just expired was Louis Lichaire; it was not against him, but against his nephew, that the assassins had had a grudge, but finding the nephew out when they burst into the house, and a victim being indispensable, they had torn the uncle from the arms of his wife, and, dragging him towards the citadel, had killed him as I have just related.

Very early next morning I sent to three commissioners of police, one after the other, for permission to have the corpse carried to the hospital, but these gentlemen were either not up or had already gone out, so that it was not until eleven o'clock and after repeated applications that they condescended to give me the needed authorisation.

Thanks to this delay, the whole town came to see the body of the unfortunate man. Indeed, the day which followed a massacre was always kept as a holiday, everyone leaving his work undone and coming out to stare at the slaughtered victims. In this case, a man wishing to amuse the crowd took his pipe out of his mouth and put it between the teeth of the corpse—a joke which had a marvellous success, those present shrieking with laughter.

Many murders had been committed during the night; the companies had scoured the streets singing some doggerel, which one of the bloody wretches, being in poetic vein, had composed, the chorus of which was:

"Our work's well done,

We spare none!"

Seventeen fatal outrages were committed, and yet neither the reports of the firearms nor the cries of the victims broke the peaceful slumbers of M. le Prefet and M. le Commissaire General de la Police. But if the civil authorities slept, General Lagarde, who had shortly before come to town to take command of the city in the name of the king, was awake. He had sprung from his bed at the first shot, dressed himself, and made a round of the posts; then sure that everything was in order, he had formed patrols of chasseurs, and had himself, accompanied by two officers only, gone wherever he heard cries for help. But in spite of the strictness of his orders the small number of troops at his disposition delayed the success of his efforts, and it was not until three o'clock in the morning that he succeeded in securing Trestaillons. When this man was taken he was dressed as usual in the uniform of the National Guard, with a cocked hat and captain's epaulets. General Lagarde ordered the gens d'armes who made the capture to deprive him of his sword and carbine, but it was only after a long struggle that they could carry out this order, for Trestaillons protested that he would only give up his carbine with his life. However, he was at last obliged to yield to numbers, and when disarmed was removed to the barracks; but as there could be no peace in the town as long as he was in it, the general sent him to the citadel of Montpellier next morning before it was light.

The disorders did not, however, cease at once. At eight o'clock A.M. they were still going on, the mob seeming to be animated by the spirit of Trestaillons, for while the soldiers were occupied in a distant quarter of the town a score of men broke into the house of a certain Scipion Chabrier, who had remained hidden from his enemies for a long time, but who had lately returned home on the strength of the proclamations published by General Lagarde when he assumed the position of commandant of the town. He had indeed been sure that the disturbances in Nimes were over, when they burst out with redoubled fury on the 16th of October; on the morning of the 17th he was working quietly at home at his trade of a silk weaver, when, alarmed by the shouts of a parcel of cut-throats outside his house, he tried to escape. He succeeded in reaching the "Coupe d'Or," but the ruffians followed him, and the first who came up thrust him through the thigh with his bayonet. In consequence of this wound he fell from top to bottom of the staircase, was seized and dragged to the stables, where the assassins left him for dead, with seven wounds in his body.

This was, however, the only murder committed that day in the town, thanks to the vigilance and courage of General Lagarde.

The next day a considerable crowd gathered, and a noisy deputation went to General Lagarde's quarters and insolently demanded that Trestaillons should be set at liberty. The general ordered them to disperse, but no attention was paid to this command, whereupon he ordered his soldiers to charge, and in a moment force accomplished what long-continued persuasion had failed to effect. Several of the ringleaders were arrested and taken to prison.

Thus, as we shall see, the struggle assumed a new phase: resistance to the royal power was made in the name of the royal power, and both those who broke or those who tried to maintain the public peace used the same cry, "Long live the king!"

The firm attitude assumed by General Lagarde restored Nimes to a state of superficial peace, beneath which, however, the old enmities were fermenting. An occult power, which betrayed itself by a kind of passive resistance, neutralised the effect of the measures taken by the military commandant. He soon became cognisant of the fact that the essence of this sanguinary political strife was an hereditary religious animosity, and in order to strike a last blow at this, he resolved, after having received permission from the king, to grant the general request of the Protestants by reopening their places of worship, which had been closed for more than four months, and allowing the public exercise of the Protestant religion, which had been entirely suspended in the city for the same length of time.

Formerly there had been six Protestant pastors resident in Nimes, but four of them, had fled; the two who remained were MM. Juillerat and Olivier Desmonts, the first a young man, twenty-eight years of age, the second an old man of seventy.

The entire weight of the ministry had fallen during this period of proscription on M. Juillerat, who had accepted the task and religiously fulfilled it. It seemed as if a special providence had miraculously protected him in the midst of the many perils which beset his path. Although the other pastor, M. Desmonts, was president of the Consistory, his life was in much less danger; for, first, he had reached an age which almost everywhere commands respect, and then he had a son who was a lieutenant in, one of the royal corps levied at Beaucaire, who protected him by his name when he could not do so by his presence. M. Desmonts had therefore little cause for anxiety as to his safety either in the streets of Nimes or on the road between that and his country house.

But, as we have said, it was not so with M. Juillerat. Being young and active, and having an unfaltering trust in God, on him alone devolved all the sacred duties of his office, from the visitation of the sick and dying to the baptism of the newly born. These latter were often brought to him at night to be baptized, and he consented, though unwillingly, to make this concession, feeling that if he insisted on the performance of the rite by day he would compromise not only his own safety but that of others. In all that concerned him personally, such as consoling the dying or caring for the wounded, he acted quite openly, and no danger that he encountered on his way ever caused him to flinch from the path of duty.

One day, as M. Juillerat was passing through the rue des Barquettes on his way to the prefecture to transact some business connected with his ministry, he saw several men lying in wait in a blind alley by which he had to pass. They had their guns pointed at him. He continued his way with tranquil step and such an air of resignation that the assassins were overawed, and lowered their weapons as he approached, without firing a single shot. When M. Juillerat reached the prefecture, thinking that the prefect ought to be aware of everything connected with the public order, he related this incident to M. d'Arbaud-Jouques, but the latter did not think the affair of enough importance to require any investigation.

It was, as will be seen, a difficult enterprise to open once again the Protestant places of worship, which had been so long closed, in present circumstances, and in face of the fact that the civil authorities regarded such a step with disfavour, but General Lagarde was one of those determined characters who always act up to their convictions. Moreover, to prepare people's minds for this stroke of religious policy, he relied on the help of the Duc d'Angouleme, who in the course of a tour through the South was almost immediately expected at Nimes.

On the 5th of November the prince made his entry into the city, and having read the reports of the general to the King Louis XVIII, and having received positive injunctions from his uncle to pacify the unhappy provinces which he was about to visit, he arrived full of the desire to displays whether he felt it or not, a perfect impartiality; so when the delegates from the Consistory were presented to him, not only did he receive them most graciously, but he was the first to speak of the interests of their faith, assuring them that it was only a few days since he had learned with much regret that their religious services had been; suspended since the 16th of July. The delegates replied that in such a time of agitation the closing of their places of worship was, a measure of prudence which they had felt ought to be borne, and which had been borne, with resignation. The prince expressed his approval of this attitude with regard to the past, but said that his presence was a guarantee for the future, and that on Thursday the 9th inst. the two meeting-houses should be reopened and restored to their proper use. The Protestants were alarmed at, having a favour accorded to them which was much more than they would have dared to ask and for which they were hardly prepared. But the prince reassured them by saying that all needful measures would be taken to provide against any breach of the public peace, and at the same time invited M. Desmonts, president, and M. Roland-Lacoste, member of the Consistory, to dine with him.

The next deputation to arrive was a Catholic one, and its object was to ask that Trestaillons might be set at liberty. The prince was so indignant at this request that his only answer was to turn his back on those who proffered it.

The next day the duke, accompanied by General Lagarde, left for Montpellier; and as it was on the latter that the Protestants placed their sole reliance for the maintenance of those rights guaranteed for the future by the word of the prince, they hesitated to take any new step in his absence, and let the 9th of November go by without attempting to resume public worship, preferring to wait for the return of their protector, which took place on Saturday evening the 11th of November.

When the general got back, his first thought was to ask if the commands of the prince had been carried out, and when he heard that they had not, without waiting to hear a word in justification of the delay, he sent a positive order to the president of the Consistory to open both places of worship the next morning.

Upon this, the president carrying self-abnegation and prudence to their extreme limits, went to the general's quarters, and having warmly thanked him, laid before him the dangers to which he would expose himself by running counter to the opinions of those who had had their own way in the city for the last four months. But General Lagarde brushed all these considerations aside: he had received an order from the prince, and to a man of his military cast of mind no course was open but to carry that order out.

Nevertheless, the president again expressed his doubts and fears.

"I will answer with my head," said the general, "that nothing happens." Still the president counselled prudence, asking that only one place of worship at first be opened, and to this the general gave his consent.

This continued resistance to the re-establishment of public worship on the part of those who most eagerly desired it enabled the general at last to realise the extent of the danger which would be incurred by the carrying out of this measure, and he at once took all possible precautions. Under the pretext that he was going to-have a general review, he brought the entire civil and military forces of Nimes under his authority, determined, if necessary, to use the one to suppress the other. As early as eight o'clock in the morning a guard of gens d'armes was stationed at the doors of the meeting-house, while other members of the same force took up their positions in the adjacent streets. On the other hand, the Consistory had decided that the doors were to be opened an hour sooner than usual, that the bells were not to be rung, and that the organ should be silent.

These precautions had both a good and a bad side. The gens d'armes at the door of the meetinghouse gave if not a promise of security at least a promise of support, but they showed to the citizens of the other party what was about to be done; so before nine o'clock groups of Catholics began to form, and as it happened to be Sunday the inhabitants of the neighbouring villages arriving constantly by twos and threes soon united these groups into a little army. Thus the streets leading to the church being thronged, the Protestants who pushed their way through were greeted with insulting remarks, and even the president of the Consistory, whose white, hair and dignified expression had no effect upon the mob, heard the people round him saying, "These brigands of Protestants are going again to their temple, but we shall soon give them enough of it."

The anger of the populace soon grows hot; between the first bubble and the boiling-point the interval is short. Threats spoken in a low voice were soon succeeded by noisy objurgations. Women, children, and men brake out into yells, "Down with the broilers!" (for this was one of the names by which the Protestants were designated). "Down with the broilers! We do not want to see them using our churches: let them give us back our churches; let them give us back our churches, and go to the desert. Out with them! Out with them! To the desert! To the desert!"

As the crowd did not go beyond words, however insulting, and as the Protestants were long inured to much worse things, they plodded along to their meeting-house, humble and silent, and went in, undeterred by the displeasure they aroused, whereupon the service commenced.

But some Catholics went in with them, and soon the same shouts which had been heard without were heard also within. The general, however, was on the alert, and as soon as the shouts arose inside the gens d'armes entered the church and arrested those who had caused the disturbance. The crowds tried to rescue them on their way to prison, but the general appeared at the head of imposing forces, at the sight of which they desisted. An apparent cam succeeded the tumult, and the public worship went on without further interruption.

The general, misled by appearances, went off himself to attend a military mass, and at eleven o'clock returned to his quarters for lunch. His absence was immediately perceived and taken advantage of. In the: twinkling of an eye, the crowds, which had dispersed, gathered together in even greater numbers and the Protestants, seeing themselves once more in danger, shut the doors from within, while the gens d'armes guarded them without. The populace pressed so closely round the gens d'armes, and assumed such a threatening attitude, that fearing he and his men would not be able to hold their own in such a throng, the captain ordered M. Delbose, one of his officers, to ride off and warn the general. He forced his way through the crowd with great trouble, and went off at a gallop. On seeing this, the people felt there was no time to be lost; they knew of what kind the general was, and that he would be on the spot in a quarter of an hour. A large crowd is invincible through its numbers; it

315

has only to press forward, and everything gives way, men, wood, iron. At this moment the crowd, swayed by a common impulse, swept forward, the gens d'armes and their horses were crushed against the wall, doors gave way, and instantly with a tremendous roar a living wave flooded the church. Cries of terror and frightful imprecations were heard on all sides, everyone made a weapon of whatever came to hand, chairs and benches were hurled about, the disorder was at its height; it seemed as if the days of the Michelade and the Bagarre were about to return, when suddenly the news of a terrible event was spread abroad, and assailants and assailed paused in horror. General Lagarde had just been assassinated.

As the crowd had foreseen, no sooner did the messenger deliver his message than the general sprang on his horse, and, being too brave, or perhaps too scornful, to fear such foes, he waited for no escort, but, accompanied by two or three officers, set off at full gallop towards the scene of the tumult. He had passed through the narrow streets which led to the meeting-house by pushing the crowd aside with his horse's chest, when, just as he got out into the open square, a young man named Boisson, a sergeant in the Nimes National Guard, came up and seemed to wish to speak to him. The general seeing a man in uniform, bent down without a thought of danger to listen to what he had to say, whereupon Boisson drew a pistol out and fired at him. The ball broke the collar-bone and lodged in the neck behind the carotid artery, and the general fell from his horse.

The news of this crime had a strange and unexpected effect; however excited and frenzied the crowd was, it

316

instantly realised the consequences of this act. It was no longer like the murder of Marshal Brune at Avignon or General Ramel at Toulouse, an act of vengeance on a favourite of Napoleon, but open and armed rebellion against the king. It was not a simple murder, it was high treason.

A feeling of the utmost terror spread through the town; only a few fanatics went on howling in the church, which the Protestants, fearing still greater disasters, had by this time resolved to abandon. The first to come out was President Olivier Desmonts, accompanied by M. Vallongues, who had only just arrived in the city, but who had immediately hurried to the spot at the call of duty.

M Juillerat, his two children in his arms, walked behind them, followed by all the other worshippers. At first the crowd, threatening and ireful, hooted and threw stones at them, but at the voice of the mayor and the dignified aspect of the president they allowed them to pass. During this strange retreat over eighty Protestants were wounded, but not fatally, except a young girl called Jeannette Cornilliere, who had been so beaten and ill-used that she died of her injuries a few days later.

In spite of the momentary slackening of energy which followed the assassination of General Lagarde, the Catholics did not remain long in a state of total inaction. During the rest of the day the excited populace seemed as if shaken by an earthquake. About six o'clock in the evening, some of the most desperate characters in the town possessed themselves of a hatchet, and, taking their way to the Protestant church, smashed the doors, tore the pastors' gowns, rifled the poor-box, and pulled the books to pieces. A detachment of troops arrived just in time to prevent their setting the building on fire.

The next day passed more quietly. This time the disorders were of too important a nature for the prefect to ignore, as he had ignored so many bloody acts in the past; so in due time a full report was laid before the king. It became know the same evening that General Lagarde was still living, and that those around him hoped that the wound would not prove mortal. Dr. Delpech, who had been summoned from Montpellier, had succeeded in extracting the bullet, and though he spoke no word of hope, he did not expressly declare that the case was hopeless.

Two days later everything in the town had assumed its ordinary aspect, and on the 21st of November the king issued the following edict:—

"Louis, by the grace of God, King of France and of Navarre,

"To all those to whom these presents shall come, greeting:

"An abominable crime has cast a stain on Our city of Nimes. A seditious mob has dared to oppose the opening of the Protestant place of worship, in contempt of the constitutional charter, which while it recognises the Catholic religion as the religion of the State, guarantees to the other religious bodies protection and freedom of worship. Our military commandant, whilst trying to disperse these crowds by gentle means before having resort to force, was shot down, and his assassin has till now successfully evaded the arm of the law. If such an outrage were to remain unpunished, the maintenance of good government and public order would be impossible, and Our ministers would be guilty of neglecting the law.

"Wherefore We have ordered and do order as follows:

"Art. 1. Proceedings shall be commenced without delay by Our attorney, and the attorney-general, against the perpetrator of the murderous attack on the person of Sieur Lagarde, and against the authors, instigators, and accomplices of the insurrection which took place in the city of Nimes on the 12th of the present month.

"Art. 2. A sufficient number of troops shall be quartered in the said city, and shall remain there at the cost of the inhabitants, until the assassin and his accomplices have been produced before a court of law.

"Art. 3. All those citizens whose names are not entitled to be on the roll of the National Guard shall be disarmed.

"Our Keeper of the Seals, Our Minister of War, Our Minister of the Interior, and Our Minister of Police, are entrusted with the execution of this edict.

"Given at Paris at Our Castle of the Tuileries on the 21st of November in the year of grace 1815, and of Our reign the 21st.

"(Signed) Louis"

Boissin was acquitted.

This was the last crime committed in the South, and it led fortunately to no reprisals.

Three months after the murderous attempt to which he had so nearly fallen a victim, General Lagarde left Nimes with the rank of ambassador, and was succeeded as prefect by M. d'Argont.

During the firm, just, and independent administration of the latter, the disarming of the citizens decreed by the royal edict was carried out without bloodshed.

Through his influence, MM. Chabot-Latour, Saint-Aulaire, and Lascour were elected to the Chamber of Deputies in place of MM. De Calviere, De Vogue, and De Trinquelade.

And down to the present time the name of M. d'Argont is held in veneration at Nimes, as if he had only quitted the city yesterday.

CONTENTS

Lightning Source UK Ltd.
Milton Keynes UK
UKHW010044170223
417092UK00003B/144